"Captain, this is Duke Sandoval. Open 'Mech launch chute one."

"Damn," was the only reply from the ship's bridge, except for a muttered curse. The bay lurched around them, and he could feel them descending again, more rapidly this time.

"Captain, this is the Duke! Open the launch chute!"

"We're—busy up here."

"Open the chute!"

No answer.

He jockeyed the 'Mech's controls to move them forward. He could see cracks in the main bay door in front of them, sunlight streaming through some of them. Meters above, he could see the main door actuators, one broken loose and waving as the ship rocked.

He activated the twin lasers on either side of the cockpit. He aimed manually and fired. The actuators began to glow red, then white.

They snapped, and abruptly the entire bay door peeled away, leaving them standing in front of a gaping hole in the hull. Hurricane winds ripped around them, sucking out anything that wasn't tied down, with the obvious exception of the fifty-ton *Black Hawk*.

He could see the gulf below them. The water looked perilously close.

There was another explosion below them, and the ship started to roll over. The hatch in front of them turned downward to face the whitecaps on the waves below. Instinctively, Aaron stepped the 'Mech forward and they dropped into open air.

DARK AGE

FORTRESS OF LIES

A BATTLETECH® NOVEL

J. Steven York

A ROC BOOK

ROC
Published by New American Library, a division of
Penguin Group (USA) Inc., 375 Hudson Street,
New York, New York 10014, U.S.A.
Penguin Books Ltd, 80 Strand,
London WC2R 0RL, England
Penguin Books Australia Ltd, 250 Camberwell Road,
Camberwell, Victoria 3124, Australia
Penguin Books Canada Ltd, 10 Alcorn Avenue,
Toronto, Ontario, Canada M4V 3B2
Penguin Books (N.Z.) Ltd, Cnr Rosedale and Airborne Roads,
Albany, Auckland 1310, New Zealand

Penguin Books Ltd, Registered Offices:
80 Strand, London WC2R 0RL, England

First published by Roc, an imprint of New American Library,
a division of Penguin Group (USA) Inc.

First Printing, February 2004
10 9 8 7 6 5 4 3 2 1

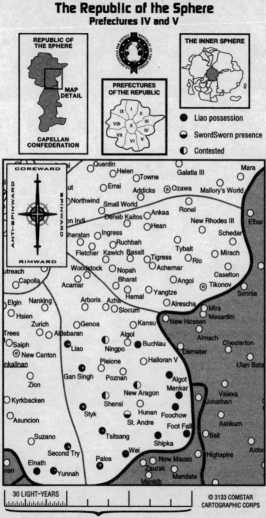

The Republic of the Sphere
Prefectures IV and V

REPUBLIC OF THE SPHERE
MAP DETAIL
CAPELLAN CONFEDERATION

PREFECTURES OF THE REPUBLIC

THE INNER SPHERE

● Liao possession
◐ SwordSworn presence
◑ Contested

COREWARD
ANTI-SPINWARD
SPINWARD
RIMWARD

Quentin · Helen · Towne · Galatia III · Mara
Errai · Addicks · Ozawa · Mallory's World
Northwind · Small World · Ankaa · Ronel
Deneb Kaitos · New Rhodes III · Elbar
Indi · Hean · Schedar
Sheratan · Ingress · Ruchbah · Tybalt · Mirach
Fletcher · Kawich Basalt · Tigress · Rio · Schedar
Woodstock · Nopah · Achernar · Caselton
Outreach · Capolla · Acamar · Bharat · Angol · Tikonov
Nanking · Arboris · Azha · Hamal · Yangtze · Sonnia
Elgin · Slocum · Alrescha · Mira · Mesartim
Hsien · Genoa · Kansu · New Hessen
Zurich · Aldebaran · Algol · Buchlau · Almach · Chesterton
Trees · Saiph · Liao · Ningpo · Halloran V · Demeter · Ulan Bata
New Canton · Pleione
Inkalinan · Gan Singh · Poznan · Algot · Menkar · Valexa
Zion · New Aragon · Jonathan
Kyrkbacken · Shensi · Hunan · Foochow · Ashkum
Styk · St. Andre · Foot Fall
Asuncion · Tsitsang · Shipka · Bell · Axtor
Suzano · Wei · Highspire
Second Try · Palos · New Macao
Elnath · Zaurak · Mandate
Waren · Yunnah · Menkib

30 LIGHT-YEARS

© 3133 COMSTAR CARTOGRAPHIC CORPS

90 LIGHT-YEARS OR 20.1 PARSECS

Aloha Agricultural District
Glastonbury continent, New Aragon
Prefecture V, The Republic of the Sphere
1 September 3134

The bombs fell on New Aragon, their shock waves sending out ghostly rings of tortured air. Aerospace fighters streaked overhead, black arrows against a red sky, bloody with the smoke and dust of three weeks of unending battle.

The ground was pocked with craters, the huge footprints of forty-ton BattleMechs and lined with tracks recording armored battles decided days before. In the near distance, wrecked tanks smoldered, trailing black smoke. Crushed battle-armor lay scattered on the raw earth like broken eggshells, black jelly that might once have been men oozing through the cracked metal.

Thankfully, Erik Sandoval could not smell the battlefield in the filtered air of his cockpit. Only the stink of his own sweat, the ozone smell of overheated circuitry, and the tang of hot metal reached his nostrils.

This, reflected Erik, was the terrible beauty of war. The unspeakable wonder, the sights that could never be forgotten, burned into the brain to emerge in the nightmares of old men and women—those who were foolish enough, or unlucky enough, to live that long.

Such was the loss of perspective that came from thirty-three days spent primarily in the cockpit of a 'Mech, striding high above the battlefield. It came from watching lesser combatants scrambling ahead, from forgetting your humanity, and simply becoming a walking, twelve-meter-tall engine of destruction, facing more targets than you can shoot—more targets than you have time to chase down or ammo to kill. Small targets that shoot back, sometimes with enough force to sting even a mighty BattleMech. Small targets that, if a MechWarrior got sloppy or inattentive or simply overwhelmed, could even kill him.

A movement caught Erik's eye, and he pivoted his *Centurion,* gyros whining. The weakened left leg, damaged in a brawl with a modified MinerMech three days earlier, caused his humanoid 'Mech to limp slightly. In the distance, the upright insect form of a green and gold *Spider* BattleMech strode from behind a hill—a shaft of sunlight glancing off its bubble cockpit, carbon scoring streaking its extended wings. It moved rapidly to Erik's right, perhaps not seeing him. He zoomed in with his optics, placed his targeting reticles over the exposed flank and squeezed off a laser burst.

There was a flash, and a jagged streak of molten armor appeared across the *Spider*'s right shoulder. A hiss of disappointment escaped Erik's lips. He'd been aiming for the damaged lower torso, hoping for a critical hit on the reactor. A week earlier he might not have missed, but such subtleties of battle were for fresher warriors and fresher 'Mechs. At this range, he knew he should have been glad to get a hit at all.

The *Spider* whirled and began running backward, lasers flashing with return fire—a clean miss—the House Liao pilot perhaps rattled by the unexpected attack. The 'Mech spun again and sprinted away from Erik. The broad wings sprouting from the 'Mech's shoulders presented a tempting target, but Erik knew where the machine's critical systems were hidden—knew the distinction between an easy shot and a victorious one.

He considered following up with a missile before remembering that his tubes were empty. He'd been leading his formation back to the command DropShip for resupply, repair, and perhaps a warm meal and a few minutes of fitful sleep. That would have to wait now.

So would the kill shot. The *Spider* was fast. He had to slow it down if he hoped to do more significant damage. Erik thumbed back to his lasers, targeted, fired another shot. A flash against the *Spider*'s lower right leg left glowing traces but did only superficial damage. The *Spider* fired its jump jets, staggering into the air from amid a cloud of plasma-blasted debris. It managed to make it to the top of the nearest hill before the jets flickered and died, dropping it heavily to the ground. The 'Mech stumbled, and for a moment Erik thought it would fall. Then it got its footing and vanished over the hill. He instinctively reached to shove the throttle forward and give chase.

"Commander."

The *Spider* was fast, but given its damage, and possibly disabled jump jets, he should be able to overtake it.

"Commander."

After weeks of hard-pressed fighting, the forces of

House Liao were on the run. In the far distance, a dark sphere rose over the horizon, trailing a column of almost blindingly brilliant fire. It was another *Mule*-class DropShip fleeing New Aragon. Targets, once lined up from horizon to horizon, were now hard to find. This might be his last chance to take down a 'Mech before—

"Erik!"

He blinked and ran his tongue across his dry and cracked lips, feeling the edge of the day-old stubble growing above them. He blinked again, rewinding the last few moments in his brain, finally recognizing the voice crackling in his headset.

"Captain Cutler?"

"Begging pardon, sir, you're ranging awfully far forward of the formation. We can't offer much cover for you back here."

"Cover?"

"Yes, sir. The patrol is spread out pretty far, and we can't watch your six and protect our armor at the same time. Can you give us a few minutes to close up?"

"Formation." He took a deep breath, shook off the tunnel vision that had locked his entire being on the fleeing *Spider*. "Sure, Hank. He's too badly damaged to be worth the chase. Besides, he's doubtless forming up with some friends. I'm out of missiles and too hot for that kind of skirmish."

"Yes, sir. Here come the bikes."

A pair of hoverbikes flashed by on either side, curving in front of him to pass each other and begin counterrotating orbits around his position. They were ungainly-looking things, but fast and hard to hit, capable of lightning in-and-out harassment attacks on an enemy. One of the riders flashed a quick salute as he zoomed in front of Erik's 'Mech.

A moment later they were joined by two squads of

Purifier battle armor arching in gracefully on jump jets. They settled in front of him like a flight of tan-and-green wasps, leaving just enough of a gap in their formation so he could move past them, if necessary, without trampling them under his 'Mech's thundering feet.

The wheeled and tracked vehicles would be farther back, he knew, still scrambling to catch up, another squad of Purifier battle armor guarding their flanks. He looked at the hill where he'd last seen the *Spider* and sighed.

This was modern war. There had been a time, long before he was born, when countless 'Mechs would have ruled the battlefield, when two 'Mechs meeting in combat would have squared off, like colossal gladiators, for a fight to the death.

That day was gone. Once he had established The Republic of the Sphere, Devlin Stone had done his best to create a state based more on commerce than on warfare. He had never been entirely successful, but during his tenure as Exarch, many BattleMechs had been decommissioned or scrapped, and even the capacity to manufacture replacements had nearly been lost. Now 'Mechs were rare, too precious to send out alone, vastly outnumbered by more conventional armor, attack vehicles, and infantry. Now a MechWarrior, even a commander, had to think like a team player, trusting others to watch his back and compensate for his valuable 'Mech's few weaknesses.

Erik dreamed wistfully of those lost times and wished he could have lived then, when MechWarriors were royalty, needing to trust only themselves, fully in control of their own destinies. But that was then.

'Mechs and their pilots were still the kings of the battlefield, for their relative scarcity. But there was a subtle change in how they were treated. Now the tankers and infantrymen knew that battles were rarely won by 'Mechs alone, and with this knowledge came a growing sense of their own importance. A few, when well lubricated with liquor and when they thought they were out of earshot of any MechWarrior, would even voice the idea that they didn't need 'Mechs at all.

It was a foolish notion, of course, though perhaps only a little more foolish than pining for days long gone. For the foreseeable future, winning battles would require a balance of forces, each playing their role. Even as Erik was nostalgic for the old times, he was a realist. These men and women who entered the battlefield without the awesome armor and firepower of a 'Mech well deserved his respect.

To Erik's mind, the military was a unique social order. While there was a clearly defined chain of command, in a sense all warriors were, on some level, equals. They had all paid their dues of danger, pain, and fear. They had stood together, literally or figuratively, shoulder-to-shoulder on the field of life and death.

Even the greenest and most untested recruits had pledged their lives to that service, and the smell of death waited for them up the road. There was a brotherhood and sisterhood of arms that no civilian could ever really understand. From the lowest private to a battle commander, they were bound by blood.

Yet it was from the role of commander that Erik now saw this war against the Liao incursion, and it chafed at him. He longed not just for the days of old, but the freedom to fight as a true warrior. If 'Mechs were too rare to risk alone on the battlefield, his status made him even less expendable. He did not hold himself apart from the men and women under his command—not at all. Rather, he was held apart from them.

Erik checked his heading back to the DropShip, and started a wide turn that the formation would find easier to follow. A row of cracking noises worked their way up the side of his 'Mech, from waist to shoulders, the last making a loud report against the ferro-glass canopy next to his head.

Small-arms fire. Nothing to trouble a 'Mech, but close enough to be worth his attention. The squad was too close to the grounded DropShip, and he didn't like to see this level of enemy activity. He thumbed his com to address the whole formation. "I'm picking up some plink, from the south-southeast I think. Bikers, watch yourselves. Let's get the scout car out there for a look. I'll watch your six. The rest of you group up and hug cover."

"Yes, sir."

He recognized the voice as Dallas, pilot of the formation's Fox armored car. The unit moved past him on the right, hoverskirts flapping as it turned, sun glinting off its bubble cockpit. He throttled up to follow, taking a slightly different path to cover more ground and give him a clear shot at any threat.

The low rolling hills offered ample cover for enemies, allowing for attack from almost any direction. The flat expanses between had once been swampland, before the early settlers drained most of the planet's two major continents through a vast network of trenches, dams, and artificial waterways. Small streams were everywhere, and many of the lowlands still flooded in the spring rains.

He saw movement along the horizon, but it was only a fleeing herd of Geef, thousand-kilogram grazing amphibians whose appearance fell somewhere in a combination of toad, buffalo, and alligator. These were probably from a commercial herd, escaped as the result of fighting, or perhaps released by their owners to fend for themselves until the hostilities were over.

New Aragon was no stranger to war. Agriculture,

ranching, and the ecosystem itself had only just recovered from the damage done by Blakist chemical weapons decades earlier.

Now war was here again. It was unclear if it had come to stay.

The *Centurion*'s limp was more pronounced at this speed, making the cockpit lurch with every second step. He could hear the frayed fibers of synthetic muscle in the bad leg twang, like an amateur plucking randomly at some huge guitar. The heat indicator, which had been falling since his last laser shot, now began to slowly climb again. That shouldn't be happening. Clearly there was damage somewhere that wasn't showing up on his diagnostics.

His eyes scanned ahead, looking for the hidden infantry that was the likely source of fire. A stand of trees, most smashed and broken off to stumps by earlier action, offered an excellent potential hiding place, but a gully to his right and some rocks uphill beyond the trees were also possibilities.

He heard the chatter of a light machine gun in his helmet's earphones, and sparks danced across the cockpit of the Fox. "There they are," yelled Dallas, "in the rocks."

"I'm on it," said Erik, turning the *Centurion* to wade through the stand of fallen trees. He put his crosshairs on the rocks, but could see no obvious target. "Get me some infantry support here, and get the tanks in position to pound those rocks."

There was a whistle as the *Fox* disappeared in an explosion of earth and shattered metal. Just that fast, Dallas was gone. "Artillery!" Erik swung the humanoid 'Mech's torso looking for a target, but the artillery was likely out of sight behind one of the nearby hills. "Bikers, get out there and find those guns!"

"Incoming!" Cutler's voice broke in. "Incoming!"

Erik pulled up a rear camera, and saw explosions

around and among the armor. "Damn, damn. Spread out! Make them work for it!"

The column began to scatter, but it was too late for an M1 Marksman Tank that was nearly swallowed in an explosion. When the dust began to clear, he could see one front track flopping loose, the other track on that side apparently frozen. The unit spun helplessly in a circle, the still functional turret restlessly searching for a target.

A movement far below alerted him to a more immediate threat. From the trees, soldiers in Purifier battle armor swarmed. While several units trapped him in a circle of laser fire, two others fired their jump jets to leap onto his 'Mech. He managed to lash out with the 'Mech's right arm, smashing one out of the air with a satisfying bang, but the other landed on his right shoulder, too high for him to easily reach. He lost sight of the unit. Then there was a loud hammering at the hatch behind him.

They're trying to take my 'Mech!

Helplessly, he looked around. Neither his weapons nor his arms could reach his tiny tormentor. Then he had an inspiration.

His 'Mech began to run, breaking free of the circle, heading directly for the rocks that had been his original target. If the machine gun opened fire on him, all the better. They'd be more of a threat to the Purifier than to him. If not, he'd overrun them.

But that wasn't his primary intent. Through the neurohelmet that controlled the 'Mech's balance, he stopped fighting the limp and leaned into it, causing the 'Mech to lurch and stagger sickeningly with each step. He began flailing the *Centurion*'s massive arms, twisting the torso, swinging it forward and back. His stomach lurched at the chaotic motion of the cockpit. How much worse must it be for his "passenger"?

He couldn't reach the infantryman on his neck, but

he could slam the arms wildly against the 'Mech itself, making the entire structure ring like a massive bell. He cringed as the sound stabbed into his ears, overwhelming the noise-canceling effect of the headphones. He could feel it in his chest, in his bones.

He dug the 'Mech's heels in, simultaneously whipping the torso from side to side, slamming into the stops at either extreme. Then he swung the *Centurion* forward at the waist, almost toppling it. Above him he heard a scrambling noise, followed by a thud, as the Purifier, its hold loosened by the movement and noise, flipped over the 'Mech's head. The infantryman tried to fire his armor's jump jets, but it was too late, and his attitude was all wrong. He landed at an angle and crashed hard into the ground.

The trooper struggled weakly to rise, but Erik was moving again. It was only a second before he dropped his right foot on the struggling man and pressed down. The 'Mech's foot settled onto the rocky ground.

Erik turned. The other Purifiers were fleeing as fast as their jump jets would take them. The artillery fire had stopped, and he heard one of the bikers calling in a bearing on their location.

In the confusion, they were moving right toward Erik's formation, and Erik would quickly be within range of their guns, helpless. While not as satisfying as taking out a 'Mech, Erik would be happy to settle for taking out what must be several units of House Liao artillery. To his right, he could see the crew of the crippled M1 transferring to an Armored Personnel Carrier, as the rest of the column charged after the artillery. He radioed in a recovery unit for the M1. Then he fired the *Centurion*'s jump jets. The nozzles in the 'Mech's legs blasted out streams of glowing plasma, sending the 'Mech in a high arc over the formation, allowing him to take point. At this moment,

Erik Sandoval wanted to kill something. He wanted to kill a lot of somethings.

Duke Aaron Sandoval leaned back in his couch overlooking the DropShip *Victory*'s command center. In the center of the crowded room, a holotable flashed three-dimensional maps of the ongoing battles, the view changing every ten seconds or so as the display rotated through the various hot spots scattered around New Aragon's two continents.

Around the room, a dozen combat controllers sat at individual consoles, relaying orders and situational data to the field commanders. The room buzzed with many voices talking at once, yet it was also strangely calm as each controller focused intently on their own console.

A few supervisory controllers walked the room, observing and stopping to intervene with some detail. Occasionally a runner would come through to hand a document or a cup of coffee to one of the controllers.

From Aaron's seat, he could look down on the controllers and their consoles, as well as on a ring of holodisplays that surrounded his position. He seemed quiet, but nothing escaped his attention.

There was one overarching pattern: The red icons representing House Liao forces were all on the retreat, falling rapidly back to beachhead areas where DropShips waited to spirit them away, or to the spaceport in the capital city of Argos, still nominally under their control.

To a casual observer, the victory for Duke Sandoval's forces seemed decisive and overwhelming. But the Duke fully appreciated how fragile the situation was. As House Liao forces fell back nearly as fast as the Duke's forces could follow, they collapsed their own supply lines in front of them, even as his were stretched ever thinner.

House Liao seemed on the verge of withdrawing from the planet, but Aaron had studied just enough Aikido to know how an attacker's own energy could be turned against him. The greater it was, the more it could be used to the attacker's disadvantage. His troops—his SwordSworn—were pushing hard to keep up with the retreat.

The door to the room slid open with a hiss, and a handsome woman with streaks of gray in her shoulder-length brown hair entered the room. She wore a trim black suit with pale blue piping; loose sleeves framed her carefully manicured hands. Her perfume was musky and, to Aaron's taste, rather unpleasant. Apparently the scent was quite popular among both women and men on New Aragon, but he had heard some of his troops jokingly refer to the scent as "swamp cabbage."

Her makeup was immaculate, but she looked tired. Like many people, she apparently had trouble sleeping under stress, a problem Aaron had never shared. Ostensibly, she had no business in the command center. This was a military matter, not a civilian one. Another military commander might have asked her to leave, especially at such a critical juncture, but Aaron's political sense would not allow it. New Aragon would not always be at war, and Marilou Grogan was the planetary governor, after all.

He repressed a sigh. She remained his major stumbling block to bringing New Aragon under his influence—a possibility that had seemed remote when they'd first arrived. To Aaron's distress, he discovered that Prefect Shun Tao, Prefecture V's supreme military commander, had stationed himself on New Aragon in order to be closer to the line of resistance against House Liao's invasion.

While Shun Tao was in no position to refuse Aaron's aid, he was a fierce Republic loyalist, and justifiably suspicious of the Duke's motives. Aaron was well outside his own Prefecture, meddling without invitation from the local government. From Aaron's standpoint, it was as though he'd been caught with his hand in the candy jar. Their relationship had been chilly, and Aaron knew that his presence on New Aragon would be welcomed only so long as his forces were militarily necessary.

Then there had been an astounding reversal. The official reports said that Shun Tao had been wounded in early fighting. The Prefect had been evacuated from the planet, and simultaneously the Prefecture's forces had begun pulling back, abandoning the world to the House Liao advance. Aaron suspected there was more to Tao's withdrawal than that. Perhaps the man had been recalled, or had simply cracked under the strain.

Though he was too pragmatic to put much stock in such things, Aaron could not help but think of it as divine intervention—a sign that his campaign was meant to succeed. He would repel House Liao's aggression, and bring many new worlds under his banner, ultimately to pledge them to the renewed glory of House Davion, from which his family had drawn power and prestige. The Republic, though a noble experiment, was rapidly proving itself a failed one, and Aaron wanted to be ready when its remains were divided.

But every journey was a series of steps. Divine intervention or not, the traveler could stumble, or even fall. First, he had not only to win New Aragon, but to gain its continued allegiance to his cause. The ongoing battle with Liao would justify the alliance for the foreseeable future, but Aaron hoped for more than that. He could see The Republic crumbling around them, Prefecture V more than most. If the people of New Aragon could not count on their own Prefect and Lord Governor for protection and stability, they would turn elsewhere. Hopefully they would turn to him.

Much could go wrong. Much had gone wrong already. Aaron tried not to let it concern him. His grandmother had been fond of telling him that, "For the wise, each failure teaches fifty lessons, and with each setback comes fifty opportunities." He had always tried to live his life by those words, seeing each day, good or bad, as a springboard to an infinity of bright tomorrows.

This philosophy had led many to criticize him as being a reckless dreamer. He suspected that some even thought him mad. He didn't care. He had noticed that those criticisms became more muted each time his power and status increased.

With Shun Tao out of the picture, a new range of possibilities had opened, and Aaron was quick to position himself in response, establishing relations with the remaining local powers. He'd had no trouble with the Legate, New Aragon's military commander. He'd immediately seen the Duke's forces as the saving grace they were, and he had no desire to try and step into the Prefect's shoes. Aaron had put him in charge of operations on the other continent, and the Prefect willingly placed himself under Aaron's authority, a neat arrangement that kept him out of Aaron's hair.

The Governor, on the other hand, had no real authority over the military, which was Aaron's immediate concern, and yet she was too politically valuable to ignore. Should their forces be successful in this theater, Aaron would later have need of the resources, manufacturing capabilities, money, and public support that were within her sphere of influence.

Yet she remained a cipher to him. The extent of her loyalties to The Republic and her own Lord Governor were unknown, and it was unclear to Aaron whether she would respond better to diplomatic seduction or simple intimidation. Perhaps he would try a little of both.

A narrow aisle separated the raised platform, on which he sat, from the rest of the room. She walked purposefully over to stand in front of him. He glanced down at her and smiled what he knew, from hours of practice in front of a mirror, was a reassuring smile. "Things are going well, Marilou. With luck, we may have the capital firmly back in our control by tomorrow afternoon."

She flinched slightly when he used her first name. She evidently did not enjoy his familiarity, but was in no position to object. It was the sort of subtle display of power and authority that the Duke enjoyed.

"I would prefer to be in the capital myself, instead of cowering here in your DropShip."

He raised an eyebrow. "And do what? Get yourself shot? I don't know if you're more concerned about your people or political appearances, but trust me, neither of them would have been served if you'd stayed in the capital and gotten killed or captured. Nothing will speed the return of New Aragon to normality when this is over than a big parade through the center of Argos to the Capitol Building, celebrating your triumphant return."

"If your intelligence reports are accurate, one wing of the Capitol is a burned-out hulk, and the dome has collapsed. Some celebration that will be."

He grinned. "Then you'll stand on the ruined steps, praise the courage of the New Aragon people, and vow to rebuild, bigger and grander than ever, with a memorial park for the war dead right in front."

She pursed her lips and considered. "You have an answer for everything, don't you, Duke Sandoval? Even the New Aragonians who are dying out there can be stacked up as a neat political platform."

He frowned slightly. "You make me sound cold,

Governor. We fight the best war we can fight, and nothing will bring back those who perish. I'm merely practical. Their sacrifice can be given additional meaning, if it helps to strengthen our Republic in its time of trouble." He studied her face at the mention of The Republic. He saw no reaction; perhaps she wasn't a loyalist after all. He thought perhaps that her first loyalty might be to herself. If so, that was good news. Greed and self-interest were readily exploited. He smiled.

"If I've learned anything in my years, it's that any disaster, no matter how grim, can be given a political spin," he said. "There are no defeats—only opportunities. There are no casualties—only fallen heroes."

"I won't be happy until I have my capital city back, no matter the condition that it's in." She studied the maps, her face showing a great deal more comprehension of the abstract symbols than he would have expected. She blinked, then looked up at him with a slight frown of puzzlement. "Couldn't you have taken the city already? It seems that you have more than enough forces in place in the suburbs."

He nodded. "But if I were to take the city, logically my first action would be to sweep up along the north-south arteries and take the spaceport."

The frown deepened. "And? That seems like a good thing."

"The spaceport is speeding their retreat. If I took it, the forces in the area would be cut off. They'd have to try to retake it and make a fighting retreat to another staging area, or House Liao would have to redeploy forces to support them."

"Still, shouldn't you then be able to crush them?"

"In theory, if everything went perfectly, I could wipe out a good part of their forces and put a dent in their aggressive advance across this part of space."

"Again, this seems a good thing."

"It's a trap. Even if it wasn't intentionally set, it's just as easy to fall into. I have no reserves left to back up such an attack. None." *Or at least none that could be moved without leaving us critically vulnerable somewhere else.* "If things didn't go as planned, or if some of House Liao's retreating forces doubled back to hold Argos, then this entire war could turn in the course of a few hours." He looked into her eyes. "You *do* want your planet back, don't you?"

Her eyes widened as she grasped the situation. "Of course I do. I'm sorry, Lord Governor, for questioning your judgment. Of course I'm grateful that you've come to our aid. With the Prefect injured—perhaps even dead—and our own forces overwhelmed, your unexpected arrival was little short of a miracle—one I'm not inclined to question. I'm just tired, and concerned about my people and my planet."

And about getting your cushy office back as well, I'll wager. Duke Sandoval smiled slightly and turned his attention back to the holotable.

She stood there for a moment. Then, realizing that he was quite through talking, she walked over to the railing where she could observe the holotable.

Aaron relaxed a bit. They were getting close to the issue of what would happen if the battle turned on them—something he didn't want to get into with the Governor. That was, of course, the difference between her and him. This planet was everything to her. To Duke Aaron Sandoval, it was—it had to be—merely one strategically placed chess piece in a game that spanned light-years and many star systems.

Taking advantage of the chaos that had reigned since the collapse of the Hyperpulse Generator—the faster-than-light HPG interstellar communications network—House Liao forces had swept across the outskirts of The Republic, having taken nearly half of one Prefecture, and encroaching on a second. They had succeeded in conquering a handful of worlds and thrown countless others into panic and chaos. Sandoval's game was not to protect any particular world, but to kill House Liao's momentum, bloody their noses, and hope that forces could be rallied to stand against them.

New Aragon was simply the right world at the right spot on the stellar map: a place where the Duke's limited forces would be enough to turn the tide of battle, and where winning that battle might be seen as having real importance. It was The Republic's last remaining sizable military base in the region, the rest having fallen to the Liao invasion. Alone, unprepared, it was powerful enough to put up a good fight, but nothing more. Now, thanks to the Duke's forces, the invaders were being repelled, and the base might now serve as a staging area for a counterattack.

The next twenty-four hours would be critical. By then, New Aragon would either have expelled the bulk of the invaders or would be facing another round of battle that could not be won.

If that reversal came, Aaron had little doubt as to what he would do. While he didn't mind playing the role of gallant savior of New Aragon, the world was merely a pawn. And pawns were—regrettably for them—expendable.

To the Duke's mind, such decisions weren't cruel. Cruelty required malice, and he had none. He was simply concerned with the greater good of House Davion. If New Aragon could be saved and brought under their banner, so be it. Otherwise, it was simply an unfortunate circumstance and not his concern.

Justin Sortek, senior officer of the watch, looked up from his console. "Lord Governor, you asked to be informed when Commander Sandoval's unit returned. They've just entered the bays, and Commander Sandoval is parking his 'Mech."

He nodded and stood. "Very good, Major. I'll be going down to debrief him. You have the watch for the moment. I'll have my earset on in case you need to consult me."

As Aaron stepped down from his platform, he passed near Sortek's console and leaned close to his ear. "Make sure the Governor stays out of trouble while I'm gone. If the fighting heats up, have her escorted out. Any pretense will do."

The Duke slipped into the elevator and watched the blast doors slide closed in front of him. His stomach fluttered slightly as the lift abruptly dropped toward the deck of the 'Mech bay below. He had a rare moment of privacy, and despite his best efforts, he felt the pressure of his situation bearing down on him. He leaned back against the railing, feeling its cool duraplast under his palms. He squeezed tightly, as though he could crush the plastic with his bare hands, trying to drive his doubts and emotions back into the dark recess where he kept them hidden. So much depended on this battle, the decisions he would make, and the ones to which he had long ago committed.

The door slid open, and the sights, sounds, and especially the smells of the 'Mech bay washed over him. He sniffed the odor of hot hydraulic fluid and lubricants, burned powder, rocket exhaust, ozone, sweat, and a slight stink of fear. It mixed with the smells of New Aragon: crushed vegetation, stagnant water, a hint of salt from a nearby marsh.

Once again, the eyes of others were upon him, and Aaron realized he needed to project the proper authority due his rank. He straightened, back stiff, shoulders squared, chin high, doubts forgotten. He stepped through the doors, hearing the chatter of air tools, loudspeakers droning orders, warning buzzers, the whir of electric motors, and the occasional thunderous footsteps of a 'Mech moving across the deck.

Through the open doors he could hear the distant chatter of gunfire and muffled explosions. DropShips were normally kept far behind the front lines, but the current rapid enemy movement had caused Aaron to cut that margin somewhat. The line was moving again, and soon it would again be time for the *Victory* to leapfrog its contingent of troops, armor, and 'Mechs in one five-minute hop.

Despite the powerful equipment moving all around him, Duke Sandoval moved through the 'Mech bay with the confidence and assurance that comes only from experience. Even old hands were known to cower a bit when a fifty-ton BattleMech passed a little too close to them on the bay floor, but the Duke had confidence that, battle weary as they were, his Mech-Warriors would stay within the painted walkways—the lines beyond which men and lesser machines were always subject to trampling. These were, after all, members of the elite Davion Guard, who saw themselves as being among the best-trained and best-equipped MechWarriors in The Republic, perhaps even rivaling the Knights of the Sphere. They prided themselves on their courage, professionalism, discipline and, above all, precision.

Thus, he found himself sighing as he looked at Erik's *Centurion*—its heat sinks still giving off shimmering columns of hot air—which stood in the support structure in front of him.

Commander Erik Sandoval carefully stepped his *Centurion* backwards and heard the clunks and scrapes as various hard-points and support umbilicals lined up on his 'Mech. A final clunk caused his cockpit to lurch, and he heard footsteps scrambling on his hull. He pulled the hatch release.

In a moment it swung open, a blast of cool air entering the sauna-hot cockpit from a duct deliberately positioned above. Erik saw parts of a tech's green coveralls and brown leather gloves reaching in and patting him on his neurohelmet. In response, Erik relaxed the 'Mech just enough to lock it into the support structure, then shut the reactor down.

He pulled off the neurohelmet, flipped the quick-release on his harness, and slumped in the seat, basking in the blast of chilled air from overhead. He looked up at the tech, a pretty woman with a few curls of honey-colored hair peeking from under her ball-cap and ear protectors. She smiled and gave him a thumbs-up.

He smiled back weakly. That was the good thing about techs: as long as their 'Mechs were brought back more-or-less in one piece, they didn't judge. It had not been one of his better days at the office.

He released the harness that held him in the ejection seat, squeezed past it in the narrow confines of the cramped cockpit, and climbed out the narrow hatch in the back of the humanoid *Centurion*'s head. He stepped out onto the metal grid of the catwalk, then turned back to inspect his 'Mech. Erik ran his finger along a series of new dents in the hatch's lock housing, dents that would fit the fist belonging to a suit of Purifier battle armor. He grunted and continued to the end of the catwalk.

From there, he could look down across the *Centurion*'s broad shoulder structure and its massive arms, bristling with lasers on the left and a huge Gauss rifle on the right. Though he couldn't see it from where he stood, he knew the long-range missile rack mounted in the left side of the 'Mech's torso was now empty.

As he watched, techs swarmed over the 'Mech like lime-green ants, throwing open access ports, refilling ammo bays, patching damaged and missing armor.

The *Centurion* would be, if not good as new, at least fully battle-ready again within an hour. It would likely take the pilot a bit longer to recuperate.

A sharp movement on the bay floor ten meters below caught his eye: a group of techs flashing a salute. It took another moment to identify the reason for that salute: Duke Aaron Sandoval, striding purposefully toward the 'Mech. Erik Sandoval-Groell let a little grunt of exasperation slip from his lips.

Short of climbing back in his 'Mech and marching half-loaded back onto the battlefield, there was no avoiding this encounter. Erik ran his fingers through his sweat-soaked hair, feeling the stubble that told him it was past time to shave the sides of his head, then checked the top-knot—a style that he shared with his uncle, and a tradition for Sandoval males. Straightening the thin combat jumpsuit—the maximum a MechWarrior might wear into combat—he squared his shoulders and stepped onto the man-lift platform. It started with a slight lurch, then dropped smoothly to the floor of the bay, decelerating only at the last second, so that he had to bend his knees to absorb the shock.

He stepped onto the painted metal of the bay floor just as Aaron arrived at the lift. Deciding this was no time for family informality, Erik flashed a quick salute.

It was not returned. Instead, the Duke just stood there, his eyes locked on Erik's, a slight frown of disapproval on his square, unconventionally handsome features. Duke Aaron Sandoval was a large man, just short of two meters tall, big boned, muscular, broad shouldered. Erik was by no means a small man himself, but he found Aaron physically intimidating.

Most maddening about dealing with his uncle was Erik's difficulty holding his perceptions in the present. On his own, Erik was a MechWarrior, elite and respected even on his worst day. When he was in Aaron

Sandoval's presence, he felt like a child: unworthy, insecure, *small.*

Erik was twelve when his father sent him to live in Aaron's palace on Prefecture IV's capital world, Tikonov. He'd been resentful at the time, forced to leave his family and home. His father told him it was necessary; Erik was part of the distaff line of the Sandoval family. While his father had some measure of wealth and privilege, Erik's place in the family couldn't offer him power, opportunity, or even citizenship in The Republic, so connections were used, old favors called in, and Erik was placed under Aaron's care.

It was a curious relationship. Though Aaron was actually his cousin, Erik had been instructed by his father to honor him by calling him "Uncle" instead. At first it had seemed odd, even unnatural, but later Erik had become comfortable with it, and eventually came to think of his older relation in those terms.

"Cousin" implied that they were contemporaries, and though there was not a huge span in their ages, that had never been the case. When Erik had arrived, a tall but still gawky teen, Aaron was already well into his missile-quick rise to power and wealth. Erik had been in awe of Aaron's confidence, poise, and sophistication—elusive qualities that Erik strongly desired to emulate and still often struggled to find in himself.

Aaron became as much a father figure to Erik as his own sire, pushing him to develop himself as a scholar and a warrior. The title "Uncle," first offered as a sign of respect, became one of admiration and affection—though that affection was rarely returned. Instead, Aaron treated Erik like a weapon or tool, to be honed and sharpened to a razor's edge, then to be used. As soon as he was old enough, Erik's abilities were put to use, acting as Aaron's surrogate eyes, ears, and hands in dealings across the Inner Sphere.

As Aaron's star ascended, so had Erik's. Erik had been the Duke's aide, military advisor, courier, diplomat, and general. He'd visited dozens of worlds, conferred with leaders at the highest level, and traversed the halls of power countless times. And yet, Duke Aaron Sandoval's approval always seemed to escape Erik's grasp.

Erik sensed that this day wasn't going to be any different.

The Duke's left eyebrow rose quizzically. "I understand you nearly lost another 'Mech today."

Erik tried to hide his reaction, but he could feel his face redden. Months earlier, as the result of an act of family treachery, Erik had lost a war, most of the forces under his command, his personal 'Mech, and the planet of Mara. Forgiveness had been a long time coming, and annoyingly, though Aaron seemed to be over the rest of it, he never let Erik forget the loss of his 'Mech.

He'd once told Erik of some ancients—the Romans, or the Greeks perhaps—who had a saying: "Return with your shield, or upon it." He'd had to explain to Erik that during that time, a man's shield would be used as a stretcher on which to carry his dead body home from battle. It struck Erik as a foolish—as well as inappropriate—comparison, as his 'Mech had been hijacked rather than taken in combat. Still, the memory of the incident filled Erik with shame.

"There was a capture attempt, yes. We repelled it quite easily. My 'Mech was never in any real danger."

"There were losses," said the Duke. "You let yourself be led into a trap."

Erik wondered how Aaron already knew the details of the encounter. Had the battle been observed by a scout, or did he have a spy in Erik's patrol, reporting back on some secret communications channel? It would be typical of "Uncle," who, though he trusted

Erik more than almost anyone, didn't trust him very much at all.

"I would have thought," Erik replied dryly, "that you'd have better things to do than keep tabs on my every move, Uncle. I've heard there's a war on."

The corner of Aaron's mouth twitched upward for just a moment, a tiny flinch that anyone else would likely have missed. Even Erik couldn't be sure if the suppressed smile was one of amusement or annoyance.

"Walk with me," Aaron said, spinning on the ball of his foot and heading back toward the elevator to the crew decks. Erik double-timed until he was walking at his uncle's side. "Yours wasn't the only 'Mech they tried to take today, or the only guerilla-style ambush set. There were half a dozen similar incidents."

Erik's eyebrows rose. *Damn you, Aaron—why didn't you say that to start with?* "That's not good," he finally said aloud.

Aaron stopped in front of the lift doors and pushed the call button. He turned to look at Erik. "On the contrary, it's encouraging news. I believe that if House Liao were sending reinforcements for a counteroffensive, they wouldn't be taking such reckless chances to shore up their forces. I hate to be an optimist about such things, but I think we finally have them. New Aragon will be ours, with most of her military and production assets intact."

Despite his mood, Erik smiled. The lift opened and they stepped in. "That's excellent, then. We were due for a victory."

But Aaron's face remained grim. "It's too late. Our entire offensive at this point is mainly bluff and bluster. While the Prefecture's forces won't hinder us, we can't count on them for assistance, either. The Lord Governor has pulled them all back to Liao and a few nearby worlds, effectively ceding control of the rest of Prefecture V to anyone who can take it. I'd prefer it to be the SwordSworn rather than House Liao, but right now our position is tenuous.

"We have no reinforcements. Parts, fuel, and supplies are low and our troops are exhausted. If the damned Cappies managed to push back at all, we wouldn't last a week. Fortunately, they don't seem to know that." He pushed the button that would take them to officers' country. The elevator started up with a gentle whoosh of air.

The Duke turned back to Erik. "That's why I'm leaving."

"Leaving? When? To where?"

"Immediately. The flagship is in orbit, and a shuttle is arriving within the hour to take me there. There's a waiting JumpShip charging its drive right now, so I'll be able to jump almost as soon as we link up. I'm going to New Canton, to talk with that fool Jose Sebhat. He's convinced his Lord Governor that they can avoid conflict with House Liao by ceding territory. It's idiocy. You don't hold a wild dog at bay by feeding it your fingers. If I could convince him of that, and make a mutual-defense pact with Prefecture VI, it could change everything."

Erik had met Sebhat, Prefect of Prefecture VI, several years before at a Republic summit. At the time, Erik had thought him a fainthearted man to hold a post of such military importance. Now his instincts were being verified.

"Frankly," continued Aaron, "New Canton's control over their Prefecture's worlds isn't much better than here. I'm not even entirely sure they're worth the bother. But if I can at least bring in the Prefect's personal forces to our cause, and stop them from handing Liao gifts on a platter, that will be something."

The doors of the lift opened, and they stepped out into officers' country, where Aaron and Erik were both quartered. In the hallway beyond, a steward was cleaning a bulkhead, the smell of disinfectant strong in the air. Aaron flashed him a silent look that told him he wasn't wanted here. The steward saluted, even as he scurried for the lift, slipping through the doors just before they closed.

"Worse," continued Aaron, "every world House Liao takes without a fight frees up more forces to continue their offensive into Republic space. They've been allowed to take far too many worlds, to win too many battles already. They have momentum on their side, and that's a difficult thing to resist, not only militarily, but in terms of public perception. Battles can be won and lost in the hearts of the people. If a planet believes that capture by the Cappies is inevitable, then that planet is already lost to us.

"We can't win alone, and we wouldn't want to if we could. Both as a condition of victory, and as part of my long-term goals, I need to build a coalition of worlds fighting under our banner. I'm starting with New Canton in hopes that we can bring many worlds into our fold with one agreement—but if that fails, there are many worlds here in Prefecture V that might answer our call."

They entered Aaron's quarters. His valet, Deena Onan, greeted them at the door, taking Aaron's officer's jacket and handing him the tailored civilian tunic that he preferred.

Erik watched as she disappeared into the adjacent bedroom with the jacket. The quarters were tiny and rather plain by the Duke's usual standards, even though they were considered large for a military DropShip. The fortunate part about their relatively small size was that Deena would have to either work very hard to stay out of sight, leave outright, or simply go about her business where Erik could watch her. He sighed inwardly. Deena was a lovely woman: tall, athletic yet shapely, with waves of auburn hair that cascaded loosely over her shoulders. Despite his long-standing interest, she seemed oblivious to all Erik's overtures toward her. Still, he could look and dream.

Aaron settled into the combination easy chair/acceleration couch bolted into the corner of the little sitting room. There were two other chairs just like it in the room, and a small folding chair in front of a writing desk; Erik wasn't invited to sit down, and therefore remained standing.

Deena passed through the room, giving Erik a whiff of her musky perfume. She dropped several orange courier folders full of documents on the desk before vanishing again. The papers were likely dispatches from the Duke's extensive personal and military empire, a power base that had become increasingly hard to manage after the failure of the HPG interstellar communications network. Now business, war, and diplomacy all had to be carried out in person, by long-delayed courier dispatches, or through surrogates. Everything had changed.

"I'm leaving you in charge," Aaron said. "Hopefully, all you're looking at is mopping up, making sure that the local government—and their allegiance to us—is solid, then preparing our forces for the next counteroffensive."

Aaron looked at Erik, something obviously unsaid.

Deena appeared in the bedroom doorway again. She glanced at Aaron, but he did nothing to indicate that she should leave. She was one of the few people on his staff who had his absolute trust in matters of security.

Aaron took a deep breath, then continued. "If I'm wrong about the situation, if there is any sign of a counterattack, you're to withdraw our forces immediately. Minimize our casualities and losses at all cost."

"We could—"

Aaron held up a finger immediately to silence him. "You will do nothing. If this planet falls, it falls, and we won't lose one of our boys or girls unnecessarily in its defense. We can't afford to. I am trusting you, Erik, to follow my orders without hesitation. Understood?"

Erik clenched his jaw, but nodded.

"Very good, then. Get down to the command center and prepare the ship to jump forward with the lines as soon as my shuttle is away." He looked at Erik for a moment. "Go."

Without another word, Erik slipped past Deena and out into the hallway. He heard the security door lock behind him. He stood there for a moment, his stomach in knots. *He's trusting me? Well, the people of New Aragon are trusting us, too, and God willing, they'll never know how ready we were to abandon them.*

2

DUKE AARON SANDOVAL SEEKS INTER-PREFECTURE PACT—New Aragon. Even as his troops mop up after a stunning reversal against House Liao forces, Duke Aaron Sandoval, Lord Governor of Prefecture IV, has announced that he will proceed to New Canton and seek a pact for the mutual protection of all Republic territories, including Prefecture V, against the Capellan Confederation incursion.

Responding to critics who state that the Duke is "out of his jurisdiction" in bringing his forces deep into Prefecture V, he responded, "Neither I nor the leaders of Prefecture VI can ignore the chaos just across our borders in Prefecture V. The unprovoked and unjustified attacks by House Liao against our territories cannot be ignored, nor can we allow outmoded notions of Prefecture sovereignty or protocol to determine how, and especially where, we choose to act."

—AP Courier News Services

Lord Governor's Palace
Merrick City, New Canton
Prefecture VI, The Republic
9 October 3134

Duke Aaron Sandoval sat quietly in the soft leather of the meeting room chair, his fingers wrapped around the polished mahogany of the chair's arms, their ivory inlays cool against his skin. The table was carved mahogany as well, the top inset with thick slabs of green-tinted glass. At the far end of the table sat General

Divos Sebhat, Legate of New Canton, the focus of the Duke's attention and his quiet ire.

Sebhat was a tall man, trim without really looking fit, his head shaved and polished under his wide cap. He wore a green woolen uniform that matched the cap, lushly decorated with gold buttons and cording, his chest layered with enough unearned ribbons and medals to stop a cannon shell. A nickel-plated automatic handgun was holstered at his side—a decorative touch. Despite superficial appearances, Sebhat was a peacetime general, more politician than warrior—a man who preferred to settle disputes with talk, or treachery, rather than battle.

In that, Aaron could not fault him, as it mirrored his own preferred methods. But unlike Aaron, Sebhat had never backed up his words with weapons. He lacked the skills of a true warrior. For someone who wore any uniform, much less the theatrical spectacle Sebhat wore, Aaron found that unforgivable.

Still, for over a week, since his arrival on New Canton, Aaron had treated Sebhat with the utmost respect and decorum, even as their negotiations dragged on, producing no real results. Every day Aaron left the guest quarters in the palace's north wing and met Sebhat at the oak-covered blast doors that protected the conference room. And every day they sat across the table and exchanged empty proposals that never quite meshed.

It had become torture. Aaron knew every line of Sebhat's face, the grating and obviously false smile he often wore, the way his left eye twitched when he was bored, which in Aaron's presence seemed to be often.

Aaron also knew every detail of the room. He had memorized the geometric pattern woven into the deep carpeting, studied each of the paintings that surrounded the room: the formal portraits of past Lord

Governors and Prefects and the large impressionistic battle scene that hung behind Sebhat's chair—done in dark blue, black, orange, and gold—featuring a hundred-ton *Atlas* 'Mech, guns blazing as one mighty foot crushed the torso of a fallen *Panther*.

He'd seen the Prefecture's Lord Governor, Harri Golan, only once, at the ceremony marking the Duke's arrival at Capital Spaceport. There had been a brief speech, a cool handshake, a few empty pleasantries, and then the Lord Governor was in his motorcade and gone. If he was even in the palace where the meetings were taking place, Aaron had seen no sign of him. He was uncertain if Sebhat was the real power behind the throne—wondering if he had been passed off to an underling with no authority to negotiate. In any case, no progress was being made on the negotiations, and the precious time Aaron needed to build his coalition was slipping away.

Every morning had been the same.

Except this one.

Aaron's stomach knotted slightly, as he realized this day would be much different.

It was the little things that made Aaron uneasy. The expected silver coffee and tea service was absent, as was the tray of colorful yet bland sweet-cakes normally set out on the sideboard under a great mirror. The secretary, who usually sat at a small table in the corner taking notes into a computer pad, was also missing, replaced by two ceremonial guards who stood at attention behind Sebhat, ivory-colored rifles clenched in their white-gloved hands.

But the thing that was most disturbing of all, the thing that had placed the knot in his stomach, was the little self-satisfied smirk on Sebhat's face. It was a smirk he'd only seen hinted at before—a small, private expression quickly quelled, but now openly and brazenly displayed. Sebhat no longer cared what Aaron thought of him—there would be no more pretense of talk.

Aaron regretted allowing himself to be convinced that the palace security would protect him, that his usual full retinue was neither necessary nor welcome. It was a chip played in the cause of diplomacy, and obviously a misstep on his part.

Aaron sensed a movement behind him, as someone stepped close to the right of his chair. He glanced up to see the muscular figure of Ulysses Paxton, his personal bodyguard and chief of security—at least Aaron had insisted that Ulysses be permitted to stay as a driver. Aaron drew some comfort in his presence. The bodyguard was very good at what he did, and Aaron wondered if he might have use of his skills very soon.

"There will be no talks today," announced Sebhat, unable to hide the glee in his voice. "There will be no talks at all."

Like a skilled actor, Aaron kept absolute control of his public self—every gesture, every expression. He leaned back, giving the appearance of being calm, and placed the fingertips of both hands together in front of him. He waited. Sebhat smiled. Obviously, Aaron was expected to make the next move.

"May I ask why?"

"We will not be joining your coalition, if indeed any such entity comes to pass, as Lord Governor Golan has just signed a nonaggression pact with House Liao."

Sebhat seemed startled when Aaron began to laugh. Not a polite chuckle, but an honest belly laugh that had him slapping his thigh. A minute or more passed before the laughter faded, and Aaron wiped a bit of moisture from his right eye. "A nonaggression pact? And what concessions did you make in order to secure this valuable piece of paper?"

Sebhat's smile was gone. He looked down his nose

at Aaron, seeming, if anything, slightly offended. "There were no concessions."

Aaron laughed again, but in a more controlled manner this time. "House Liao agreed to bypass your fat, juicy, under-defended little Prefecture out of the goodness of their hearts? I don't believe for a second they'd even *pretend* to make such an agreement without some major tribute thrown their way.

"What was it? Bases on New Canton? Maybe"—he grinned in a manner calculated to provoke—"the Lord Governor's virgin daughter?"

"That's enough." Sebhat was close to shouting as he stood, pushing his heavy chair back so that it almost toppled over. His hands flared out at his sides, like a fictional frontiersman reaching for his pistols. Aaron wondered if the nickel-plated monstrosity of an automatic in his holster was even loaded, and if Sebhat could hit the broad side of a DropShip if it was.

"I was just asking," said Aaron, his voice even.

Sebhat's eye twitched. He let out a deep breath, air whistling through his nose. "If you must know, the Lord Governor has gifted the Capellans with the worlds of Second Try and Yunnah, a small concession to avoid open warfare on the capital world."

Aaron snorted. "If you met a wolf, Sebhat, would you try to placate him by hacking off pieces of your own flesh? You're only delaying the inevitable, and saving Chancellor Daoshen the trouble of crushing your inferior forces before rolling past. They'll be back, and you'll be licking the Chancellor's boots by December."

"You're a fine one to talk, Sandoval. House Liao has won battle after battle, world after world. You expect us to rally round the banner of House Davion, or whoever you *really* serve, after one victory?"

Aaron maintained his best poker face when Sebhat

mentioned House Davion, but he was surprised. If Sebhat knew, or even suspected, that Aaron was no longer loyal to The Republic, so might others. It was inevitable that it would eventually become common knowledge, but Aaron had hoped to control that. Perhaps he had waited too long.

Sebhat sneered. "You're a fool, Sandoval. You're finished, and you don't even know it yet." He drew himself up to his full height, tugging at his uniform coat to straighten it. "You have one hour's safe passage to have your DropShip clear of New Canton soil. After that time, you will be considered an unwelcome hostile and held for collection by House Liao."

It was Aaron's turn to look indignant. He stood and leaned forward on the table with both hands, feeling a slight slick of sweat between his palms and the cool glass. "That's barely time to get through traffic to the spaceport, much less pack."

"One hour. This is more courtesy than you deserve. Your DropShip has already been notified to make ready for takeoff upon your arrival."

The Duke felt Paxton's powerful hand on his shoulder. "My Lord, we should leave."

Aaron turned and nodded to his bodyguard, then glanced back at Sebhat. "You're the Capellans' lapdog now, Sebhat. I hope they at least feed you well."

Paxton's hand tightened slightly, giving the distinct impression that its full force could break bones. *"My Lord."*

"Fifty-nine minutes, Sandoval."

Aaron allowed Paxton to push him toward the door. He noticed that Paxton shielded him with his body from behind, then at the moment they reached the door, brushed past him to move through first. Suddenly clarity returned, and he remembered why he'd hired Paxton, and why he dreaded the thought of losing such a skilled protector.

They rushed down the palace's corridors, Aaron close to the wall, Paxton looming over him like an umbrella, whispering instructions into a hidden microphone in his sleeve, watching every doorway and potential hiding place with professional suspicion.

Aaron felt himself relax, becoming no more than a parcel in Paxton's capable care. Whatever happened next, it was out of his hands. That realization freed part of his mind to review those last moments in the meeting room.

He cursed his own weakness. He'd allowed emotion to get the best of him, lost control in his desire to get the last word. It was beneath him to covet such a meaningless gesture. Sebhat's day would come very soon, he knew. He'd make sure of it.

They turned a corner, and Deena Onan fell in with them, a small leather overnight bag clutched in her hands. Doubtless she had scooped up a few of his personal belongings from the palace guest suite, those items with some sentimental or historic value that could not easily be replaced. To Aaron's recollection, he had arrived at the palace with two steamer trunks, four suitcases, and probably a half-dozen smaller cases and portable items, not counting Onan's or Paxton's personal luggage. He added those items to the mental ledger sheet that he was tallying against New Canton.

Paxton pushed him firmly through the two-story lobby attached to the side entrance. A ground limousine waited outside. Paxton pushed Aaron against a door pillar before stepping outside briefly to assess the situation. Then he pulled them out into the open air. Aaron could smell apple blossoms and hear motor traffic beyond the palace walls. The sky was a cloudless blue-green, and New Canton's largest moon was a ghostly crescent just above the gates.

Paxton put his hand on Aaron's head, pushing him down into the car. Paxton was next, holding Deena's hand as he pulled her in after him. She slipped into the seat next to Aaron, and Paxton lighted—he wasn't settled enough to call it sitting—on the jump seat across from Aaron. He half-turned and tapped on the ferro-glass that separated them from the driver. The ground car lurched out of the portico with a screech of rubber, whipped up the curved drive, and rushed through the gates while they were still opening.

The car merged into heavy morning traffic, moving rapidly, but boxed in on all sides. Paxton glanced at his watch, then gestured at the seat belts. "Fasten yourselves in. This could get exciting."

Brakes squealed as they cut off another car getting on the expressway. There was a crunch and the sound of breaking glass behind them as the swerving car struck another in the next lane. Their limousine smoothly accelerated away from the accident.

"Do tell," said Aaron.

The glacial lake was breathtakingly beautiful, surrounded by towering walls of striated rock as raw and jagged as though they had been thrown out of the ground only yesterday. The water was still and dark— a mirror that reflected the cloudless sky, making the 'Mech-sized icebergs look as if they were floating in air.

Erik Sandoval was not here to sightsee. Recon patrols had found fresh 'Mech tracks in the high mountain valley below here. There was reason to believe a few isolated Capellan units, separated from their column during the previous day's fighting in the pass a thousand feet below them, had retreated into this frigid wasteland.

Erik would have loved to appreciate the lake for its own sake, and perhaps someday he'd return here for just that reason. But today he saw the lake only in strategic terms: a potential heat sink, a place where he could plant his 'Mech and empty his weapons with no fear of overheating.

Out in front of him, a *Spider* trotted, wings glinting in the sun, jump jets occasionally flaring just long enough for it to bounce over a stream or crevasse. To his right and left, slightly behind him, a pair of *Hatchetmen,* their mighty namesake in time with their steps, paced his *Centurion.* In his rear camera, he could see a recently captured *Thor* bouncing over the caramel-colored rocks, its shoulder-mounted missile canister ready to back them up with ranged fire.

It was exciting to have the rare opportunity to field a brace of 'Mechs, leaving their conventional forces to hold rearward positions. Erik could almost imagine they were in the glory days before The Republic, and the flexibility of the 'Mechs, unencumbered by conventional forces, made it easier to do what had to be done.

Though final victory had been slow in coming, the last stronghold of House Liao on New Aragon had been broken. All that was left were scattered pockets of resistance, isolated forces that had to be eliminated before Erik's forces could move on. He knew that was the real strategy here: a delaying action. It had worked for a while, but they were almost done.

"Commander! Twelve o'clock high!"

The voice in his headset was Angie Chelsy, commander of the Ghost Legion, pilot of the *Hatchetman* to his right.

He raised his eyes to find himself looking right down the tubes of a seventy-five-ton *Tundra Wolf*'s blazing jump jets.

Erik staggered his *Centurion* to the side so rapidly that he nearly toppled into the lake, the gyros whining as the 'Mech struggled to stay upright. The *Tundra Wolf* landed with a thunderous report, almost within

'Mech-arm's reach. Erik backpedaled, his brain running as fast as a computer to assess the situation.

The *Tundra Wolf* was primarily a long-range fighter with terrible heat efficiency—not the sort of 'Mech that wanted to be caught alone. The heat issue explained why the pilot had sought out mountain lakes. But why hadn't he attacked from a distance?

The answer had to be that he was low on missiles, perhaps even out. That left him with a good suite of lasers, but not enough to deal with a brace of 'Mechs. He had jumped to the high walls surrounding the lake, hoping to take out Erik with his "death from above" attack. Then he could wade into the lake and put his lasers to work on the rest, perhaps scatter them.

It hadn't worked. What, Erik wondered, was plan B?

He smiled grimly. There was no plan B. It was an act of desperation by an outgunned 'Mech. Though the *Tundra Wolf*'s original Clan-designed weapons had no minimum range, Erik knew that in many of that model, if not most, those weapons had been replaced for lack of parts. Assuming this was the case, Erik was now inside his enemy's minimum firing range. It was a calculated risk, but a good one.

Erik spun his 'Mech's torso, bringing his own light Gauss rifle to bear. Even at this range, it wouldn't do much against the heavily armored *'Wolf* except keep him off balance.

That was the point. The two *Hatchetmen* moved in from either side, their massive weapons raised high. They crashed into the *'Wolf* in a shower of sparks; their deadly blades fell again and again, sending chunks of armor flying in all directions. Erik stepped in close to join the fray. He smashed his 'Mech's fist into the *'Wolf*'s already mangled left arm. It ripped off with a shriek and tumbled into a snow bank, trailing sparks.

Past the 'Wolf, Erik could see the Thor in the distance, lining up for a shot. He shouted, "Clear!"

All three of his 'Mechs stepped back at once, and for a moment the Tundra Wolf stood alone. Then a pair of missiles from the Thor ripped into its back, and pulse lasers from the Spider raked across its front armor and cockpit. There was a flash of escaping plasma before the 'Wolf's damaged reactor detonated its remaining ammunition.

Erik instinctively turned his cockpit away as pieces of the shattered 'Mech slammed into his right-side armor. He heard Angie's victory whoop in his headphones as her 'Mech trotted in front of him, hatchet held high, shreds of armor still dangling from the top of its blade. "Look at that baby burn!"

He turned back to see the shattered hulk of the defeated 'Mech, engulfed in flames and glowing plasma.

"One down," she said, "and none to go."

Erik nodded to himself. They hadn't seen any other tracks in hours. "That's a good day's work, people. Let's get back to base." He pushed his throttle to CRUISE, set a way point for their waiting DropShip, and settled back to enjoy the ride. He surveyed his damage display. The explosion had cost him some armor, and he'd damaged his 'Mech's left leg slightly avoiding the Tundra Wolf's attack, but nothing more serious.

Angie's Hatchetman fell in at his left shoulder. "Well fought, Commander. It took courage to go toe-to-toe with the 'Wolf the way you did. Or to time the Thor's attack as you did."

"It was nothing, really."

"You take risks, Commander. Not that you're foolhardy—far from it. But you have a warrior's heart, and you don't lead from the rear. I appreciate it. The troops who serve under you appreciate it. I wanted you to know that."

"Thank you, Angie. That means a lot, perhaps com-

ing from you more than one of the Davion Guard."
Erik liked Angie. Her Ghost Legion was full of tena-
cious fighters whose loyalty to the Duke was far more
tenuous than the Davion Guards Erik more often
fought alongside.

The Ghost Legionnaires said what was on their
minds, Angie most of all. Erik found it refreshing.
"Angie, go to a private channel." He switched channels and activated a scrambler to keep their conversa-
tion private.

"What's up, Commander?"

"This is warrior to warrior. Call me Erik."

"Erik, then. What's up?"

He took a deep breath, held it for a moment while
he thought, then let it out slowly through his nose.
"What do you think of my uncle?"

"The Duke? That's a very loaded question, you
know. You could get a girl in a lot of trouble."

"This is just between us. Soldier to soldier—what
do you think?"

She chuckled. "I'm not sure how well I know him.
My direct contact with the Duke has been brief and
rather—intense."

Something about the way she said that made Erik
wonder if he'd put his trust in the wrong person, but
she quickly allayed that fear.

"In some ways, I don't think I know him at all,
and yet, I probably know him much better than you
realized." She chuckled again. "You don't have to
worry, Commander; I said this was between us, and
no matter what might happen in the future, it will
remain that way.

"Actually, when you ask what I think of the Duke,
I have to ask *which* Duke. He's like a fine diamond,
different from every angle, in every light. It's a quality
he shares with other members of the Sandoval
family."

"What do you mean?"

"I hope this isn't too impertinent, Commander, but you aren't at your best around him, and he seems to be at his worst around you. You're a warrior, a leader, a man of many talents, yet the Duke fails to treat you with the respect that you deserve. The troops speak of it in whispers.

"Don't get me wrong. They're loyal to the Duke, of course. He's a dynamic leader, and he treats us well. But those who have served with you are loyal to you, too. When they see the Duke dressing you down like a buck private, it distresses them. It's as though he's belittling them personally."

Then it isn't just me. Nor is it just a personal matter. It's hurting troop morale. Yet still Erik felt the need to apologize for Aaron. "The Duke holds me to very high standards."

"He holds everybody to high standards, but most people under his command get the carrot. You just get the stick. My opinion."

"I'm not just somebody under his command. I'm a Sandoval."

"That's exactly the problem, Commander. You're both Sandovals, and your conflict is a family conflict. But it's spilled over into your professional conduct. If you had a junior officer whose family problems intruded into their battlefield performance, would you allow it to continue?"

"No, of course not. I'd insist that they resolve it, keep it outside their duty hours, or I'd reassign them."

"Well, there you go."

"It's not that simple."

"It never is."

"I can't 'reassign' my uncle, and I can't resolve this problem, either."

"But you reassign yourself every chance you get."

He considered. It was true, he'd long welcomed assignments that took him out of his uncle's direct sphere of influence, spending as much time away from the capital on Tikonov as possible. He'd been avoiding confrontation with the Duke. And when he couldn't avoid it—

"I've allowed this to go on, haven't I?"

"As I said, you're not at your best around him, either." She laughed. "Look, the Sandovals are big players—money, power, position in The Republic, ties to the Davion crown and all that. But family loyalty doesn't seem to be a strong suit. Seems like the Sandovals spend more time fighting each other than they do fighting their enemies. And it seems to me that he shouldn't expect your loyalty just because you have the same last name."

"But I *am* loyal. He's done a lot for me over the years."

"From what I can see, you've done a lot for him, too. Family is irrelevant to that. You deserve respect for your accomplishments. Hell, Erik, you're not just an officer or a noble, you're a *MechWarrior*. We sit in the high seat. People should give us respect. Even dukes. Even uncles."

She was silent for a minute. Finally, she said, "Why do you even care what he thinks, Erik? What is he to you?"

Erik licked his lips. "I don't know. He practically raised me, or more exactly, I was raised in his house. He helped earn my citizenship, taught me to be a man, how to carry myself like a noble."

"So you owe him? Fair enough, but what about you? What do *you* want? Power? Riches? Glory? A title of your own?"

Erik sighed. "All of that, and none of it. What I really want. . . . I-I want to be my own man. I want to steer my own destiny. That's all, really."

Angie chuckled. "I'll drink to that."

*   *   *

"Morning, Clete." The guard at the spaceport maintenance facility barely looked at Cletus Wyoming's security pass as she waved it under the scanner and handed it back to him. Why should she? It was just the same as it had been, five days a week, for the last three years.

It was strange, he thought, as he hung the ID lanyard back around his neck, that it was the last time he'd ever go through this little ritual. Cletus Wyoming was exactly one day away from a very early, and rich, retirement.

It had been no surprise when, an hour before, a text message calling him in to work early had arrived on his 'puter. He'd been sitting at the kitchen table in his small apartment, dressed and waiting impatiently for it, since before dawn.

The people who had hired him had told him when he'd be called, where he'd be going, what he'd be doing. They'd given him the lunchbox that he carried in his left hand, externally identical to the one he'd carried to work every day of those three years. Internally it was the same too, except for the fake vacuum bottle packed with a powerful high-explosive charge. A built-in detonator could be armed by twisting the cap.

As Clete walked across the asphalt toward the waiting maintenance truck, he knew it would be taking him to the Union-class DropShip looming on the pad a mile beyond the maintenance building. He knew exactly what last-minute adjustment would be his excuse for going aboard, and he knew just how he'd route himself through the ship's engineering compartments to pass near the fuel-expansion couplings. He knew precisely where he'd plant the bomb from his lunch kit—a place that would guarantee a secondary fuel explosion that would cripple the ship, if not destroy it outright.

He jumped into the passenger seat of the electric truck and nodded at the driver. The truck accelerated quickly down into a service tunnel leading to the *Union*'s pad. They'd be there in less than two minutes. He would be in and out in five.

Then Clete would feel a flu bug coming on—one that would require him to leave early and never come back. When thirty-five hundred tons of fully loaded DropShip came crashing back down, he didn't want to be anywhere close by, and he certainly didn't want to be anywhere he could be found.

The greenish lights of the tunnel flashed past, and the whir of the truck's motors bounced off the walls. The air was pungent with oil, paint, and solvents. Most days it smelled like hell. This morning, it smelled like perfume.

Clete pulled the brim of his cap down over his eyes and leaned back in his seat. "Drive faster," he said.

3

This is the emergency hatch release. This is the harness quick-release. Most importantly, this is the eject lever. They'll be different in every 'Mech cockpit, so get to know where yours are and how to use them.

Know how to find and use them automatically, in smoke or darkness or underwater. Know how to find and use them with the noise of combat blasting through your earphones. Know how to find and use them with either hand, just in case one gets blown off.

Most of all, know when to ignore your pride and use them. All warriors eventually find themselves on the losing side of a battle, where they can do nothing more for anyone but themselves, and their cockpits suddenly stop being the safest places on the battlefield.

That's the time to get out. No MechWarrior ever won a battle by standing still and getting hacked to pieces with his dead 'Mech.
—"Flight to Victory," MechWarrior Training Video #13

Capital Spaceport
Merrick City, New Canton
Prefecture VI, The Republic
9 October 3134

The limousine spent five agonizing minutes at the spaceport gate, while a pair of scowling, black-uniformed security guards with automatic rifles scrutinized their paperwork. Crosstown traffic had been heavy, as expected, and time was short. It galled Aaron to run like a scared rabbit, but he'd be a fool to put himself in danger over false pride. He sensed the Prefect was up to something, and Aaron didn't want to give those intentions even a hint of legitimacy by overstaying his welcome.

Ulysses Paxton was listening to his headphone. He turned to Aaron. "They just had somebody do a last-second swap-out of a balky guidance module, but they're fueled, preflighted, and ready to lift off as soon as we're aboard."

One of the guards finally passed back their clearances. "This looks to be in order. Have a nice trip."

Paxton nearly growled as he snatched the papers back and signaled the driver to move on. The tires squealed as they headed across the apron toward their waiting DropShip. It was a *Union*-class, an eighty-meter-plus sphere sitting on four massive landing legs. She wasn't a luxury craft—her quarters small and unpleasant for such an important passenger—but her hull was heavily armored, and weapons bristled from turrets around her waist and on her nose. Huge sliding doors covered two loaded 'Mech bays, including the Duke's personal 'Mech, and a third bay that could hold a pair of escort fighters.

Once aboard, they would be well protected, which was why the last kilometer seemed to take forever. At the base of the ship, a squad of Davion Guards in winged Kage battle armor covered their approach. The car slid to a stop, and the troops surrounded the door. Paxton pushed Aaron and Deena out of the car and into the protective circle, then into the elevator that lifted them into the belly of the ship.

The driver of the car, one of Paxton's men, followed, climbing into the lift with them. The car was abandoned on the vast concrete blast-deflector beneath the ship's immense fusion thrusters. That made Aaron grin. The car had been provided for them by the New Canton government. Knowing it would be blasted into wreckage didn't do much to balance the scales, but it made him feel better.

He lost sight of the car as the lift ascended into the ship and continued up another forty meters. It passed through the smaller 'Mech bay where his personal gold-and-white *Black Hawk* was stored. It quickly passed through the roof of the bay and stopped on the crew deck above. Paxton pushed them out of the car and into a nearby emergency crash-couch. There would be no time to get to the Duke's quarters.

Paxton didn't seat himself. He simply locked his legs, feet apart, and held onto an overhead support with one muscular arm. He lifted his other arm and barked into his sleeve. "The Duke is secure."

The captain's answering voice came from an overhead speaker, as well as Paxton's hidden earphone. "Davion Guards are aboard and secure. Hatches sealed. Core preheat cycle is complete. Ready to lift off."

"Lift off," said Paxton.

The deck under their feet shuddered and began to vibrate. There was the whine of turbo-pumps spooling up, followed by a rumble, like a vast waterfall, then a clap of thunder as the huge engines reached temperatures as hot as hellfire. Plasma erupted from the engine bells, and the huge craft began to move.

Aaron wondered about the car. Did it melt? Was it vaporized? Pulverized? Or just tossed away like a leaf in a gale? He wished he could have seen it.

Acceleration pushed them gently into their seats as the ship lifted off. Paxton's knees flexed slightly with the G-forces, and he seemed intently focused on the sounds of the launch.

The engines dulled to a roar as they gained altitude, the sound no longer echoing back from the ground to pound against their armored hull. After a few seconds, the deck groaned again, then shuddered as the landing legs retracted into the ship's lower skirt.

Thirty meters below them and fifty meters over in the direction of the number two landing leg, an accelerometer in the detonator of Clete Wyoming's "retirement-fund" triggered a solid-state relay. A timer began, its settings based on the typical launch profile of a *Union*-class DropShip and the designated departure pattern of the Capital Spaceport.

The ship climbed out at 1.5 gravities, moving eastward over the snow-white dunes of the shoreline and the Gulf of Emeralds beyond. By now, its course would have taken it five kilometers out to sea, to an altitude of six thousand feet.

That was far enough. That was high enough.

It would be a darned shame about the fish, though.

The bomb exploded.

The explosion tossed Aaron painfully against his harness. The whole compartment seemed to buckle around them, decking and bulkheads rippling like cardboard.

Paxton was tossed off his feet and, for a moment, hung by his hands from the overhead support. Aaron watched with horror as the angle of Paxton's body shifted dramatically, a human plumb bob defining a "down" that changed moment by moment.

It was like being in a building that was slowly falling over on its side.

There was another explosion, louder than the first, and something ripped through their compartment. Aaron looked over to see the car driver slump over in his seat. His upper harness was severed by a wrist-thick shaft of steel that had been driven through the back of his seat and straight through his chest. Aaron watched the light of life fade from his eyes, his expression not one of pain or fear, but surprise.

Aaron felt . . . nothing. Or perhaps a perverse kind of relief, releasing the tension that had been building since his confrontation with Sebhat back at the palace. There was no more waiting. Now what happened would happen.

"All hands to crash stations," the captain's voice came, muted, from down the corridor, the speaker over their head having been silenced. "We've lost the turbopumps on the number six thruster. Number five has shut down from secondary damage!"

The sound of the motors changed. Aaron's stomach lurched as though he were in a falling elevator.

"Shutting down two and three to balance thrust!" The falling slowed, and the floor seemed to pitch back toward level.

Aaron barely was aware, lost in a fugue state. It was the same feeling he'd had when he committed himself to battle, when the cockpit of his 'Mech sealed and the warrior took over for the diplomat.

He saw Deena's face, white with fear. He'd seen her confront mortal danger before without flinching, but the circumstances had been different, more under her control. This was different.

He smiled at her. How could he make her understand? In danger there was clarity. These were the moments when one was most alive, facing death, fighting fate for every moment of life.

He glanced over at Paxton, thinking he at least would understand, but Paxton was looking around like a caged animal. This was not the kind of threat he could fight. He could protect his Duke against bullets, but not gravity. He looked like a man who had just realized he was about to fail.

Deena looked at Paxton desperately. "Escape pods?"

Aaron answered for him. "They're unreliable in the atmosphere, and we're not going up anymore. Lifeboats would work, but a *Union* doesn't carry any."

"Can we land?"

The captain's voice came from the speaker again, sounding almost as desperate as Deena's, as defeated as Paxton's expression. "Number two landing leg is jammed. Negative deployment on two. We're going to come down hard."

Paxton looked at Deena and shook his head sadly.

Aaron blinked and looked at the elevator, which now stood with doors ajar. The elevator car was visible, jammed halfway down to the lower deck. Next to it was an open shaft with a ladder in it. He reached up to his chest and twisted the buckle to release his harness. "If you want to live," he said, "follow me."

He ran to the shaft, glanced in to make sure it was clear, then started climbing down as fast as he could. He looked up to see Deena, then Paxton, following him. He counted steps and calculated. Forty meters give or take. Maybe two rungs per meter.

Half a dozen steps and they emerged through the roof of the 'Mech bay. The far end of the bay was a shambles, the bulkhead blasted open to expose twisted metal trusses that were probably part of the crippled landing leg. The farthest 'Mech was twisted and melted almost beyond recognition. The next, a *Centurion*, was heavily damaged, a ceiling crane having fallen and wrapped itself around the 'Mech's shoulders.

But the two 'Mechs on their end were intact, including his *Black Hawk*.

He glanced down. Just below them, the ladder passed through a maintenance catwalk and ran next to the *Black Hawk* at shoulder height. Good. They wouldn't have to go all the way to the bay floor and climb back up.

He dropped to the grating of the catwalk. He smelled hot metal and burning plastic. A stream of smoke came from somewhere in the wreckage and whistled out through a breach in the bay door. He reached up to help Deena down as Paxton dropped the last two meters and landed lightly on his feet.

Aaron glanced at the 'Mech and considered his options. A 'Mech was a one-person vehicle. He should be able to squeeze Deena into the cramped cockpit in the space behind his command couch, but there'd be no room for Paxton. The *Black Hawk* had been left in midservice, cockpit hatch open, missile bays empty, the missile loading hatch on the right arm open. Down the catwalk, the crate for a replacement gyro sat open and empty, having been hastily tied down to the metal grating before liftoff. Draped over the edge of the crate were blue padded packing blankets.

He pointed. "Paxton, grab those and get down to that missile hatch. Climb inside, slam the hatch, and try to wrap yourself in padding. It's going to be a rough ride. Deena, you come with me."

Her eyes went wide. "What are you going to do?"

"We're going to jump," he said calmly.

"You're insane!"

"Then stay here and die." He climbed over the railing and dropped down next to the open hatch. "I'll miss you. You're the best valet I've ever had."

She hesitated only a moment before climbing down after him. He was already in the cockpit, strapping himself in. He fitted the neurohelmet over his head with one hand, flipping switches to initiate an emergency startup sequence with the other. It was a risk, cold-starting the 'Mech's fusion reactor like this, but there was no choice. If it didn't work, they'd only be as dead as if he hadn't tried.

He glanced over to see Paxton, a huge bundle of

blankets under one arm, climbing into the missile hatch. He reached down into a compartment next to his seat and pulled out one of the headsets sometimes used to communicate with ground crew in the field.

"Deena, throw this down to Ulysses." He tossed the headset over his shoulder and heard Deena grab it, then throw it down. Ulysses caught it one-handed, then ducked down and shut himself inside the 'Mech's arm.

Deena squeezed in behind Aaron.

"Dog that for me," he snapped, then heard the door cycle shut, and Deena grunt in the tight space.

The 'Mech started to come alive around them. The computer lit up. "Voice authorization required."

"Duke Aaron Sandoval," he said, followed by his code-phrase, *"The hand is the sword; the sword is the hand."*

"Authorization recognized. 'Mech systems on-line."

The 'Mech shifted around them, hard-points clunking against the restraining clamps. There was no ground crew to release them. He pushed the throttle forward and wiggled the stick. There was a whine, followed by a series of reports as the clamps snapped one by one.

"Captain, this is Duke Sandoval. Open 'Mech launch chute one."

"Damn," was the only reply, except for another muttered curse he couldn't understand. The bay lurched around them, and he could feel the DropShip descending again, more rapidly this time.

"Captain, this is the Duke! Open that launch chute!"

"We're . . . busy up here."

"Open the chute!"

No answer.

He jockeyed the 'Mech's controls to move them forward. He could see cracks in the main bay door in front of them, sunlight streaming through some of them. Meters above, he could see the main door actuators, one broken loose and waving as the ship rocked.

He activated the twin lasers on either side of the cockpit. He aimed manually and fired. The actuators began to glow red, then white.

They snapped, and abruptly the entire bay door peeled away, leaving them standing in front of a gaping hole in the hull. Hurricane-force winds ripped around them, sucking out anything that wasn't tied down, with the exception of the fifty-ton *Black Hawk.*

He could see the gulf below them, the shallows dappled with patches of pale green, the deeper water in blues ranging from pale to indigo. The water looked perilously close.

He hated to land in the water. The 'Mech would survive, if he could land softly enough, but he wasn't sure Paxton's compartment would be watertight under the circumstances. He doubted it. The bodyguard could drown before they reached land, and that would be a regrettable loss.

The ship rolled on its axis, and on the horizon Aaron could see a large island, one shore ringed with high-rises, the other with warehouses and docks. In the middle, another spaceport sprawled, dotted with huge freighter ships.

Aaron tried to remember the maps he'd seen of New Canton. What was that island called? Barosa? It was the planet's major transfer point for bulk space freight, as cargo was transferred to and from oceangoing ships and barges that serviced the rest of the planet. The island looked far away. Then Aaron noticed a light-colored finger extending out from the island in their direction.

A reef.

"Ulysses, we're going wading. I'll do my best to keep you dry, but this is going to be a hard ride."

"Do it," was the unhesitating reply.

There was another explosion below them, and the ship started to roll over. The hatch in front of them turned downward to face the whitecaps on the waves below. Instinctively, Aaron stepped the 'Mech forward and they dropped into open air.

He let the 'Mech free-fall to get clear of the DropShip. He glanced up through the canopy. Above them, he could see the ship starting to roll as another thruster sputtered. They had to get out from under it.

A *Black Hawk* was a powerful 'Mech, but if a thirty-five-hundred-ton DropShip landed on top of it, it would still splatter like a bug.

Whatever primal part of his brain the neurohelmet tapped into was ahead of his conscious mind. The gyros whined as the *Black Hawk* tumbled forward. He aimed his crosshairs in the direction of the reef, then hit the jump jets.

His stomach did a flip as the 'Mech went from free-fall to three Gs in an instant. It didn't help that the angle of acceleration was nearly at a right angle to the surface of the gulf that was rapidly coming up to meet them. He realized he was looking down into a huge circular shadow on the water below, a reminder that, although he could no longer see the DropShip, it was very close behind him.

He watched the heat indicator climbing, and a cluster of yellow lights appeared on the jump jet status panel. It was fortunate, he thought, that he valued mobility on the battlefield so highly. He'd used much of his money and influence to have the *Black Hawk* fitted with experimental jets that increased power and firing duration by about sixty percent, but he was going to need to push them well past their limits today.

It helped that the 'Mech was running light, with no missiles in its ammo bays, but Aaron had no idea if that would be enough.

He heard Deena grunt and gasp as she tried to find a less painful position, and he reached up to swat her hand as it strayed too close to the yellow-and-black striped ejection handle over his head. It occurred to him he could probably survive by ejecting right now, but the ejection would kill Deena, and Paxton would fall to his death.

He reached over and flipped the command couch breaker to OFF. There would be no accidents.

She spoke. "We're going to die, aren't we?"

"That remains to be seen." Aaron glanced out at the water below. He saw his 'Mech's shadow now, well separated from that of the DropShip.

Wind whistled past the cockpit. This would have to be far enough. If he waited any longer, they'd never survive the landing.

The *Black Hawk* rolled back again as he pushed the jump jets into overload. Red lights began to flash on his panel. Burning insulation stung his nose and eyes. The cockpit started to feel like a furnace, but that would be the least of their problems when they were in the water.

"Hold on," he heard himself say.

Aaron had gone skydiving in his younger days, and his instructor had warned him not to trust his eyes when it came to opening his chute. "Your eyes will fool you until it's much too late, and then I'll have to pour your high-blood out of your boots." He knew that things would look fine, and suddenly he'd realize how close the ground was, and it would come up to smack him.

That's exactly what happened, except it was shallow water coming up far too fast. He moved the stick just a little, aiming for the deep water just past the reef. "Ulysses!" he yelled into the mike. "Hold your breath!"

Then they hit.

Deena yelped with pain as she was slammed down in her narrow refuge, metal digging into her body in a dozen places. There was a roar, like a waterfall turned inside out and backward. For a moment they were actually looking up at the sky from a hole they'd made in the water.

The gulf slammed in around them, and there was a grinding crunch as they slammed into the coral-covered bottom. The legs howled in protest, folding until every joint slammed against its stops.

Then they were still: green water surrounding the canopy, metal moaning and shrieking from the pressure and sudden cooling, bubbles from the heat sinks and red-hot jump jets making it impossible to see anything—even which way was up.

He didn't need to see.

MechWarriors called it situational awareness. He'd oriented himself coming in. He knew where the reef was. He knew how far it was. He knew that Ulysses might have only seconds to live if he didn't get up there.

He pushed the throttles and pulled the stick over hard. The legs moaned and hesitated. Then they were standing, moving, running across the bottom, up an underwater slope.

It grew brighter above his head, changing from green to wavering blue. His cockpit breached the surface, water streaming down the armorglass.

He raised the arm to where Paxton was hidden and opened the missile exhaust chutes loading hatch, hoping that any water that had gotten inside would quickly flow out. So much water was running off the 'Mech, it was impossible to tell how successful this was.

"Ulysses, are you with us?"

Nothing.

"Ulysses!"

There was a choking cough in his headset. "Still here, Lord Governor."

The *Black Hawk* continued up the bank until they were on top of the reef. The water there was no more than a meter deep—barely enough to cover the 'Mech's feet.

Aaron set the throttle at one quarter and started a slow trot toward the island, watching for dark water ahead that might require him to leap from one colony of coral to another. There was no telling what sort of environmental damage he was doing, but it couldn't be helped.

Deena pushed her face close to the canopy.

"My Lord!"

He wasn't sure if she was calling for his attention, or for her savior. He followed her gaze, just in time to see the crippled DropShip plunge into the gulf. White-hot metal met warm tropical water with explosive results. Fusion reactors detonated, spewing plasma, causing a rapid cascade of secondary explosions as the magazines went off.

The hull of the ship, what part they could still see of it, shattered like a dropped Christmas ball, and a ghostly hemisphere of shock wave moved out from the crash. It washed over them, shuddering the 'Mech with its force.

But that was only the beginning. Even as the broken bulk of the DropShip vanished into the gulf, a huge, white wall of water rose up, towering higher than the 'Mech's cockpit. Aaron bit his lip. The jump jets were fried. The wave roared toward them, and there was no avoiding it.

And as it swallowed them, ripping the 'Mech off its feet like a toy, he remembered Deena's question, and his answer:

That remains to be seen.

*   *   *

The entry bell on Erik's cabin door rang, followed by an urgent pounding. He groaned, threw back the covers, and squinted at the holoclock display hovering over his bed. The floating green numbers told him he'd been asleep for two hours.

More pounding, followed by a woman's muffled voice. "Commander! There's been a flash-news report from New Canton, regarding the Duke!"

He considered ignoring the voice, but realized he was already awake. He reached over, clicked on the reading light, and pushed the hidden button that released the door's security lock. "Come."

The door slid open, and he recognized the uniformed woman standing there as Captain Malvern, the watch intelligence officer. "I'm sorry to disturb you, Commander, but we've just received a report that I knew you'd want to hear immediately."

He asked skeptically, "A flash-news report? Do you people actually read that stuff?" Since the breakdown of the HPG, reliable news of distant events usually traveled no faster than a JumpShip could traverse the same distance, taking weeks or months to cross any substantial part of The Republic.

Even though jump travel was in itself instantaneous, logistics limited the speed of any physical object traveling between star systems. JumpShips had to recharge, people and cargo had to load and unload, DropShips had to undock from one JumpShip and transfer to another, or fly between jump points and the planets themselves.

In theory, information suffered no such limitations. The limiting factors for information travel were the speed of sound or data, in-system light-speed delays as the information was passed along from ship to ship, and the availability of the next charged ship which would leave the system to pass the information on to the next.

Occasionally, by random chance, a long chain of such rapid transfers would take place, information traveling rapidly from one arriving JumpShip to a departing one, and so on, system by system. By this method, news could travel across a Prefecture in days or hours instead of weeks, flashing over like an electric arc crossing a gap.

The problem was that information travel was completely unpredictable and notoriously unreliable. Information was almost certain to travel via an indirect and circuitous route, through an unknown number of relay stations of unknown reliability. Even in the best of times, the information tended to "drift" and change as it was passed along, and the potential for malicious manipulation was unlimited. Some in the communications and intelligence community had started calling the phenomenon of rapid information transfer "flash-news," but still others called it the "new HPG," which in this case stood for "Hyper-Pap Generator."

Even if the random tidbit was of potential interest, Erik didn't see how it could be trustworthy. Yet Captain Malvern seemed sincerely to believe that this flash-news was important. He couldn't see her face clearly while she was back-lit from the hallway, but she looked grave.

He sat up in bed, suddenly feeling wide awake. "Out with it."

"The report said that Duke Aaron Sandoval's DropShip had an accidental thruster explosion and crashed into the Gulf of Emeralds shortly after takeoff from the Capital Spaceport."

"Survivors?"

She lowered her head. "All hands were said to be lost."

"It could just be a rumor," he said, "even misinformation planted by the Cappies." But even as he said it, he sensed there was at least some truth to the report.

Erik felt his body turn to ice. *The Duke is dead? What should I do now?*

He wasn't sure what bothered him more: that the report might be true, or that grief was only the third or fourth emotion he felt upon hearing it.

4

It is with deep regret that the Government of Prefecture VI reports the tragic death of Duke Aaron Sandoval, Lord Governor of Prefecture IV, in the crash of his DropShip shortly after departing the capital of New Canton.

Early analysis indicates that a faulty fuel pump may have exploded. The Duke inexplicably walked out on negotiations with high officials on New Canton, and prepared to launch in haste. It's possible that he may have bypassed preflight inspections that would have identified the problem before launch. In addition to the Duke, all passengers and crew on the ship perished.

The Lord Governor sends his deepest regrets to the survivors, the people of Tikonov, and of Prefecture IV. "It is hoped that after an orderly transfer of power is completed, another representative will be dispatched from Tikonov to continue negotiations, assuming the rapid advance of House Liao forces through Prefecture V does not render such negotiations redundant.

"As always, the bond and respect we share with Prefecture IV, its worlds, and its people, is undiminished."

—Official release from the palace on New Canton,
9 October 3134

Barosa Island Spaceport
Barosa Island, New Canton
Prefecture VI, The Republic
9 October 3134

Every radio in the Barosa Island Spaceport had been tuned to the emergency frequency, listening to the desperate distress calls from the Duke's DropShip. Captain Gus Clancy was hearing it, and watching it, magnified on the viewscreen on the bridge of the *Excalibur*-class spherical DropShip *Tyrannos Rex*.

He leaned back in his chair, hearing its familiar squeak—the worn leather of the armrests soft under his calloused fingers, and looked around the bridge. His navigator, helmsmen, and flight engineer sat quietly at their respective stations, eyes locked on the doomed ship. He knew they were with the other crew in spirit, and when it crashed, part of them would die with it, too.

That was the bond all spacefarers shared. Clancy also felt it, more so perhaps, since he'd spent much of his childhood on a *Union*-class DropShip much like the one he was watching now.

The bridge of Clancy's vessel towered more than a hundred meters above the launch apron. He could see clearly out into the gulf, see the Union's thrusters as they failed one by one, watch the captain try desperately to keep the craft under control. It was a DropShip captain's worst nightmare, a ship that could neither fly nor land, stuck deep in the maw of the bitch called gravity.

The *Union*'s captain had made a good show of it, Clancy thought, tried every trick that Clancy could think of. But it wasn't enough, and in the end time and gravity had to win.

The crash was a terrible thing. The resulting wave swamped miles of shoreline, sweeping away blue-collar vacation homes, fishermen's shacks, and low-rent hotels as though with a great broom. He could only imagine the public outcry, the calls for new flight patterns, increased launch safety, or maybe even absurd suggestions that the cargo spaceport be closed.

It didn't matter to him, though. Very shortly, Captain Clancy and the *Tyrannos Rex* were leaving New Canton, cargo holds empty. Pockets, too. He didn't expect ever to be back.

The voyage had turned into a bitter disappointment—one that might cost him his ship. The government had declared his scheduled cargo of manufacturing tools "war materiel," impounded it, and given him twenty-four hours to leave the planet.

A huge cloud of steam boiled off the gulf, exposing pieces of wreckage that dotted the water. The waves were receding, and he could see the flashing lights of rescue vehicles winking as they drove toward the stricken coastline, emergency helicopters swarming like mosquitoes.

He should leave. The ship was fueled and ready to lift. His twenty-four hours were almost up. Logic said there was nothing to be gained by staying here. Clancy's gut told him something else.

That DropShip had belonged to Duke Aaron Sandoval, Lord Governor of Prefecture IV, and one of the richest men in The Republic. Clancy had heard the scuttlebutt: he had been ejected by the Lord Governor of New Canton, and there was a falling out. It was the same political shift that had probably cost Clancy his cargo—and now the Duke was dead.

Most likely.

Clancy wasn't sure, but he thought he'd seen something separate from the DropShip before it made its death plunge. A small separate plasma flare had descended into the gulf.

Clancy thought it was a 'Mech, and if so, it might have survived. Whoever was in it was likely loyal to the Duke and would want to get away from New Canton as quickly as possible. They'd head for the spaceport, where Clancy just happened to be sitting with an *Excalibur*-class DropShip and three empty cargo bays, ready to launch.

He had nothing. Nothing but an idea, and a hope, and the guts to try and pull things off if his idea turned out to be the truth. He stood and grabbed his neurohelmet.

"Stand by to lift on my order, but open bay one, and have LoaderMech Alpha ready when I get there." He stepped into the lift that would take him down through the core of the ship, then hesitated. "Keep watch on the spaceport perimeter in the direction of the crash. You see anything unusual at all, you call me right away, you hear?"

He ran the lift at emergency speed, descending so fast he had to hold onto the rail to keep his feet on the floor, then flex his knees to absorb the sudden deceleration at the bottom.

The yellow LoaderMech's diesel engine was already clattering as he climbed up the support gantry. Lieutenant McComb, the ship's loadmaster and the 'Mech's regular pilot, was standing by the open cockpit. Clancy jumped into the seat, donned his neurohelmet and plugged it in, gave McComb a thumbs-up, and then slipped both hands into the waldos that controlled the manipulator arms. The LoaderMech was a prototype that Clancy had picked up in a card game a couple of stops back, and he was still getting the feel for it. Its drive controls were all designed to be operated by the pilot's feet and knees, freeing the hands for other work. It was an unusual setup, tricky to learn, but allowed for fast and precise loading. It also meant that the 'Mech was flexible enough to do many things it was never designed for.

He tapped the throttle-up toggle with one knee, heard the diesel engine roar, and guided the machine clear of its gantry using the steering pedals. He flexed the fingers on the ends of the manipulator arms through the waldos—each finger equipped with an extendible "fingernail" blade like the tine of a forklift.

He activated the com. "Bridge, this is Clancy, what do you see?"

"Cap'n"—it was Sanchez, the engineer—"there are two spaceport security 'Mechs headed toward the south perimeter, moving fast."

"What are they headed *for*?"

"I don't see—I—Damn!"

"What?"

"A 'Mech just ripped through the south security fence, three police helicopters in pursuit, lasers blazing, and I'll swear it's wearing half the seaweed in the gulf!"

Duke Aaron Sandoval felt as though he were in a ground car with no springs and no brakes, running down a washboard road that never ended. The 'Mech cockpit was hot as blazes, and the *Black Hawk* seemed to be trying to tear itself apart with every step. But he didn't back off the throttle. He couldn't.

He'd figured out by now he was a dead man walking—an embarrassing corpse that had crawled out of the ocean and had to be buried before anyone beyond New Canton noticed. He was certain his DropShip hadn't gone down by accident, and his survival was an inconvenience that somebody was going to try to cover up as soon as possible.

He guessed that the two light 'Mechs headed his way were there to finish the job.

Behind him, he could hear Deena muttering to herself. "Ulysses, I think Deena is praying. You are welcome to join her if you have nothing better to do."

He was answered with fatigued laughter. Ulysses' voice was slurred and uneven. "I'm too busy, my Lord, bleeding out into my bruises and trying to put my teeth back into their sockets. Will this hellish ride be over soon?"

"The good news is that one way or the other, it will be."

Ordinarily the *Black Hawk* would have been a good match for its opponents, but damaged, lacking missiles or jump jets, and already carrying too much heat, the situation didn't look good. There was only one thing left to do: Negotiate.

He switched his radio to broadcast on all civilian channels. "This is Duke Aaron Sandoval, Lord Governor of Prefecture IV, on a diplomatic mission. I claim diplomatic immunity. I demand free passage off-planet."

"Unidentified *Black Hawk,* this is Spaceport Security One. Duke Sandoval is dead. We don't know who you are, but we have orders to take you dead or alive. Dead is fine with us."

Both 'Mechs opened fire, and autocannon shells peeled off a line of armor below the cockpit. Deena's muttering grew louder.

Time to change strategy.

"This is Duke Aaron Sandoval to any listening ship in port. I am being illegally attacked and detained by the government of New Canton. I offer my eternal gratitude, and five-hundred thousand C-Bills, for aid and safe passage off-planet."

There was no reply. He hadn't expected any captain there to have the courage to challenge the local authorities, but it was worth a try. He angled between the converging 'Mechs, hoping they'd have to cease fire for fear of hitting each other.

"I don't lift for under a million C-Bills."

"Who said that?" There were half a dozen cargo ships in port, spheroid and aerodyne. It could have been any one of them, or even a trick.

"A man who's asking a million Cs. Plus expenses."

A pulse laser cut into the *Black Hawk*'s arm, uncomfortably close to Paxton's compartment.

"We can negotiate fair payment as soon as we're off-planet."

"You heard my terms. They are fair."

He sighed. "Done. My honor as Duke. What ship are you?"

"You'll see," said the voice.

Abruptly, to his north, Aaron was surprised to see the waist turrets around an egg-shaped *Excalibur* flash to life, spitting a stream of lasers and missile fire between the *Black Hawk* and its pursuers. Aaron managed a grim smile. A converted military ship, but not entirely toothless. His would-be savior was full of surprises.

Another voice crackled in Aaron's earphones. "DropShip *Tyrannos Rex,* you are in violation of Port Security Protocol One. You are ordered to cease fire and surrender your ship, or face military retaliation."

There was a scratchy laugh. "With all respect, Control, bite my thrusters."

Aaron was making the best speed he could toward the waiting *Excalibur.* The door of what had at least started out as a 'Mech bay was open, boarding ramp extended. They were almost home. He could see the ramp just ahead of them.

The cockpit shook violently, and a ball of fire swallowed the *Black Hawk*—probably a short-range missile. Red lights flickered all over Aaron's panels, and the 'Mech's left leg froze.

In his rear camera, he could see the two security 'Mechs closing in for the kill. Then one of them exploded as a volley of missiles slammed into it. The other was soon covered with glowing stripes as lasers swept over its light armor. It angled away from the big DropShip, seeking cover.

Aaron flinched as he spotted another 'Mech nearly upon them. He realized it was an IndustrialMech, a loader, apparently from the *Excalibur*-class vessel itself. The little yellow 'Mech swept past him, close enough that he could almost count the gray whiskers on the pilot's chin, then it disappeared behind him.

Then Aaron realized the 'Mech was towing a cable.

There was a scraping noise, and the LoaderMech came back around the other side. Aaron saw a large hook in the 'Mech's manipulator hand. The pilot expertly slipped the hook over the cable, forming a loop around the *Black Hawk*'s waist, yanking it tight with the LoaderMech's other hand. It turned and charged back up the loading ramp.

"Take slack, then full power till she's in," came a voice on the radio. It sounded like the *Excalibur* captain's voice again.

The cable shifted, went taut. Then the *Black Hawk* started to tip over. Using what little control he had left, Aaron shifted the big 'Mech to land on its back. The impact threw him against his harness and slammed his helmet against the side of the command couch. He heard Paxton curse somewhere. Deena was very quiet.

Metal squealed against metal as the powerful cargo winch dragged them up the loading ramp. Despite the agonizing sound, Aaron started to relax.

Then the second security 'Mech came out from behind the ship's massive landing leg, guns blazing. Aaron watched the armorglass canopy in front of him craze and finally shatter. Something ripped into his chest and made him hurt straight through to his back, where he felt something warm and wet.

His last thought was that he hoped it didn't get Deena, too.

5

*"My grandmother was a huge influence on my life.
Health problems kept her bedridden from the time
I was ten, but her mind never lost its edge. I would
sit by her bed for hours as she told me the most
wonderful and amazing stories. She knew the whole
glorious history of the Sandovals: every name, every
title, every treaty, every conquest, every battle. She
taught me what it meant to be one of them—something I'm not sure all of my relatives fully
understand.*

*"When she died, I did not mourn her, because
she told me that there was a special place in Heaven
for loyal Sandovals—a palace where those true to
the family ideals and traditions would rule forever.
I'd like to think that if such a place exists, I'll see
her again there someday."*

—Duke Aaron Sandoval, quoted in *The Lords of
Tikonov,* published 3130

Excalibur-*conversion-class freighter* Tyrannos Rex
Outbound from New Canton
Prefecture VI, The Republic
12 October 3134

Before the strokes had left her a bitter cripple, young
Aaron Sandoval's grandmother would receive him at
her summer estate on the southern shore of Lake Tikonov. It had been a magical place, with warm beaches
for swimming, miles of open coastline he could ex-
plore with his little hydrofoil, endless trails through
fragrant cedar where the head groundskeeper taught
him to bow-hunt deer and wild boar. A place where

fresh game and blue potatoes roasted in the massive stone fireplace became the finest meal in the Inner Sphere.

Sometimes when it was late and he couldn't sleep, or when the storms blew down from the north and filled the lake with foam-flecked whitecaps, he would retire to the mansion's extensive and little-used library. There, he would dig through the dusty volumes and stacks of data cards so old they only worked in an antique reader that sat on a corner desk.

It was there he had discovered an ancient holovid dating back to Old Terra—no, just a vid actually, since it was only two-dimensional. Parts of it were even curiously lacking in color. It was only a fragment of the original, a few cheerful songs, actors in silly costumes, a few scenes of campy melodrama, yet it had somehow fascinated him, and he'd watched it again and again.

It was curious how, as consciousness rejoined him, accompanied by the smell of antiseptics, the electronic chirps of medical machines, a distant throbbing of drug-dulled pain, and the familiar low rumble of a fusion drive, that his first thoughts were of that ancient video-relic. He parted his dry lips and heard the raspy sound of his own voice. "Toto, I don't think we're in New Canton anymore."

"He's awake!" The voice was Ulysses Paxton's.

"He's delirious," said Deena Onan, a tone of concern in her voice.

He opened his eyes a little, squinting against the stinging brightness. Deena's face leaned in front of him, and she spoke slowly and loudly, as though he'd been pierced through the eardrums instead of the chest. "My—name—is—not—Toto!"

He chuckled, and it came out as a rasp.

Deena held a straw to his lips, and he sipped, sloshing the water around his mouth to wash away the cotton. "How long?"

"My name's *never* been Toto, Lord Governor."

He looked at her. She was a mess—a large purple bruise on her left cheek, the bridge of her nose taped, and a half-healed cut on her lower lip. Her skin looked red and slightly parboiled.

Ulysses looked even worse, with bandages seemingly covering half his body, and bruises the rest. His eyes still looked red and irritated—from seawater or smoke, Aaron couldn't tell—and the big man occasionally emitted a deep liquid cough. There was a brace around one knee and another around one wrist, but nothing appeared to be broken.

Nothing appeared to be overly healed either. He hadn't been unconscious too long, then. He wondered how bad he looked, then decided he didn't want to know.

A medic in a green-and-white jacket checked his pulse. Aaron glanced up at the man's chiseled profile and cleft chin, and decided that he must be a doctor.

Aaron was startled when the doctor turned to shine a penlight into his eyes, and he saw the man's full face for the first time. A jagged pink scar extended up from the right corner of his mouth to his forehead, crossing his right eye socket. The eye on that side was a silvery artificial orb with a black lens in the middle. He could see something moving beneath the glass as the eye changed focus.

The doctor's eyebrow rose as he saw Aaron's reaction. "Not much to wake up to, I'll admit, but it's lucky for you. If it wasn't for this scar, somebody with my qualifications would never let themselves be stuck on a tramp freighter."

A shorter, older man with a gray beard stepped forward. "Hell, Doc, you love it, and you know it."

The doctor glanced at the bearded man, but didn't argue. He turned back and examined the red-tinged bandage taped to Aaron's chest. "The shard of ferro-glass missed your aorta and your spine and only nicked a lung. You're a lucky man, Lord Governor. There are a lot of ways you could have been dead."

You don't know the half of it. Aaron looked past the doctor to study the bearded man. He wore a blue merchant marine shirt, untucked at the waist, and a white cap with captain's bars pinned in the middle. The only decorations on the shirt were a pair of gold DropShip wings and a stylized set of tank treads crossed with a red lightning bolt. *A tanker's pin. Why does a DropShip captain wear a tanker's pin?* He recognized the face as the man who had piloted the LoaderMech that had come to their rescue.

The bearded man stepped forward, studied Aaron for a moment, then wrinkled his nose. "Don't *smell* like a duke," he said.

Paxton stepped in close to him, frowning. "Respect!"

The captain didn't flinch. He looked up into Paxton's eyes. "Well, he's not *my* duke." Then he looked back at Aaron and shrugged. "Still, he's a customer. Don't pay to be too rude to a customer, long as *they* pay."

Aaron grinned. He liked the man's pluck. "You'll get paid, Captain . . . ?"

The captain tugged at the brim of his cap briefly. "Captain Gus Clancy of the DropShip *Tyrannos Rex.*"

"I'll ask again. How long have I been out?"

"Three days," said Paxton. "We're well on our way to the JumpShip."

"No one is coming after us?"

Paxton smiled slightly. "We pulled six Gs getting off New Canton. I would have never believed an *Excalibur* could do that without shredding apart. I'll hand it to Captain Clancy; this ship is *much* more than it seems.

"We had some planetary defense fighters dogging

us, but Captain Clancy put some missiles across their bows and then pulled a high-G slingshot maneuver around the third moon that had us all wondering if we were going to clip a mountaintop. But nobody tried to follow us after that, and things cooled off."

Aaron nodded. "The assassination attempt failed, and their attempts to correct that mistake were getting increasingly messy. They finally cut their losses."

Captain Clancy seemed to remember something, and dug a folded piece of paper out of his shirt pocket. There was a ring-shaped coffee stain on the back. "I reckon that might explain this. Came in for you on the datafax from New Canton an hour ago."

Paxton glared at Clancy. "You *read* it?"

Clancy looked indignant. "It's my blasted datafax."

Aaron glanced at the doctor, his practiced eyes neither avoiding the man's scarred face, nor staring at it. "Doctor, will you excuse us for a moment? Apparently I have nothing to hide from Captain Clancy, so he can remain."

"Well, ain't that nice," said the captain sarcastically.

Aaron looked at Deena. "Read it."

She took the paper, her eyes widening as she saw the name at the top. "It's from the Lord Governor.

" 'My dearest, Duke Sandoval. It is with great horror and regret that I apologize for the unfortunate events that befell you during your hasty departure from New Canton. Imagine my delight when I learned that you had miraculously survived the accidental crash of your DropShip. Let me assure you that, despite some miscommunication with the local authorities, you were never in any danger.' "

Aaron saw Paxton's mouth curl into a sneer.

Deena continued reading. " 'Although present circumstances divide us politically, let me assure you that I have nothing but the highest personal regard for the

Duke and his family. Perhaps in another time, we will yet again be allies.

" 'Lord Governor Harri Golan,' blah, blah, etc., etc."

Aaron chuckled. "Covering his ass."

Deena looked puzzled. "How so, Lord Governor? He's allied himself with our enemies, and he's trying to be cordial?"

"He fears I'll seek personal revenge, or worse—that Liao's incursion will ultimately be repelled, leaving him alone and in a very embarrassing position. He knows it was an assassination attempt, probably by that toad Sebhat, not the Lord Governor himself—not that it matters to me. He knows I know. He knows I have enough money to hire many assassins."

Paxton looked concerned, probably imagining an escalating war of assassination attempts. "And will you?"

"What would be the point? I'm above petty acts of revenge. Better to make him worry and fret about it, lying awake every night listening for footsteps outside his door, torturing himself, until one day when I approach him. That day, he will beg to find my favor again. Isn't that better in the long run?"

Paxton nodded. "The Duke is wise."

Aaron grinned. "The bodyguard is diplomatic. I wonder what you'd have said if I'd put a price on the bastard's head?"

Paxton just looked at him and cocked an eyebrow.

"Lord Governor," said Deena, leaning in close to look at his face, "you look tired." She turned to the others. "He looks tired."

Clancy crossed his arms over his chest. "Tired, is he? When we've still got business to attend to?"

"He's tired," she insisted.

"Excuse me," said Aaron. "Do I get a say in this? Hello? Still the Duke."

Deena looked embarrassed. "With apologies, my Lord, I forgot my place."

"No." He grimaced as he tried to shift position without dislodging any of the various tubes that ran in and out of him. "I forgot mine, which is horizontal in a bed with a hole through my chest. I *am* tired, but I do have business with Captain Clancy that can't wait."

Both Deena and Paxton looked unhappy.

"I'll make it brief. Besides, you people look like you need rest as much as I do. I know you lost friends on the DropShip. So did I. Go take some personal time."

Deena's eyes clouded slightly when he mentioned lost friends, and he noticed the muscles of Ulysses' jaw clench. She nodded, and headed for the door. "I'll be back to check on you later."

Ulysses didn't move. "With respect, Lord Governor, it would be better if I stayed with you. I've disgracefully subjected you to too much danger already."

"You're not my mother, Ulysses. I put myself in danger, and you scramble to get me out. My job is always easier than yours"—he grinned—"and I'm better at it."

He looked at Captain Clancy, who stood at the foot of his bed. "Ulysses, do you trust this man?"

Ulysses blinked. "Yes, Lord Governor, I believe I do."

"Captain Clancy, am I safe here?"

"Doc is the best sawbones in the merchant fleet. He's patched me and my crew together from worse than the likes of you. I've got two of my most loyal men outside watching the door, and except for a dozen or so short-timers who haven't proved themselves yet, I'd trust my life with any of my crew."

Clancy nodded. "Yeah, you're safe here as you can be."

Aaron bobbed his head in the direction of the door. "Go. Sleep. You're no good to me the way you are, Ulysses. Don't come back till you're halfway presentable."

Paxton nodded and reluctantly headed for the door. He stopped in the door to inspect the two guards and, apparently satisfied, made his leave.

Doc looked at Clancy. "Captain, he *should* rest."

Clancy waved him away. "Don't you got some pills to go try out or something? Let us talk a minute, then I'll get out."

The doctor shrugged and wandered into an adjacent office cubicle.

"As I said, Captain, you've set your price, and you'll get paid."

"Aye, you can bet your blue blood that I will. But that's not what I'm here to talk about."

"I owe you a debt beyond that, Captain. You saved my life out there, all our lives. I don't know if I'd have done the same thing in your place."

"I can't say I know you well enough to judge that. I had my reasons."

"Beyond money?"

"Reason enough, but it was a chance to give it to those bastards on New Canton who screwed me."

"I don't understand."

Clancy waved his hand like he was swatting a mosquito. "Long story. They impounded my scheduled cargo. It takes a lot of C-Bills to lift this big tub, and I can't afford to go running empty."

"You've got paying passengers now, Captain. Do you mind passengers?"

"Machine parts, they don't talk back, complain about the chow, or try to tell me how to run my ship."

"It sounds like they also barely pay the bills, Captain. Tell me, how'd you like to sell your ship?"

"Sell? The *Tyrannos Rex?*"

"What's an *Excalibur* worth these days? Seven hundred fifty mil?"

"The *Rex,* she's worth more. Like your buddy Ulysses says, she ain't what she seems."

"Nine hundred mil?"

"She's not for sale."

"A Gigabill? Surely she's not worth more than that."

"She *ain't* for sale!"

"Mind you, I'd want to hire you and your entire crew to stay on."

"She ain't for sale, blue blood. Some things ain't got a price."

"That hasn't been my experience, Captain. Besides, you've got bills to pay, and once we leave, you're right back where you started, except that you're no longer welcome on New Canton."

"She's not for sale." He leaned back and licked his lips. "She's for hire though, if the price is right."

Aaron smiled. Negotiations had opened. "I'd need a long-term contract. You give me reasonable numbers and I won't say no."

"Contract? To haul what to where?"

"To haul me, to wherever."

"This isn't some bloody pleasure yacht, Sandoval. The grub is good, but plain, and the beds are soft, but the cabins are small. You think you can live with that?"

"I've had worse, Captain, believe it or not. The accommodations will do for now, but I'll be putting in some new ones as soon as circumstances allow."

"You ain't hacking into my ship."

"In a cargo hold then. One for my quarters, one for 'Mechs and vehicles, one for supplies and consumables. Maybe you can still haul some cargo on the side."

Clancy looked skeptical. "And I get to haul you all over the Sphere?"

"That's the plan. Good pay, dependable work."

"What about the ship?"

"Ulysses says she's good. So do you."

The captain's eyes narrowed. "She could be better. I got lots of ideas I just ain't been able to afford. Better weapons, armor, upgraded systems all over. I take you on board, half the galaxy is going to be gunning for us. I got to know we'll have what it takes to survive."

"That and more. No expenses spared." Aaron extended his hand. "Shall we shake on it?"

Clancy just looked at his hand. "I'll sleep on it and get back to you." He turned toward the door, then hesitated. "Until then, where are we going, Duck?"

6

*DUKE SANDOVAL LIVES!—In an exclusive ho-
lorecording obtained by an INN Courier-News cor-
respondent on Liao, the Duke himself appeared to
deny erroneous reports of his own death. Expert
analysis of the holo leaves little doubt that it is genuine, and the content makes it clear that it was recorded after his alleged death.*

*Sandoval reports that he survived the crash of his
flagship with only "minor injuries." He described
the incident as a "bungled assassination attempt, in-
dicative of the disorder and lack of central control
that has infected Prefecture V, and now Prefecture
VI as well. While I must return to Prefecture V and
continue the struggle there against the Liao incursion, the threatened people of Prefecture VI should
know that when the time is right, I will return to
their aid."*

—Interstellar News Network

Fortress-*class* DropShip Madras
***SwordSworn Fleet Staging Area, near Pleione
jump point***
Prefecture V, The Republic
20 October 3134

Erik Sandoval floated down the corridor of the
DropShip, warning Klaxons echoing in his ears as he
pulled himself hand-over-hand toward the bridge.
More experienced crew members, easily identifiable
by their orange coveralls, rocketed past him in all directions, gracefully pushing off at one end to sail the
length of a corridor, bouncing skillfully from wall to

wall in a zigzag pattern, or simply scrambling along them like hyperactive spiders.

Erik was still getting his space legs, and could never hope to be as proficient as these people who almost lived in space. He was content to hand-walk along, being passed like a ninety-year-old man on the hoverway.

"Unscheduled JumpShip arriving in two minutes," the captain's amplified voice echoed through the ship. "All hands to emergency stations. This is no drill."

This was another of the unfortunate results of the collapse of the HPG network. Now, unless arrangements were made far in advance, every incoming ship was "unscheduled," and therefore a matter of concern, given the current state of war.

The ship could be friend, foe, or neither—and even if it was an enemy, the old traditions might allow it to slide past without shots being exchanged. Still, the arrival of any unexpected ship created tension, and was cause for a full alert, just in case.

The armored bridge doors were just ahead. A marine stood at guard outside, assault rifle across his chest, back rigid, feet held to the deck by Velcro tabs. Erik didn't envy him. It was work to keep your body at attention without gravity. A full watch could be agony.

The human body liked to assume something called the "neutral position" in space, but to the military mind, that was more appropriate for a floating corpse than a trained soldier. So "attention" was still the order of the day.

The marine recognized him and saluted—another formality that wouldn't have been practical for a floating guard. Erik glanced at the weapon—a standard model except for the blue stripes on the barrel, stock, and magazine, indicating it carried fragmenting ammo that would shatter before penetrating the ship's hull or ferro-glass windows.

Erik held his security pass near the lock, and the door slid open. He slid through the blackout curtains and felt the elastic closures snap shut behind him.

The lights on the bridge were dim and red, to protect the crew's night vision. The bridge crew was strapped into acceleration couches. Only Captain Ricco floated free, watching a computer display that Erik knew showed the point where the incoming ship would shortly appear.

In one of those quantum-mechanical paradoxes associated with hyperdrive travel, while they knew where, and approximately when, the ship would arrive, it actually hadn't left yet. The trip, from their point of view, was instantaneous. It was one of those technical curiosities Erik had long ago stopped trying to wrap his head around.

The captain held his position with one hand, hanging from a grab bar over his head. He looked over at Erik. "Could be a big one, Commander. Big enough to be a threat."

Erik felt his stomach tighten. He knew it was probably nothing. Even if it wasn't, his little fleet awaiting transport numbered six full DropShips—more than enough to take care of itself. Still, it was as though the fall of the HPG network had filled the universe with shadows, from which they were always waiting for something to jump out. It was getting tiresome.

"There it is," said the navigator, studying a holodisplay floating above her console. "*Merchant* class, one DropShip attached."

Erik felt himself relax a bit. *Merchant*s were normally just that, hauling cargo and virtually unarmed.

"Wait a minute," said the navigator. "DropShip is a big one, military—an *Excalibur*—and I'm not getting a SwordSworn IFF signal. I don't know whose it is."

Erik frowned. The *Excalibur* was an elliptical DropShip, the biggest military vessel of its type, capable of transporting a full combined-arms regiment in its three huge bays. In addition, it carried enough armor and offensive weaponry to be a formidable threat on its own.

The captain pulled himself over behind the navigator and ran his fingers through his blond, close-cropped hair as he studied the display. He smiled. "I know that ship. It's not military anymore, it's a freighter conversion. It's *Tyrannos Rex,* Gus Clancy's ship. Jeri, open a ship-to-ship channel."

He turned, and a flat-screen display in the middle of the bridge lit up, displaying an older man with collar-length gray hair and a beard.

"Hey, Gus," said the captain, "how's business?"

"Hey, Ricco, business is, surprisingly, pretty good. You should pull out the good china. I got nobility aboard. Paying passenger."

"Doesn't sound like your style. Who is it?"

"Duke Aaron Sandoval, the high and mighty Lord Governor himself."

Despite himself, Erik gasped. Once again his emotions were complex. Since receiving the erroneous reports of Aaron's death, he had publicly downplayed the possibility, but privately acted on the assumption that his uncle was gone. He'd been working on plans to keep the SwordSworn from falling apart, to salvage what he could of the action against House Liao, and of course, to gain personal control of as much of his uncle's assets and power base as possible. Now, in a stroke, all those half-formed plans were swept away.

Yet he was relieved as well. Rationally, those plans had little hope of success, at least not without striking alliances with other parties, notably other members of the Sandoval family. Though Aaron's death would have given him the opportunity to have everything he ever wanted, it was far more likely that he would have ended up with nothing. Or perhaps with a knife in the back.

The captain's mouth opened, but nothing came out. The bridge crew members were all looking at each other, grinning, but Erik wasn't ready to believe it yet. He leaned in front of the captain. "Are you sure? There were reports he was killed on New Canton when his DropShip crashed."

Clancy scowled out of the screen, his eyes narrowed. "Who in blazes is asking? Guess you must be Sword-Sworn or you wouldn't be on Ricco's bridge, but you ain't nothing to me."

"Commander Erik Sandoval-Groell."

Clancy nodded. "Family, then. Guess that gives you the right. He's got a few holes in his hide, but he put his thumb out on New Canton and I was going his way. Picked up a couple of his hired hands, too. Never too busy to help somebody who actually works for a living."

Erik felt his jaw tighten. This Clancy was annoyingly impertinent. Maybe he was intentionally digging at Erik. In any case, it was working.

"Is he conscious? Can I talk to him?"

"Hell if I know, and even if he is, I don't know if Lord high-and-mighty is taking calls. Reckon I'll ask him." The screen went blank.

"Wait," sputtered Erik, but the channel was already closed. "Call him back."

"That, Commander," said Captain Ricco, apologetically, "would only annoy him. I've dealt with this guy before. He's all right, but he's not much for protocol. You've got to do things his way."

Lord almighty, how did Uncle Aaron hook up with this lout? He must be badly injured, or he'd have thrown the man out an airlock long ago.

A light flashed on the navigator's console. "Call from the *Tyrannos Rex*. Putting it on-screen."

The screen lit up, and Erik was delighted to see Aaron's face; bandaged, unshaven, and battered, but still recognizable. "Uncle, you're alive!"

"Thanks for the update, Erik. I've traveled all the way from New Canton for that INN news flash."

"We'd heard reports you were dead—that your ship had an accident on takeoff."

"Except for the 'dead' part and the 'accident' part, that's reasonably accurate. The ship was sabotaged. A clumsy assassination attempt—the messy sort that kills nearly everyone but the target." He sighed. "We lost the *Kiwanda* with all hands. Ulysses Paxton, Deena Onan and I managed to escape in my 'Mech; I'll be needing to raid your parts stores to get it operable again. If there's a system I didn't manage to damage or overload, I'm not aware of it.

"As for the mission, obviously, we won't be getting any assistance from New Canton. Quite the contrary: they're groveling to House Liao now." His eyes drifted away from the camera for a moment. "Judging from the number of our DropShips here, the news from New Aragon is either very good or very bad."

"New Aragon is secure, Uncle. Liao has completely withdrawn from the system. We've left a token force, mainly symbolic, and returned security to the local military. In addition, they've pledged a regiment of infantry, two light armored companies, and a few IndustrialMechs to the coalition forces, with more to come as they rebuild."

"Well, there's that, then. Erik, this coalition is now more important than ever. Without an accord with New Canton and Prefecture VI, every world that signs on is vital. This can't wait for me to heal. We have to work twice as hard, and we have to start now."

"Uncle. The news about the *Kiwanda* is regrettable, but not unexpected. I'm delighted you're alive. I'll have the captain prepare quarters for you. You're well enough to be moved?"

He shook his head. "I'm not going anywhere. You're coming here. I've contracted the *Tyrannos Rex* to act as my personal flagship. This brush with death has opened my eyes, Erik. It's a new age we're living in, and a great many things are going to be changing."

The screen blanked. Erik frowned. Aaron was hardly back from the dead five minutes, and already he was ordering Erik around like a dog. *We're going to have to have a talk about that.*

Erik glanced to one side, and realized that Captain Ricco was staring at him.

"What's up, Commander? A SwordSworn DropShip isn't good enough for the Duke any more?"

Erik shook his head. "I'm as puzzled as you are. I suppose the only way to find out is to go over there and ask the Duke myself. Have a Battle Taxi made ready for launch."

"Aye. It'll be ready by the time you get to the bay."

"This Captain Clancy—who is he?"

The captain shrugged. "If by that, you mean his background, I don't have a clue. I've never understood how a lowborn ended up owning an *Excalibur*, either. But he's a tough old bird, and he runs a good ship, if that's what you mean. Beyond that, all I can say is . . . well, he's a character."

Despite his fearsome appearance, Doc, which was the only name by which anyone on the ship seemed to know him, seemed to know his medicine. Aaron had avoided complications and seemed to be healing well. His two staff members, likewise, had been well taken care of. One more reason that putting his faith in this ship seemed well founded.

Since he awoke, he'd spent most of his time consulting with Deena and Ulysses, and writing dispatches and orders to be distributed by the makeshift courier system that had been set up in the aftermath of the HPG failure. Some were bound for the capitol in Tikonov, or his palace there. Others went to his various bases and field commanders, and to outposts of his industrial and financial empire. And then there were the ever-important press releases.

There was a great deal of business to catch up on, and many changes to be made, but the dispatches took on even more importance now. Rumors had gone out reporting his death. That could destabilize his entire Prefecture, and throw his empire into chaos.

He had to make his presence felt, as soon and as widely as possible. He also knew that he was going to have to go public with his allegiance to House Davion. That was a dangerous move—one that would change his status from that of rogue Lord Governor, one who might return to the fold, to that of traitor to The Republic. But he knew that he'd already waited too long.

Even now, he was tearing up letters to key officials and replacing them with audio recordings, which would provide more tangible assurance that he was alive. He'd considered including video as well, but decided, given his appearance, that it might do more harm than good. The language of the messages was carefully chosen—peppered with mention of current events to date them past the assassination attempts. His rhetoric, without mentioning House Davion, also failed to mention The Republic. It was a first step to a more direct declaration of his loyalties.

He couldn't afford to look weak, and he certainly couldn't leave doubts about his health or control over the SwordSworn. He was entering a time when appearances were everything.

Another class of dispatches went out to brokers and

agents on the worlds he planned to visit, authorizing purchasing of fixtures and materials to be installed on the *Tyrannos Rex*. He also needed to hire workers to install his improvements, and staff to replace those lost on New Canton.

Finally, there was the most important dispatch of all—one with no signature, which described the location of a number of secret, numbered accounts, each containing a large quantity of untraceable cash. This he entrusted to Deena, and sent her to covertly deliver it via the first available transport. She would be traveling under an assumed identity—one he had previously obtained for a large sum of money, in anticipation of just such an occasion.

That left one matter to deal with before his troublesome charge, Erik, arrived. He called Captain Clancy to his cabin. Clancy took his time arriving, and made it clear upon his arrival that he wasn't at Aaron's beck and call. With the skill of a longtime spacer, he parked himself in midair just inside Aaron's cabin door, arms crossed over his narrow chest.

As soon as Doc approved it, Aaron had been moved to one of the largest officer's cabins on the *Tyrannos Rex*. Aaron had heard that the captain's quarters were slightly larger, but he wasn't going to make an issue of it.

By Aaron's usual standards, the room might as well have been a monk's cell, and taking over Clancy's quarters wouldn't have improved the situation enough to make it worth the bother. Aaron's cabin was three by three by two and a half meters, plus a small extension for a compact private bathroom and a minute closet. Most of the furnishings were designed to fold into the wall: a bed that might be big enough for two very friendly people, a table with two folding chairs, and a desk with a com station.

The metal walls were painted an institutional green,

unadorned except for a few decorative magnets shaped like tropical fruit, left by some previous occupant. Aaron had moved them to his desk area, where they currently were keeping an array of reports and correspondence from floating around the room.

A tiny nook held a water dispenser and an automatic coffee machine, both designed to operate with or without gravity; a good thing, since they were currently in free fall, and the only thing keeping Aaron from floating out of his bed was a sleeping bag attached to the frame with Velcro.

If his foot had been on the deck, Clancy looked like he would have been tapping it. "What you want, Duck? I got me a ship to run, and your big plans don't make my job no easier."

Aaron frowned. "I wish you wouldn't call me 'Duck.' "

Clancy smiled just a little. "That all you called me down here for? Then you're wasting both our time. You may be the Duke, but on *my* ship, I'm the *king,* and I calls them as I sees them."

Aaron sighed. "How about if you just hold the disrespect till we're out of earshot of guests? Appearances are very important here, Clancy."

"You got a deal, if'n you remember that on *my* ship, you calls me 'Captain.' "

"Good enough—Captain."

"That's better, Duck."

Aaron raised an eyebrow.

Clancy feigned innocence as he looked around the room. "I don't see no guests around, do you?"

Aaron chuckled and shook his head.

Clancy nodded. "We'll do that a while. Things work out all right, I might even let you start calling me 'Gus.' "

Aaron considered. "There might even come a time when I started to prefer 'Aaron' to 'Duck.' "

"I'll think about it, Duck. Now is that really all you wanted?"

"I did want to talk about names. I want to rename the *Tyrannos Rex.*"

Clancy's expression turned to one of disgust. "No, no, no way! Not for all the riches on Tikonov. Not wrapped in a purse made out of your tanned hide. No way."

"It's just for appearances again. I don't care what *you* call the ship. I just want to change the name on the hull and the registration papers. You could keep calling it anything you want."

"No. Can't be done."

Aaron sighed. He hadn't anticipated this would be more of a problem than anything else he'd negotiated with Clancy. Though Clancy made a great show of resisting, he'd ultimately been quite accommodating on any number of issues, from use of his cargo bay, to Aaron's subcontracting his off-duty crewmembers to work on his project.

Clancy was an easy man to figure out. His primary concern was always the ship, as was his secondary. His tertiary concern was probably his pride, but his pride seemed to be tied up in the ship. Aaron's plans were in the best interest of the ship, and Clancy understood that. To Aaron, he was that rarest of men: someone whose interests were simple, obvious, and for sale. As long as Aaron maintained the ship, he considered Clancy totally trustworthy.

Still, it bothered him to be surprised by a conflict. It suggested his understanding of the man might not be as complete as he thought. He had to know more. "Why is this so important? Did you name the ship?"

"Nah. She was christened with that name long before I had her, and fought through a couple wars with it on her hull. She's got a history, this one."

"But you didn't name her."

"And neither will you. Listen here, Duck. You plan to stay on this ship, or any ship, for a while, you should understand there's a bond between us spacers—a tradition. Goes back longer than your Sword-Sworn"—he sneered a bit at the name, knowing full well that Aaron's faction was brand new—"or your Republic, or your Star League, or your precious House Davion. Goes back to ships that sailed the water, and boats made out of wood and reeds.

"We men and women who sail the black abyss know how small we are, know that no matter how mighty we build our ships or how big we think we are, it could swallow us up like *that*." He snapped his fingers.

"You could call us superstitious. Me, I say we know there are forces bigger than we are—forces you got to respect if you want to live, if you want to bring your girls and boys back to port safe, to hug their spouses and babies again.

"A ship what changes its name is *cursed*. No good ever comes of it. You want a cursed ship, then fine, you change its name to anything you want. But it ain't going to be *my* ship that you curse."

"But *Tyrannos Rex*. You know what it means, don't you?"

"Tyrant King, King Tyrant, Terrible King, something like that. I'm not much for Latin. It's all Greek to me."

"I'm trying to piece together a coalition here, with me in charge. You see how that could be a problem for me?"

Clancy considered for a moment, running his tongue under his upper lip, so his moustache undulated like a silver caterpillar. "You know what I think? I think that a man with such aspirations . . . I find out he changed the name of his ship from such a thing, I'd have to wonder, what's he trying to hide? Maybe his true nature? Changing that name don't make it go away, or the worries that make it troubling to you.

"But a man shows up with a ship named like that, puts that name right out there for everyone to see. Well, you ever hear the tale of the elephant in the room—the one nobody talks about? You put their greatest worry right there on the side of your flagship, in two-meter-tall letters. And they got to think, 'Would he do that if he had anything to hide? Only a good, just, honest leader could get away with that.' And there, your elephant's gone. See what I mean?"

Aaron grinned. Damned if Clancy wasn't right. "It stays *Tyrannos Rex,* then, and we'll use its name proudly and without shame. If my enemies make something of it, then I'll simply feign innocence, and they'll look like petty fools." He chuckled, "Did you ever think of going into politics, Captain?"

He grinned back. "Duck, I'd change the ship's name first."

Erik waited impatiently in the small armored shuttle for the pressure outside to equalize. The pilot, a skinny lieutenant who was clearly bored with such a mundane assignment, sat at the helm station, humming some pop tune and passing the time fiddling with the ship's more arcane systems. He'd kept to himself on the way over, and Erik wasn't much inclined to make small talk with a junior officer.

He'd just started coming to terms with his uncle's death, and what it might mean for his place in the SwordSworn, and now things had been cast into a new sort of uncertainty.

Though he felt guilty to admit it, even to himself, Aaron's death would have created a power vacuum, one that might have pulled Erik several rungs up the ladder. Not to the top, certainly, but possibly to a place of independence and security.

The light over the door turned green, and the double doors of the lock automatically cycled open. A DropShip crewmember appeared outside, a metal snap hook at the end of a line in her hand. She snapped the hook to a ring just outside the lock, then gave the line a sharp tug. An automatic winch on the other end whirred, pulling the line taut. He saw that the other end was anchored next to a handrail, which in turn led to an interior airlock.

It appeared the bay had once been a 'Mech bay, though much of it was now equipped for cargo. A few 'Mech gantries were left intact though: some empty, some holding LoaderMechs, and one containing the Duke's white-and-gold *Black Hawk*.

He was startled to see the condition it was in—the paint scratched and scarred, laser and impact damage on the flanks, arms, and legs, much of the armor sheared away. The areas around the jump jet nozzles were blackened and partially melted. Bits of some kind of dried vegetation clung to every join and crevice. Most startling was the center panel of the cockpit—a shattered wreck with a hole in the middle. It was difficult to see how his uncle had survived. It obviously had been a close call.

One more shell or laser shot in the right place—

The woman outside the lock gave him a little wave, then pushed off sharply from the deck, sailing away into the depths of the ship.

Erik had no idea if he'd have been included in the Duke's estate—the misreporting of his death had not taken events that far. Certainly, it would have been expected, given their close relationship and Aaron's lack of heirs, that he'd receive some substantial inheritance. But he had no assurances of that, and he had to wonder. Their relationship was often troubled, especially in recent years.

He sighed, and started climbing down the line in the direction of the airlock. His mind quickly slipped back into what might have been.

An inheritance would have been only a bonus. Erik could have traded on his position, his past relationship to the Duke, the respect he had won in the military sector, and his citizenship to find a place for himself. It had been his experience that once one reached a certain social status among the elite, one never suffered from material want, even if one didn't have a penny.

Even without trading on his father's money and influence, having a member of a great family like the Sandovals begging on a street corner—or even working in some common job—would be an embarrassment none of the family elders could tolerate.

Someone would have found a board seat on a major company for him—one with a handsome stipend, stock, and other benefits attached. He had little doubt he could have these things today, were it not for the assumption that he was already provided for by Aaron.

The thought filled him with an unaccustomed resentment, and guilt. What sort of person was he, that he would resent his uncle just for living?

These thoughts haunted him as he wandered the corridors of the great ship, looking for his uncle's quarters. He'd somehow assumed he'd be met at the airlock, but that hadn't happened.

He occasionally spotted crewpeople going about their business, usually in a hurry, and often just out of earshot. He looked in vain for someone he recognized: Ulysses Paxton, his uncle's bodyguard, or the lovely Deena Onan, whom he was always glad to see, even in the darkest of circumstances.

But they were nowhere to be found, and Erik was quickly lost. Finally, he spotted a face that was, if not familiar, at least recognized. The man crossed a corridor junction a few meters in front of him, and was almost out of sight before he noticed the gray beard. "You there! Hold on!"

The man had already vanished, carried on by his own momentum, but it was only a few seconds before he reappeared, peering around the corner of the junction. "Well, if it isn't the Duck's boy."

Erik was in no mood for this, and an impertinent commoner was a natural target for his aggravation. "Listen here—Gus is your name? I'm nobody's 'boy,' except my dear departed mother's. I'm looking for the Duke."

"Listen here, *boy.* On my ship, my name is *Captain,* and you'd be wise to remember that. I been through this already today with the Duck, and he and me got an understanding. I don't bow to him, and I sure ain't bowing to the likes of you. Now, you want to know where he is, you ask nice-like."

Erik was flabbergasted, but there appeared to be little point in arguing with the old lout. The Duke had hired him; he was sure that he could discipline him as easily.

"Very well—Captain Gus."

"Captain Clancy," growled the man.

"Captain Clancy then. *Please*—where can I find my uncle?"

Clancy jerked his thumb back the way he'd come. "Go till you see the green walls. That's officers' country. Room's about halfway down, outboard. D-16. Most people couldn't miss it." He turned and braced to kick off down the hall. "You, I'm not so sure about."

Then he was gone.

Erik felt his face redden. He'd have a talk with

Aaron about this one. It would almost be fun to see what was in store for Captain Clancy.

He had little trouble finding the quarters. In fact, he suspected he had passed them once before in his wanderings. He'd somehow expected something more in keeping with his uncle's position. Judging by the distances between adjacent doors, this was no bigger than a third-class stateroom on a liner. Perhaps the former military vessel simply didn't offer anything better. He stopped at the door and rang the bell. He heard a solenoid in the lock clunk, and the door slid to one side.

He found his uncle crouched in front of a simple desk, his feet secured to the deck by loops of webbing. He was wearing utilitarian blue pajamas, and, as with his 'Mech, he was showing a lot of battle damage. He glanced up from his paperwork. "Erik. About time you got here."

Erik's heart sank. He'd been hoping that some variation of the warm family reunion of his fantasies would take place, and wash away the dark thoughts that plagued him. Obviously that wasn't to be the case. "My apologies, Uncle. I was lost briefly. It's a big ship."

He didn't look up from his papers. "It is, isn't it? Perfect for my needs. All this space. A blank canvas for my designs."

What designs? Why his sudden interest in this whale of a cargo ship?

"I'm afraid I don't understand, Uncle. I'd assumed you'd be joining us. New Aragon is ours, but House Liao's forces are moving on Halloran V and they've asked our help."

"And they'll have it, but without me. As I've told you, the coalition is our only long-term hope here. We have to build a force capable of stopping Liao and mounting a counteroffensive. That may discourage them enough to withdraw from our space, or at least impress The Republic enough to support our efforts.

"So I'll be taking the *Tyrannos Rex* to Azha to take on supplies and materials, then on to Ningpo."

Erik was surprised. "Ningpo has been none too friendly to our diplomatic overtures in the past. If time is of the essence, shouldn't you start with a more receptive world?"

"That is exactly why I should start with Ningpo, Erik. If I can get them to pledge to our cause, the other planetary governors in the region will take notice. By winning one world, I may be able to win half a dozen, maybe more."

"And how do you plan to do that?"

Aaron pulled out a data pad and scrolled through what appeared to be a financial report. "It's enough for you to know that I have a plan, Erik. I haven't got time to explain it to you. You only really need to know your part in it. In any case, it will be revealed in due time."

"I see. Then I assume I'll be continuing with our forces to Halloran V in your stead?"

"You assume wrong. I have another mission for you. A very important diplomatic mission."

Again, he was blindsided. "Uncle, our forces need leadership."

"They'll have it. I'm naming Justin Sortek as campaign commander. He's proven himself again and again with the Davion Guard. If anyone can lead them to victory, it's him."

Stunned, Erik found himself sputtering. "My Lord, am I being punished?"

The Duke looked at him blankly. "Punished?" He sighed. "Erik, you are a Sandoval. To be a competent MechWarrior is one thing. To mistake your time in the cockpit for anything that will lead to your proper station in life is quite another. You're far too much in love with the glory of battle."

"I have always served you in battle, Uncle. I carry the banner of the SwordSworn proudly. I'm not afraid to fight along with our troops in the cause of House Davion."

Aaron stuck the data pad to an adhesive strip on the desk. "I know you aren't afraid of battle, Erik. I know you'd lay down your life if it came to that. Which is why I am sending you on a mission more important to me than any battle. While I negotiate with Ningpo, you will be bringing Shensi into our fold."

"Shensi? They aren't even in the path of Liao's current thrust. Our best intelligence shows them being bypassed."

"Then your job is to convince them otherwise. They've retained a substantial army. If they aren't being attacked, it's fresh and uncommitted—just the sort of reinforcements we need right now. I am confident you can do that— It may even be easier than you think."

Erik was skeptical, and deeply disappointed that he would be left out of the coming battle. Added to all his other negative emotions was another feeling of guilt—that he was deserting their forces when they needed him most. Once again, Aaron was shuffling him to the side.

"With respect, Lord Governor, it seems that if you had confidence in me, I'd be commanding our forces in this campaign."

The Duke scowled at him. "Be careful what you say, Erik. I haven't forgotten how you've disappointed me in the past. Recently I've given you opportunities to redeem yourself—the latest on New Aragon. Your performance there was acceptable, if not exemplary.

"But you are a Sandoval. Acceptable is not enough.

If this mission is a sacrifice for you, then sacrifices must be made. You say you aren't afraid to face danger and battle, yet you never know when those things will find you." He reached up and touched the bandage on his chest. "Lord knows, I know that better than anyone.

"This is an opportunity to prove yourself to me, Erik, the greatest one yet, though you don't realize it. If you aren't up to it, then I won't force you. But if not, then I have no further use for you. In any capacity."

Erik blinked in surprise. His uncle sounded serious. Yet he couldn't just cave in. "Of course I'll do as ordered, but my objections stand." He paused a moment. "I appreciate the trust you're putting in me."

Aaron didn't seem to notice. He'd picked up another data pad, and was studying a column of numbers. "Good. Send your shuttle back to the fleet with word you'll be joining me. At Azha we'll arrange transport for you to Shensi."

Erik was puzzled by this pronouncement. The trip from Azha to Shensi would simply take him back through Pleione. "Azha's in the wrong direction."

Aaron gave him an annoyed glance. "There are things I need to take care of before we part company, and I don't want your trip attracting too much attention. Using a less direct route serves my needs. At any rate, by then, proper diplomatic credentials should be arranged. I'm having Captain Ricco send over a small contingent of officers and enlisteds to act as my temporary staff. Pick someone to act as your aide, and have them sent over as well—and of course you should have your personal items sent." He glanced at the time display on his data pad. "You've got about three hours."

Erik floated, silently, trying to take it all in, trying to think of some way around his exile.

Aaron gave him a look of annoyance. "That's all, Erik."

Erik licked his lips. At least there was one grain of satisfaction to be found in all this. "Uncle, before I go. I had a most disturbing encounter in the corridor with your Captain Clancy. His behavior was quite horrifying."

Aaron looked up and blinked. "Yes, it is." He went back to his data pad.

"Uncle, you don't understand. He was rude and insolent. He spoke of you in a disrespectful fashion. He actually made fun of your title."

"He called me 'Duck' again, didn't he? Well, I did say not to do that in front of guests. You"—he sighed deeply—"are family."

Erik bit his lip, puzzled. "You allow this sort of behavior from your subordinates?" *He'd certainly never allow it of me.*

"Only in the case of Captain Clancy. His status is special. I don't encourage it, but it isn't in my best interests to forbid it, either."

"Uncle—"

"Captain Clancy is in *my* employ, Erik. He's not part of the SwordSworn or the general staff. He's my personal concern, and I'll not have you telling me how to deal with him. He's impertinent and rude. He's also gifted and useful. Like you, he has an important place in my plan."

"But, my Lord, I won't stand by and let him—"

"Erik, what have I told you about false pride? It's the burden of fools and failures. Captain Clancy is going to be a useful and loyal servant. All I have to do is allow him this"— he swept his arms out to indicate the ship—"small domain. I'm not so petty a man that I can't bear his little insults, nor so foolish a man that I'll trade all his skills away over a few transgressions." He glowered. "Ultimately, Clancy knows his place." His eyes narrowed. "Now show me that you know yours."

Shocked, Erik left the room without another word. Had the stress of his experiences caused the Duke to become unhinged? He thought of Clancy's smug smile as he left Erik in the corridor and fumed.

This isn't over.

7

For Erik, the wait for the jump to Azha was as un-eventful as it was uncomfortable. The Duke remained sequestered in his quarters, presumably working and recovering from his injuries. But, large as the ship was, it wasn't big enough for both Erik and Captain Clancy. The wiry little man seemed to prowl the *Rex* con-stantly, like a feral cat patrolling his territory.

Nor did he avoid Erik when they saw each other. Quite the contrary. It was up to Erik to steer clear and avoid the confrontation, something that offended his pride mightily. But he felt it was necessary: the only way to avoid antagonizing his uncle further.

The time might have been more pleasantly spent in the company of his uncle's valet, Deena Onan; how-ever, although Ulysses Paxton assured him that she was alive and well, she no longer seemed to be aboard. Aaron had apparently secured separate transport for her at their last stop and sent her on some sort of courier mission. Paxton would say no more than that.

As for Paxton himself, he had always been cordial but professionally detached with Erik and, Erik suspected, anyone whose life he might be called upon to protect in the line of duty. Now he was even more so. He seemed rattled—more by the Duke's close brush with death than his own.

So Erik spent several days in his quarters reviewing debriefing reports from New Aragon, and playing Go on a magnetized board with Lieutenant Clayhatchee, the officer he'd appointed as his aide on the upcoming mission.

It was a great relief when they docked with the fully charged JumpShip and made the shift to Azha.

The system was quickly becoming a major hub of SwordSworn activity, so passage was soon arranged for Erik and his aide to travel on a fast *Avenger* assault ship. Erik received word they would be shipping out within the hour.

He was on his way into the bay to board the shuttle, when Deena Onan emerged. She seemed as surprised to see him as he was to see her.

She bowed her head respectfully. "Commander Sandoval-Groell."

He smiled. "A pleasure, as always, Deena. Did you arrive on the *Avenger?*"

"Yes, Commander, the same one you're to be traveling on. I'm told it will refuel from one of our tankers before linking up with the JumpShip for the trip to Shensi."

"My uncle told you about my mission?"

She looked uncomfortable. "Of course. I made the . . . necessary arrangements."

Erik blinked in puzzlement. She'd arranged his passage on the *Avenger?* That didn't seem right, with her just having returned.

She seemed to sense his confusion. She looked around. The bay was a busy place. There were several *Tyrannos Rex* crewmembers working within earshot. "I'm sure you've been briefed, Commander. I'm not sure we should be discussing this in such a public place. In any case, the Lord Governor will be expecting me to report in immediately."

He nodded. "Of course. I'm glad you emerged from the New Canton incident alive and well. I'd have been very upset if anything had happened to you."

"That's very gracious, Commander. Take care and have a safe journey." She seemed almost relieved as she pulled herself through the inner airlock door and disappeared down the corridor.

Erik looked after her a moment. Though she had always treated him kindly, his advances toward Deena had never gotten him anywhere. Still, he didn't understand what he'd done to make her so uncomfortable, or what that whole exchange had been about.

Again, he suspected the Duke's hand. He sometimes used Deena as an operative or messenger, and it was impossible to keep track of all his plots and manipulations. Mentally, Erik added her distress to the list of deeds for which Aaron would ultimately be held accountable.

Erik, too, would be relieved to get away from this spot, and off the *Tyrannos Rex.*

Aaron looked at himself in the little cabin's mirror. His face looked puffy, but that was a common side effect of free fall in the best of circumstances. Beyond that, his skin was regaining its normal tone, and the bruises were fading. His chest still ached constantly, despite the drugs, but Doc and the consulting Sword-Sworn physicians he'd brought aboard for consultation all told him that he was healing well and could expect a full recovery.

All he needed was time and rest—the two things that, despite his considerable fortune, he could not now afford. He resolved to push himself on, through force of will if necessary. Damn the medical consequences; he'd deal with them later.

He rubbed the whiskers on his chin. He was still toying with the idea of letting the beard grow, or at least of shaving it into a Vandyke. It would cover the jagged, still-red scar on his chin, and perhaps a few others, depending on how full he kept it. He tried to decide whether it would make him look distinguished, or merely sinister.

The door bell rang. "Lord Governor," said Paxton from outside, "Ms. Onan has returned."

He quickly buzzed her in. He was eager to hear her news, of course, but he was also glad to again have her services. He was feeling well enough to move around the ship, and being properly groomed and dressed would make him feel human again. He had to prepare himself. The day was quickly approaching when he would have to make public appearances again, no matter how he was feeling.

Deena floated through the door and clung to a grab-iron near the foot of his bed. She smiled at him as she entered. "You're looking stronger, Lord Governor."

He grinned weakly. "You lie," he said, "but you lie well."

His quip seemed to bother her. "It is what you pay me for, I suppose."

"You're back far sooner than I expected." He'd used his considerable resources to expedite her return trip, even holding a charged JumpShip for her at Styk, but her outbound travel arrangements from Liao had necessarily been haphazard. Still, amazing things could happen if you threw enough money at a problem.

"I made excellent connections to Second Try, Lord Governor, and as it happened, an outbound St. Cyr's carrier DropShip was waiting at the jump point as I arrived. In fact, it's likely the ship they'll use for our assignment. I was able to negotiate the deal with the mercenaries at the jump point, without actually traveling to the planet."

He studied her face and frowned slightly. Deena was normally a cheerful person. She seemed somehow disturbed—not like someone celebrating a difficult job well done. "No trouble, I take it?"

"No, my Lord. I successfully negotiated a hit-and-run surprise air attack on the capital city on Shensi. The arrangements and timing are as we'd planned, and it was only necessary to give them the smaller two of the three numbered accounts you provided to me. I believe they'll actually try billing House Liao for the attack as well."

Aaron laughed. "It's even possible they'll collect. There's something to be said for hiring your enemy's mercenaries. You're sure they don't know who is hiring them?"

"I gave them the distinct impression I represented Capellan business interests who wish to bring Shensi mineral rights into their sphere of influence. I implied an early attack might lead them to capitulate with their production infrastructure undamaged.

"They'll arrive at a pirate point in the system in fifteen days. The DropShip will immediately deploy toward the planet. Once in a close orbit, several wings of fighters will stage a lightning raid on the capital city, targeting primarily monuments, government buildings, and infrastructure: power, communications, water, sewer—creating as much public disruption as possible.

Then they'll rejoin their carrier DropShip, rendezvous with their JumpShip and be out of the system before Shensi has a chance to react, and they'll be sure the Shensi people know who is attacking them. The leadership there will have no reason to suppose it's anything more than a Capellan advance attack."

He smiled at her. "Well done, Deena. Once again you've proven what an asset you are to me, and how clever I was to rescue you from that DropShip."

She looked away, frowning.

"Is there something you aren't telling me?"

She hesitated before speaking. "I encountered Commander Sandoval in the bay as I was arriving. I didn't know if I should be providing him details on the timing of the attack on Shensi. He'll need to make provisions for his own safety."

Aaron stared at the wall for a moment. "You didn't tell him anything, did you?"

"Tell him, Lord Governor? I told him I'd made the arrangements for his trip. Nothing more. The meeting was far too public to talk about such an important matter freely."

He was relieved. He hadn't expected her to return before Erik left, and therefore hadn't briefed her on the possibility. It was the sort of mistake he didn't intend to repeat. "Good, good; I was worried for a moment."

She blinked rapidly, unconsciously bobbing her head. "Lord Governor, if you don't mind my asking— Commander Sandoval does know about the attack, doesn't he?"

Aaron took a deep breath and let it out slowly. "In order for this ruse to work, Erik must be as genuinely surprised by the attack as anyone."

"My Lord, the danger—"

"Erik is a big boy, Deena, capable of taking care of himself. This is no different than any other battle I've sent him into, and I've sent him into plenty."

"With respect, my Lord, the people shooting at him in those battles weren't working for the SwordSworn."

"You've never questioned my activities before."

"I'm sorry, my Lord, I've never had cause to." She immediately seemed to regret her words. "Apologies, Lord Governor. That was inappropriate. I'm merely concerned for his safety."

"He's a Sandoval, Deena. You should know, better than most anyone, that we're born survivors, hard to kill. Erik will be fine."

She still looked very unhappy. "If you don't mind, my Lord, it's been a long and tiring trip. I'd like to rest up for a few hours before resuming my duties."

He nodded. "Of course. Take as much time as you'd like. I'll see you in the morning. I'd like to work on getting back to my regular routines. It's time to start looking like a Duke again."

"Very good, Lord Governor. I'll see you tomorrow."

He watched her leave. She had doubts, but she'd come around. He was doing the right thing, the *only* right thing. This was the only way to bring the Shensi into their coalition.

In time, even Erik would tell her that.

Deena floated into the hall, cursing the zero gravity. There were times when a person just wanted to lean against the wall, to feel the cool metal against her forehead, and be alone with her thoughts for a minute. That didn't work when a person was bobbing around like an escaped balloon.

Instead, she just hung there, a hand loosely covering her eyes. Had she just arranged for Erik's death? Could she forgive herself if he didn't return?

Paxton waited at his post by the Duke's cabin door, but watched her with concern. "Deena, is there anything I can do?"

"No," she said, "nothing." But she didn't move or try to escape his attention. "You knew about my mission, and the attack I arranged?"

He nodded. "The Duke keeps very few secrets from me. Or from you, for that matter."

"Were you aware that Erik doesn't know about the plan—that he has no idea what he's walking into?"

Paxton considered the question for a moment. "I didn't know the specifics. It doesn't, however, surprise me."

"I just don't . . . How could the Duke do this?"

He smiled grimly. "Deena, you've been employed by Duke Sandoval long enough not to be surprised at this sort of thing. You know he can be ruthless when the occasion calls for it."

She chewed her lip.

He tilted his head, trying to look into her eyes. "It isn't what he's doing that's bothering you, so much as the fact that he's made us culpable."

She nodded.

"Professional detachment, Deena. It's a necessity when you work for people in high positions—for your own protection more than theirs. I think sometimes you let yourself get too emotionally involved with the Sandovals."

"I don't want to be uninvolved, Ulysses. I'm a person, not a robot."

He smiled slightly. "And I am?"

"I'm sorry. I didn't mean it that way. You're very professional, Ulysses. I admire that and in your situation, protecting lives, it may be a necessity. It's just not me."

"Then tell me, Deena, how do you feel about the Duke just this minute?"

She considered. "I feel . . . disappointed."

"You should know by now not to judge nobles by our everyday standards. They have different duties, different responsibilities, and follow a different moral compass. You understand that, don't you?"

"I suppose. It's just—this wasn't how I saw the Duke."

"Tell me, Deena, do you have feelings toward the Duke?"

"Feelings? You mean . . . romantic feelings?"

"Close feelings of any kind."

"Have I done something to make you think I have romantic feelings toward him?"

"No; and given what I know of your history, it seemed most unlikely. Still, I had to ask."

"I feel very protective of the Duke, and of Erik as well. I feel very . . . close to the Duke. I've been with him for some time—been within his circle of confidence. He saved my life, Ulysses."

"And mine as well. But it's easy to read too much into that. Both of us would be very difficult for the Lord Governor to replace." He smiled wryly. "If there's one thing I've learned about dealing with nobles: Never attribute to decency what can just as easily be explained by enlightened self-interest."

She frowned. "If you feel that way, why do you work for him?"

He chuckled. "Deena, if I could find a saint who needed a bodyguard . . ." He considered. "You know, I'd probably turn down the work. They wouldn't have nearly enough enemies to make the work interesting, and if the day ever came that I failed, how could I live with myself?"

Her eyes widened, and she grinned just a little. "So you work for the Duke because he's hated and expendable?"

"Not in so many words, but—Well, if nobles can be pragmatic, why can't we be, too?"

"Then perhaps that's why I work for the Duke as well. He's a force of nature, a power—the kind of power I'll never have. But perhaps I can steer a little of his energy to my ends, to do some kind of good in the universe. Let's face it: The power will be there whether I am or not."

"I'm not sure I can say the same if I'm fulfilling my job description. But then, perhaps my good work enables your good work. Together, we may have a net positive influence on the grand scheme of things."

"Oh," she said, fishing in the side pocket of her trim velour jumpsuit and pulling out a card. She handed it to Paxton. "This is the private intelligence firm you asked me to hire to look into the sabotage of the DropShip. They'll be communicating through a series of anonymous mail drops. I'm still not sure what the point of this is. Won't SwordSworn intelligence do their own investigation?"

"As time allows, but they're new, and their resources are limited. Gathering strategic intelligence has to be their highest priority. But a private firm, properly funded, will be able to make it their first priority, and they'll have more freedom to operate on New Canton. The Duke has instructed SwordSworn resources to concentrate their efforts inside The Republic's territory that House Liao has taken. We have a few assets there, though not many.

"The Duke believes his assassination was a condition of the agreement between New Canton and House Liao. He's hoping their failure may throw the agreement into doubt."

"You think otherwise?"

Paxton sighed and glanced around to be sure nobody else was within earshot. "I believe the Duke greatly overestimates his own importance in the eyes of House Liao. I believe that only if the SwordSworn succeed in thoroughly bloodying their noses will they even be aware he exists. New Aragon may have put him on their scanners, but that's a matter of their own priorities. The Duke would never admit it, but there are worse things than going unnoticed.

"Still, I think that New Canton's Prefect ordered the attempt with little planning, and on his own authority. It was a crime of opportunity. House Liao would have never ordered such a clumsy attempt. Perhaps, uncertain of his position with Liao, the Prefect thought he could curry some favor by delivering the Duke's head to them." He grinned. "Imagine the Prefect's surprise if he'd succeeded, went to them with his prize, and they looked at him and asked, 'You killed *who?*' "

A rumble emanated from the structure of the *Rex*, like a first peal of distant thunder. Something in the guts of the great ship was stirring to life.

"All hands," Captain Clancy's voice echoed from dozens of hidden speakers, "stand by for boost. One-G acceleration in twenty seconds from . . . mark."

"Well," said Paxton, as he pushed himself down the wall so his feet were against the deck, "I guess the commander is off, and we're on our way to Azha."

She nodded, accepting his hand so he could pull her down against the deck. "It'll be a distraction at least. I've been on the downlink most of the last day, while waiting for you to arrive, but there's still a lot to arrange before we reach the planet. Time to do some shopping."

It was a six-day round-trip from the jump point to Azha and back, and Aaron wished to maximize their short stay on the planet. For his plans to go forward, a great deal of material would have to be secured and placed aboard *Tyrannos Rex*, as well as a virtual battalion of craftsmen who would begin installing it immediately, continuing the process during the voyage.

It would have been far more reasonable, and less

expensive, to do all the work in port, but at this point Aaron had far more money than time.

There were certain matters that could only be handled while the ship was grounded, and for that Azha was well suited. The abandoned Capellan supply depot at the capital city of Casella had been equipped with excellent ship-service facilities, which had been converted for civilian use.

The *Tyrannos Rex* would need structural modifications that could not be handled in space, and she would need to be repainted.

Aaron had secured a team of the best available shipwrights and craftsmen for the modifications. As for the paint, a huge hangar there housed a system that once had applied protective hull coatings to freighters. It had been converted to a computer-controlled ship-painting system. The company that operated it boasted they could apply a custom paint job, even a complex design, to the largest vessel in less than a day.

Aaron was going to put that to the test.

Until then, the best thing most of the occupants of *Tyrannos Rex* could do was get out of the way.

A limousine arrived at the apron below the ship shortly after landing, and picked up Aaron and his entourage. Though the car came with a driver, Ulysses Paxton insisted on taking the wheel. The original driver handled opening doors, loading bags, and navigating. They were soon on an elevated expressway, headed into the capital.

The landscape was low and dry. Wide valleys covered with sagebrush, dry grass and cactus were surrounded by low hills. Low, umbrella-shaped trees with purplish leaves, probably native to the planet, were scattered among the sage.

Small herds of long-necked mammals on thick, stumplike legs—each adult bigger than the limousine—fed on the purple trees. They were no species

Aaron had ever seen, and were probably indigenous. Flocks of strange four-winged birds, pale blue and as tall as a man, flew overhead in swooping circles, or walked among the herds, looking for some mysterious food source.

To the southwest, they could see the skyline of the city—a central core of metal-and-glass towers dwarfed by a handful of massive arcologies. Beyond the city, a shimmering field of silver near the horizon marked the beginning of the southern ocean.

Aaron rubbed the leather seat cushions. They were exceptionally soft and beautiful. He leaned forward and tapped the intercom to the forward compartment, where the driver navigated while Ulysses drove. "Driver, what are these seat covers made of?"

"Tunna-beasts, those big things you saw grazing near the highway a ways back. They're not much good for eating, but the hides make the best leather in The Republic."

Aaron turned to Deena. "We'll need some of this. This car is nice, too. See if it's available in an armored model, and if so, buy two."

Deena crossed her long legs and looked at him. "Any particular color, Lord Governor?"

"I'm partial to green," he said, "or perhaps gray. One of each would be good, I suppose."

"Indeed," she said, taking a few notes on a pad in her lap.

He pushed the intercom button again. "Driver, I'm told that the Chipley Arms is the finest hotel in town. Is that so?"

"Well, my Lord, I haven't stayed there myself, mind you, but I've heard nothing but good reports from my passengers, and the travel guides give it the highest ratings. I also hear that they have the finest French-Chinese chef on the planet, perhaps even the whole Prefecture."

Aaron smiled knowingly. "I'm glad to hear that. I'm looking forward to sampling his cuisine."

The car wound its way past the arcologies and into the core of the city, through wide canyons of concrete and steel.

The Chipley Arms was a fifteen-story tower of white marble on top of a low hill, with a view of the water. Ornate trim and carved scrollwork covering the building gave it the look of a cake decorated with white frosting. A portico supported by Corinthian columns marked the entrance.

As they pulled into the drive, uniformed doormen dashed out to meet them. A red carpet was rolled out to the limousine. He was getting a good feeling about the hotel.

A slender man with thinning hair, a pointed nose, and a thin moustache met them at the door. He pressed his white-gloved fingertips together in front of him and bowed slightly at the waist. "Duke Sandoval. I am Charles Pinckard, the manager. Let me welcome you to the Chipley Arms. I can't tell you what an honor it is to have such a special guest in our hotel."

"My arrangements have been taken care of?"

"Indeed, my Lord, though it is unusual to have a guest reserve the entire hotel."

"I won't be using all of it, of course. Your best suites are on the top three floors?"

"Yes, and of course I'll be showing you our Emperor's Suite on the top floor. I hope it meets with your approval."

The manager led them to an ornate brass express elevator, which he operated with a key attached to a watch chain on his jacket. It whisked them to the top floor, and directly into the suite. "A private elevator is one of the features of the suite. There are three bedrooms with baths, plus a parlor, drawing room, library and formal dining room. Our kitchen is at your disposal around the clock."

Aaron admired the furniture. The legs were all gracefully curved, and elaborate scrollwork was deeply carved into the wood. The upholstery was done in plush burgundy velour striped with gold thread. Rich tapestries woven with stylized scenes of the desert and sea hung on the walls. Marble sculptures stood on illuminated pedestals, and mirrors in elaborate gilded frames hung on the walls. Huge carpets, woven in the same style as the tapestries, covered the marble floor.

It was a splendid space—comfortable and impeccably decorated.

He turned back to the manager. "Is there a freight elevator?"

The manager nodded. "Just down the hall, through the common spaces."

"Good. Some of my men should be waiting in your lobby by now. Please have them brought up through that elevator."

"Certainly, sir." The manager raised his hand to his cheek and spoke briefly into the tiny transmitter strapped to his wrist. "Will there be anything else?"

"This will be fine. I'll take it. I'll take it all. Now, is your second-best suite on this floor as well?"

The manager looked puzzled. "Yes, just down the hall."

"Good. I'll be staying there. Show me, please."

The manager stepped to an inlaid set of double doors and swung them open to the corridor outside. He hesitated and turned. "But, my Lord, I thought this suite was satisfactory?"

"Oh, yes, it's perfect. That's why the men are coming here."

Just then, an elevator at the end of the hall opened, and a full load of large, rough-looking men stepped out. An observant person might have recognized them from Captain Clancy's crew. They looked completely out of place in the elegant surroundings.

They marched up to Aaron. A bald man with a nose that appeared to have been repeatedly broken seemed to be the leader. He looked at the open doors. "Is this the place, Duke?"

Aaron nodded. "Strip it—carefully; I don't want anything broken or scratched—and take it all back to the ship."

The manager's eyes widened. "Strip it? I don't understand."

"I'm taking the suite, Mr. Pinckard, or rather, all its contents. I'll pay for full replacement of course, plus a generous overhead, and we'll compensate you for loss of use while the room is being redecorated."

The manager's jaw hung open. "Redecorate. But— This is impossible. These are all antiques, some dating back to the Star League."

"Which is exactly why I'm taking them. These aren't the sort of furnishings one purchases off a showroom floor. The quickest way to furnish a luxury suite is to find one that's already furnished, and remove its contents to the new suite."

The manager just couldn't seem to wrap his head around what Aaron was saying. "Move the suite?"

Two men positioned themselves on either end of a couch, bent down, and lifted it onto their muscular shoulders. The manager watched in horror as they carried it down the hall to the waiting elevator.

Aaron waved his hand in front of the man. "The second-best suite in the hotel?"

"Yes," said the manager, seemingly grateful for some task he could relate to. "This way."

Three more men walked by, one with a lamp, one with a rolled-up tapestry over his shoulder, and a third carrying a statue wrapped in a blanket.

The manager opened another set of doors. "This is the suite. Um—Will you be stripping it, too?"

"I'll be staying here for a few days while my ship is being refitted. Put my valet and bodyguard on this floor as well. The floor below will remain vacant as a noise buffer." He had a sudden inspiration. This was a fine opportunity to gain the individual loyalty of Clancy's crew. "Oh, and the gentlemen who are hauling this furniture, they'll need first-class rooms on the lower floors. There will be another forty-five or so coming from the ship as well. They should all have rooms. I'll be taking care of their meals, bar tabs, and room service. And of course I'll pay for the damage."

The manager paled. *"Damage?"*

The Duke ignored the question, turning to Deena. "Call the ship. Tell Clancy that anyone who can get shore leave is welcome, including him."

"That won't happen, my Lord. He loves that ship."

"I agree, but ask him anyway."

"Damage?" The manager worried over the word like a dog with a bone.

Deena glanced at him and shrugged. "They're sailors on leave. There *will* be damage."

The manager nodded his head sadly. "Of course."

"I understand," said Aaron, "that you have a very fine chef."

The manager brightened a little. "He is, if I may say so my Lord, exceptional. Chefs have come from throughout the Sphere to study his techniques."

"That's good," said Aaron, looking out through the suite doors as a massive dining table was carried past, "because I'll be taking him with me as well."

The manager's mouth hung open. He blinked. Blinked again. "But of course," said the manager, "but of course."

Aaron relaxed on the balcony outside his suite, feet propped on an ottoman, a fresh batch of company reports on his computer pad, a cold drink made from some sort of fresh-squeezed cactus juice in his hand. His view extended down a strip of parkland through the heart of the old city, to a dockside amusement complex that seemed to operate all day and most of the night.

He'd spent almost an hour the previous evening looking down at its colorful lights and spinning rides. Everything—even the boats that cruised the harbor— seemed to be outlined in strings and lines of colored lights. He'd even sent for a pair of binoculars, so he could watch the people from behind the ferro-glass canopy that protected him from snipers.

Part of him wanted to be down there, too. Walking the boardwalks, peering into the shops, smelling the spicy intoxicants wafting from every food stall and vendor cart. Oh, to be a fledgling cadet, feeling power-ful in his new uniform, a beautiful and deeply impres-sed young lady holding his hand, seeing those spinning lights reflected in her eyes.

He pushed the thoughts away. Such things were for overgrown children, not for men of title and power. Those days were gone. They would not come his way again. He tried to work, and suddenly found himself unable to concentrate.

He took his feet off the ottoman and climbed out of his deeply padded wicker chair. He stood next to the railing, looking out, reaching up to put his finger-tips against the cold glass. He was a long way from forty, but could he be feeling *old?*

Or perhaps just alone. There were aspects of life that were passing him by in the rush to power.

There were women, of course. Companions, flings, but his requirements for anything beyond that were very strict. He would not be merely choosing a wife, but a *duchess,* and perhaps something more than that. There was the matter of heirs as well. There was *far* more to consider than his own pleasures and whims.

He sighed. Perhaps it was merely his current project or his close brush with death that had put such thoughts in his mind—some kind of primitive nesting instinct calling to the modern man.

The phone on the table next to his 'puter chimed, rescuing him from his melancholy.

He tapped the ANSWER button, and Captain Clancy's holographic image floated above the phone. "Okay, Duck. I put up with you shanghaiing my crew, messing up my cargo bays, and painting my ship like a spaceport whore, but you got welders down there cutting a *hole* in my hull."

"Technically, they're notching into the corner of the number one bay door."

"You're putting a hole in the part that keeps the outsides out, and the insides in. Same thing, Duck."

"Trust me, Captain, I'm as concerned about that as anyone." He chuckled. "I'm one of the insides that needs to stay in. The armor surrounding the opening will be four times as thick as the hull surrounding it, and there will be four armor-plated pressure doors. It's a hole in your hull, but an exceptionally well-protected hole."

"Yeah, well, you should have consulted me."

"I would have, if there'd been time. The shipwrights are literally working without blueprints, with two structural engineers on-site designing things as they go."

"I reckon you must trust these engineers of yours quite a bit."

"They're both Republic Navy veterans. They've spent fifty years between them putting battle-damaged ships back together, under fire and in the worst of conditions. I'm certain our 'hole' will be just fine."

Clancy nodded, and the corners of his mouth seemed to twitch up almost imperceptibly. "Well then, I guess you got it covered." The almost-smile abruptly ended. "But next time you *tell* me first. This is a ship, not your blasted summer house.

"I don't even know what all this mess you're putting on my ship weighs. When we lift, I'm going to have to give her full throttle, base my weight calculations on our acceleration, then redo all my center-of-gravity adjustments and orbital calculations on the fly. It won't be no picnic, I tell you."

Aaron grinned. "Your reputation says, Captain, that for you it *is* a picnic. Kind of like making an emergency takeoff under fire, with no notice, and with fifty tons of unexpected 'Mech aboard."

"Well, yeah, I guess it's kind of like that."

"Which reminds me. We don't have time right now, but I want to upgrade the armor on that entire bay door, and possibly the interior bulkheads as well. Maybe at the next nondiplomatic port of call."

The French doors opened, and Deena stepped out onto the deck. She placed a new stack of papers on the table next to his 'puter, then stood patiently to see if he needed anything else from her.

"Maybe," said Clancy. "I'll say this for you, Duck. You keep me amused. Been laughing my ass off watching my boys hauling in this sissified furniture of yours. It's gonna look even funnier floating around in free fall."

"The style is called recoco—"

"Rococo," Deena corrected.

"Rococo," he continued, "and it will all be bolted to the floor."

Clancy raised a skeptical eyebrow. "So, for half the voyage it'll just be something to bang your head on. Coulda pointed you at a place'll sell you any kind of folding furniture you want. Quality stuff, too."

"I'm sure. And it would *look* like quality storable furniture too. Listen, Captain Clancy, it's not like I'm trying to install this on your bridge. You did say that what I did in the cargo bay was my business. Is that arrangement still true?"

"Yeah, well, 'cept for that hole in the hull. But I still gots the captain's prerogative to make fun of foolishness when I see it.

"Well, I'm gonna go keep an eye on those welders of yours. Clancy out."

The display blanked, and Aaron turned to Deena. "You're giving me that look."

"What look?"

"That skeptical, 'I can't tell him what I really think because he's the Duke' look. I do value your opinions, you know. What is it?"

"He's right about how absurdly impractical this furniture will be on a DropShip. Not to mention the carpets, the tapestries, the paintings, the art, the gourmet chef."

"Chef Bellwood served on the liner *Ian Cameron*. He's an accomplished zero-gravity chef as well."

"Which means, I suppose, we'll be installing a second kitchen for that?"

"Later. Until then, he can work out of the officers' mess when we're not under boost or on a planet."

She sighed. "Lord Governor, I enjoy interior decorating as much as anyone, but haven't you forgotten there's a war on? That people have died—continue to die—while we're playing house on a spaceship?"

"Of course not, Deena. But these things are neither for my comfort nor my vanity. They are for show. Some things are all the more impressive precisely *because* they are so extravagantly impractical. To build our coalition, we have to win the hearts of the people whose planets we visit, and those of their leaders, as well.

"This is the symbol of power, of confidence, of *victory*. They will all be drawn to this, wish to align themselves with it, hope it will rub off on them. This is the *pull* that will bring our coalition together.

"And the little show you've arranged for Shensi, that's going to be the *push*."

She frowned and tilted her head. "And this is how you fight a war?"

What was with Deena today? He didn't mind her frankness, at least in private, but it was uncharacteristic of her to be so confrontational. "Deena, have you ever wondered what the sword is in the Sword-Sworn's seal?"

"I assume it's the Sword of Davion."

"That's true enough, but there's a legend associated with it that far predates House Davion. My grandmother used to tell it to me when I was a child." He gestured at a love seat across the table from his chair. "Sit, and I'll share it with you. Ring for a drink if you'd like."

She sat on the edge of the seat and crossed her legs, hands cupped over her knee.

He sat as well, moving the stack of papers to one side. "You see, long ago, perhaps on ancient Terra, there was a dragon that emerged from a crack in the ground. It was born of fire and lava. It breathed fire, its skin was hard as stone, and molten metal ran in its veins.

"Though many brave and skillful men tried to fight it, they could not get close enough to mortally wound it, and were themselves killed. The dragon rampaged at will, killing the people and burning their homes. It seemed that very soon, men would be no more, and the dragon would have won.

"But one man had watched the others. He had seen them hesitate before the beast, so that their blades did not bite deep enough to harm him. He knew the only way to slay the dragon was to plunge a sword directly through the soft spot on his chest, deep into his flaming heart.

"It would be a terrible thing to do, but he knew that unless the dragon was stopped, everyone he knew and loved would die.

"So he put on his armor, and took up his sword, and went to face the dragon. And though the beast was terrible—the heat of its breath scalded him, and the heat of its skin burned him—he did not hesitate. He leaped upon the creature and plunged his sword, and his whole arm, into the flaming heart of the creature.

"The pain was terrible. He knew his arm would be lost, if not his life, but he had the satisfaction of seeing the beast expire before he himself fell into unconsciousness.

"The people came upon their rescuer. His arm was terribly burned. They took him back to the village to care for him. He hovered on the brink of death, until the Lady of the Stars came to him in a vision. She told him he was to be rewarded for his selfless bravery in the cause of the people.

"He found that he was well and whole again, and even his armor was restored to him, bright and polished. But what, he asked, had happened to his sword?

"The Lady of the Stars told him that, in the crucible of the dragon's heart, the arm and the sword melted together and were made one. Forevermore, the sword is in his heart, his blood, and his hand.

"He is given dominion over the people, to act as their guide and protector, and thus, anything he holds in his hand, be it a pen, a paintbrush, a hammer, or the tiller of a 'Mech, that will be his sword in this great task.

"And so he became the first Knight, the first Prince, and the first noble. He sired a lineage that lives today, and his blood runs in the veins of all nobles—even mine." He shrugged. "The *Tyrannos Rex* is my sword, Deena, as much as any 'Mech or weapon. I wield it for the greater good.

"That is the lesson of the story."

She licked her dry lips. "And is Erik your sword, too?"

"He is—and the story also shows us that you must not, for fear of losing your sword, fear to commit it."

"So if your cause is just, you think he'll be returned to us?"

He took a deep breath, and released it slowly. "He is a Sandoval. The blood is his, too. If he does not return to us, Deena, then it will be because he did not *deserve* to return."

8

Shensi was a world rich in natural resources: those of material value, such as timber and ore, but also those of the spirit—or so the locals claimed. Erik Sandoval-Groell had to admit it was a beautiful world, relatively unspoiled by the last major war.

The forests were vast and spectacular, the mountains high and jagged. Much of the northern continent was a frozen tundra—harsh, vast and savage in its beauty. The southern continent was covered with flat plains drained by wide, meandering rivers, its rich black soil dotted with farms that fed the world.

Though mining and mineral extraction were a large part of the economy, careful application of advanced mining techniques had minimized the impact on the environment. Likewise, the people of Shensi were caretakers of their forests, harvesting selectively, and in a strict rotation that kept their ecologies wild and diverse.

Like all worlds, it carried some scars from past wars, but it was perhaps as idyllic and unspoiled a world as Erik had ever seen.

He was enjoying it not a bit.

The Shensi people prided themselves on "government by consensus." At first glance, the structure was like dozens of others, a planetary Governor, a military Legate, a Parliament with three houses: Elected, Appointed, and Hereditary. As with many worlds, the Governor and the Legate shared great authority over the rest of the government, and could likely have entered into the coalition without any further approval— if both had wished to.

But only Governor Rivkin seemed at all interested. Legate Tarr felt the current advance would bypass them, and that—given their historic ties with the Capellans—a nonaggression pact was both possible and the best course of action. On other worlds, this might have resulted in a power struggle between these two dominant figures.

Not on Shensi.

Instead, the stalemate caused the issue to be passed down to the Parliament. There it was debated for two days, then voted into yet another deadlock: The Elected House supported it, the Hereditary House opposed it, and the Appointed House stalemated to an undecided result.

The situation seemed hopeless.

The Shensi Governor told Erik that he needed a hired agent called a facilitator. The Governor recommended an old family friend, and off Erik went.

The facilitator's office was located in a low granite office building just outside the city's Central Park—an easy walk from any of the houses of Parliament, and a short trolley ride from the Capitol itself. The building was quite old, and was neither run down nor meticulously restored. The wooden banisters on its stairways showed the wear of years of use, and the granite cracked in places that had not been repaired.

But the dark blue carpets were new, deep, and plush, and the potted plants that seemed to be everywhere—a signature of Shensi buildings, Erik had noticed—were green and well cared for. He found the name, OZARK KINSTON, FACILITATOR, on a directory. To his surprise there were no guards in the lobby. A series of escalators took him to the third floor.

He found the name repeated in gold-leaf letters on a heavy walnut door. He turned the glass knob and stepped inside. There was no lobby, no receptionist. Just a large desk stacked with paper and periodicals, where a moon-faced man with red hair typed on a computer with machinelike speed. The desk was surrounded by packed bookcases that ran from floor to ceiling—stacked not just with books, but with more papers, magazines, and enough gewgaws, awards, and souvenirs to stock a junk store.

The man continued typing for several minutes, during which time Erik supposed he must have typed the equivalent of several pages. He then slammed down on a key triumphantly with his right index finger, and looked up at Erik. "Commander Sandoval." He stood and extended his hand. "I was told by Marjori—the Governor—to expect you. Please have a seat."

There were a couple of wooden armchairs in front of the desk, upholstered in a rich fabric printed with burgundy and cream-colored stripes. Though none were visible, the room smelled strongly of cashews and something like spiced gumdrops. Erik was reminded of a candy store, and suspected a hidden cache of snack foods somewhere in the desk's many drawers.

The man ran his fingers through his thinning hair. "Where shall we begin?"

"I suppose I should tell you about the coalition."

"Oh, I know about your coalition and your proposed agreement. I think most everyone in the capital does. That isn't your problem."

"You're a facilitator. Is that like a lawyer?"

"Not at all. Lawyers deal with existing law. Facilitators deal in the creation and modification of law." He grinned. "Think of us as midwives."

"A treaty being just another flavor of law in your mind?"

Kinston smiled. "Exactly. I'm here to advise you, help you through the process of understanding how we do things."

"Do facilitators, like lawyers, have a rule of client confidentiality under planetary law?"

"Oh, absolutely!"

"Good, then let's just make this brief. Who do I have to bribe?"

Kinston blinked. "What?"

"Who do I have to bribe to make this happen? I'm authorized to be quite generous, if necessary. There are also other intangibles I can offer. Preferential contracts with the many Sandoval-held companies, for instance."

Kinston shook his head sadly. "Commander Sandoval, that is *not* how we do things here. It's strictly forbidden for any of our officials to take bribes. There's a death penalty on the books, and it *has* been enforced in the last decade."

"Death penalty? For the official or the person making the bribe?"

"Both," Kinston said dryly. "I wouldn't advise trying it. You'll frighten away far more support than you'll attract, and while getting caught might only get *you* deported, rather than executed, I wouldn't count on it."

"So, what do we do?"

"I'll approach certain members of Parliament with close ties to the Legate. I'll let them suggest various changes and alternate wordings of the proposal. We'll rewrite it in those terms, and you can take it back to the Governor and the Legate."

"And if the Legate still doesn't like it, or the Governor doesn't like the new version?"

"If there's a split opinion, then it goes back through the Parliament for another vote."

"I can't just rewrite it and take it back to the Governor and Legate directly?"

"Again, Commander, that isn't how things are done. If they then took action on the proposal, it would offend most of the Parliament and cause them no end of political difficulty. If a proposal doesn't create immediate consensus between them, then it *must* go through the Parliament."

"And if they're split again?"

He shrugged. "We repeat the process.

"That isn't unusual. A few years ago I worked on the Mogot slurry pipeline proposal, which made the circuit eleven times."

"And it passed then?"

He looked sheepish. "Well, no, it didn't, which I'm now convinced is a good thing. Stupid idea, that pipeline."

"Has anyone ever told you that your system of government is insane?"

He displayed a pleasantly professional smile. "Your uncle, the Duke, actually."

Erik frowned. "You know my uncle?"

Kinston looked confused. "Why, yes. It was his company that proposed the pipeline. We talked many times before the HPG network failed, and he actually visited once. I assumed that's why the Governor chose me to send you to."

"I imagine it probably was, but I had no idea."

"Well, that *is* surprising."

"Then my uncle has intimate knowledge about how your political system works. Or, from our perspective, how it doesn't."

Kinston smiled nervously. "I can't imagine he's forgotten it. He bent my ear over it more than once, I can tell you!"

Erik crossed his arms over his chest and leaned back in his chair. What had the Duke been thinking? This wasn't a negotiation, it was political flypaper. The war could be a decade over before he worked his way through this mess.

Was that the idea? Had Aaron simply sent him here to keep him out of the way? Or had he given Erik what he knew was a particularly difficult assignment as a way of testing him, or as an indication of trust? If he legitimately wanted Erik to succeed, why not at least provide him with some useful intelligence on the situation? Why not send him to Kinston or some other facilitator straight away?

Either way, Erik found himself determined to succeed. He would show his uncle what stuff he was made of—that he could be resourceful and cunning on his own. "Very well, Kinston, how can we make this happen? Not ten cycles through the process, but *this* time?"

"That's the spirit, Commander! You can't beat the system. You must join it. That's what consensus is all about!" He shuffled through papers on his desk, and picked up a computer pad to examine a calendar. He looked back to Erik. "You could just sit back and let me do what you're hiring me to do, but I wouldn't recommend it. You need to make your presence known—mingle with the people in power."

He flipped the pages of a large schedule book that

teetered on a corner of the desk. "There's a party tonight at Senator Prescott's estate. All the power players will be there."

"Including you?"

He smiled. "Why, naturally. I'll introduce you to some of the key people. Some of them you've already met, but in such informal surroundings—well, let's just say it makes a difference."

Erik was underwhelmed with the prospect. If he hadn't been so determined to return with an accord he could rub his uncle's nose in, he would have refused. He liked to party as much as the next person, but he preferred the raucous celebrations of Mech-Warriors. Stuffy political gatherings were poison—in the bland and "consensual" environment of Shensi, they sounded even worse.

"I'm looking forward to it," he lied.

"Good, then. I assume you have appropriate attire?"

"I brought my formal uniforms, if that's what you mean."

"A nice civilian suit would be less confrontational."

"I'll wear my uniform."

"Very well, then. You may already have received an invitation. It's hard to imagine that such an illustrious visitor would have been overlooked."

"It's possible. I've gotten a large number of social invitations since my arrival. My assistant has been handling them."

"Have them forwarded to me. I'll let you know which ones are worth attending. As for tonight, I'll make a call and ensure that you're on the guest list.

"There is one other matter: Shall I arrange an escort for you?"

"Escort?"

"Yes—a social companion for the evening." He saw the look on Erik's face. "Oh, *really,* Commander! It's simply a matter of appearances. It's easier to make a grand entrance with a lovely woman on your arm. I have a list of women with social ambitions—actresses and models, all women of some breeding and sophistication—who would be happy to accompany a young man such as yourself to an event such as this. It would simply be a matter of convenience for both of you."

Erik frowned. "It wouldn't be convenient for me," he said coldly.

"Well, then. If you change your mind, I'll see what I can do on such short notice. In any case, I'll make sure the invitation includes a guest. Just in case."

He left the office feeling dejected and humiliated. It seemed his uncle had sent him on a fool's errand after all. Despite his determination, his chances of salvaging the situation—at least in time to do any good against House Liao—seemed remote.

He exited the building to find his hired limousine waiting for him. It was a beautiful day, and the park spread before him—a vista of rolling green lawns, playfully arranged hedges and shimmering ponds.

He could see the tower of his hotel on the far side.

He leaned inside the car just long enough to tell the driver he'd be walking back to the hotel. The sun was warm on his face, and the beds of purple and yellow flowers were sweetly fragrant. He took off his uniform jacket, hung it from his index finger, and tossed it over his shoulder.

The brick-paved street was closed to most vehicular traffic. Only trolleys, buses, and a few cars with special VIP permits were allowed, and therefore he crossed freely in mid-block. A low stone wall surrounded the park; Erik headed for the nearest gate, a few dozen meters to the south.

He heard the sound of high heels clicking on the brick behind him, heard their rhythm shift from a fast walk to a run. Something about the urgency in those footsteps gave him pause. He was already about to turn when a voice called his name.

"Commander Sandoval?"

He turned and looked down into perhaps the most beautiful blue eyes he had ever seen. The woman standing there was tall, graceful, and athletic, yet softly round in the right places. Her long skirt was slit high up one side to display a tantalizing flash of leg, and her wraparound top was simple and elegant, fastened with a large silver pin.

She was tanned, a few freckles displayed unashamedly on her cheeks; her nose was small and upturned, her lips full, glossy, and the color of pink rose petals. Her hair was long and chestnut-colored, held back with a blue headband. When she smiled, as she was doing now, her eyes sparkled, and as she came close to him, he smelled cinnamon and vanilla.

In spite of his natural suspicion, he found himself smiling at her, and admiring the way the sunlight glinted off her hair. "Excuse me, have we met?"

"Not really, Commander, though I've seen you before. At the Governor's Palace a few days ago." She put out her hand and he took it. Her fingers were long and soft against his battle-roughened skin. "My name is Elsa—Elsa Harrad. I was having lunch with one of the senior staff, and I saw you going into a meeting. As I recall, you looked unhappy."

"That could describe most every meeting I've had here. I wish I'd noticed you. I'm almost certain it would have made my disposition a little brighter."

She beamed, and he found himself enjoying it. A lot.

"You flatter me, Commander. Though I did find myself wondering why such a handsome man wasted himself on unhappiness, and what I could do to change that."

She was laying it on pretty thick, and Erik was buying none of it. A man in his position attracted a certain type of power-hungry female, gold-diggers seeking some advantage. He usually sent them packing immediately—and even when he didn't, he'd quickly catch them making eyes at the Duke.

He sensed this woman was *not* one of those, despite her obvious attempts at manipulation. A politico of some kind? A reporter? Some sort of financial player seeking a hook into his family fortune? Well, whatever she was, he found her exceedingly pleasant, and a game of cat and mouse could be just the sort of distraction he needed to keep this planet from driving him mad. *Besides,* he thought with a smile, *in a game of cat and mouse, sometimes you get the cheese.*

"You know my name."

She laughed, and it was like the ringing of tiny bells. "I'm a frequent visitor to the mansion, and everyone there knows you by now. Everyone talks about your proposed accord. Not all positively, I'm afraid."

"What about you? What's your opinion on the matter?"

She looked apologetic. "You were walking somewhere. I interrupted you. I'm very sorry."

"To my hotel, the Fairview." He gestured.

"I know where it is. Do you mind if I walk with you? I love the park this time of year."

A likely story. "I'd be honored," he said.

They struck out along a curving walk that snaked among the low hills. It wound halfway around the shore of a pond, whose waters were navigated by native waterfowl and remote-controlled sailboats piloted by children on the banks.

The hotel, which had seemed very far just a few minutes before, now looked altogether too close, and he tried to slow his pace. "You were going to tell me how you felt about my accord?"

She laughed again, and it made him feel warm all over. "Actually, Commander, I don't have one. I'm very apolitical, and not even local. I'm an art student, and my parents run an interplanetary mining conglomerate. It's just that somehow I've fallen in with a political crowd here."

No one just falls in with a political crowd.

She continued. "Even if I don't care much for the politics themselves, I find the people fascinating."

"I imagine they find you fascinating as well." *I can lay it on thick, too.*

She blushed slightly and averted her eyes. "My social calendar is often very full, I'll admit."

"Then I imagine you'll be at Senator Prescott's party tonight." He grinned. *"Please tell me you'll be at the party tonight."* Somehow he didn't doubt for a moment that she would be.

"I think I have an invitation somewhere. But to be honest, the Senator's parties are a crashing bore."

He groaned theatrically. "You've just delivered a death sentence. I'm told it's a political necessity that I attend, and I was grasping at straws."

She looked up at him and grinned. It made her lower lip pucker in a most appealing way. "You know, Commander, if there's one thing I've learned, it's that one's enjoyment of an event depends almost entirely on the company one keeps."

"Am I being too hopeful, or was that an invitation to make an invitation?"

"It might have been."

"Then please, would you do me the honor of allowing me to escort you to tonight's boring party?"

"I'll allow you to escort me," she said, "but it won't be boring."

It was raining when Erik's limousine pulled up in front of Elsa's apartment—an elegant little brownstone perhaps a kilometer from the Capitol complex. A uniformed doorman held an umbrella over her as she slipped gracefully into the car, and Erik couldn't help admiring how her simple black dress showed off her legs. He felt his heart rate kick up a little, like a soldier going into battle.

She wore diamonds. A choker, earrings made from clusters of smaller stones, and a bangle bracelet on her right wrist—the sparkles sharp against her tan skin. Her hair was still down about her shoulders, but held back from her face by a pair of diamond hairpins. The complex elegance of her jewelry beautifully offset the simplicity of her dress. He wondered what those diamonds represented. Family heirlooms? A wealthy lover's gift? The spoils of ill-gotten gain?

He looked at her. How could anything so beautiful also be so dangerous? Yet the potential danger was part of what made her exciting. Or was it her at all? He'd known warriors who stormed headfirst into danger, simply for the glory and excitement of it. He'd never thought of himself as timid in battle, but throwing himself into danger for its own sake—simply for the thrill, and consequences be damned? He'd never understood such suicidal behavior. Until now.

But if his interest in Elsa was about courting danger, it also served his legitimate purposes. His mind flashed ahead to the coming party. He thought about what Kinston had said about making an entrance, and smiled. Everyone would be watching him. Everyone.

"I'm just a simple soldier, Elsa. I don't have words that can do you justice."

She smiled, and for a moment outdazzled every diamond she was wearing. "Commander, you are a soldier, but simple? Never. You honor me." She settled back in the limousine as casually as one might in a comfortable armchair. She was clearly used to such comforts.

"That seems to be quite a nice apartment you have. When you said you were an art student, I might have imagined more spartan quarters. Your family—"

She seemed embarrassed. "People of a certain breeding are not allowed to live in hovels. Part of me wishes I could, just for a year or two. It would be part of the 'experience.'"

He laughed. "I understand more than you know. A MechWarrior doesn't live like a foot soldier, of course. But I'm pampered, pulled from the heat of battle to run," he waved his arms, "diplomatic *errands* like this one. I'd like, just once, to actually be a simple soldier, answerable only to fate, the fellowship of my equals, and my own skill in battle."

"Your uncle keeps you on a tight leash, doesn't he?"

He laughed. "Again, you seem to be one step ahead of me. How is that?"

"The Sandovals are hardly a low-profile family. Plenty of information in the public databases—a great deal more about your uncle than you, I'm afraid. Of course, anything since the HPG network went down is sketchy."

"I thought you weren't interested in politics?"

"I'm interested in *people*, Commander. I find you *very* interesting."

"Would you stop calling me 'Commander'? I feel like I should be asking you to salute. 'Erik' would be fine."

"Erik," she rolled the name off her tongue. "I like the way it sounds."

So do I. He glanced out the car window. They were headed out of the center of the city. "Where are we going? I assume you've been there before?"

She nodded. "Senator Prescott lives in the High Bluff neighborhood. Very exclusive, old money. He's in the Hereditary House, and it shows. It also explains why I warned this could be a dull party."

"I don't understand."

"It's related to the success of your accord. The Hereditary House of Parliament is conservative in all respects. Skeptical of change, *terrible* dancers. Of course they voted against you."

He laughed.

She continued. "Elected House: mostly new money, self-made men and women, reactionary, volatile, and most can cut a rug with the best of them. They voted with you."

"And the Appointed House?"

"A mixed bag, dominated by whatever the political flavor of the moment is. The current group? Bad dancers coming in, good dancers on the wane, but still holding a power base."

"So my real strategy should be teaching people to dance?"

It was her turn to laugh. She put her fingertips to her lips for a moment, and when she lowered her hand, it fell casually, and lightly, on his knee. "That's not really my area, but if you want to meet people, that I can help with."

"I've hired this fellow, Ozark Kinston. You know him?"

"'O'? Certainly. We move in much the same circles here."

"Do you think he knows his stuff?"

"I believe he does. He has a good reputation among the Senators. I will warn you of one thing though." She leaned toward him, narrowed her eyes and whispered conspiratorially, "He has two left feet."

They laughed together.

"Commander," interrupted the driver, "we're approaching the address."

Erik tore his gaze away from Elsa to look out through the windows. The rain had stopped, leaving slick pavement on the steep, winding, tree-lined street. The houses were large, and widely spaced. The street-lights were mounted in filigreed housings, atop slender columns. Ahead, one house in particular was brightly lit, and he could see a large number of people inside.

"Fashionably late," said Elsa.

Erik smiled. "The better to make an entrance," he said.

The car pulled to a stop under a temporary awning, set up to protect arriving guests from the intermittent rain. An attendant opened the door, and Erik stepped past Elsa to exit first. He then took her hand and led her from the car. They climbed a short run of red-carpeted steps and passed through an open set of French doors. Ahead, he could hear live music.

A tuxedoed butler stood at the door, a storklike guardian with his pointed nose. He glanced at a computer pad. "Ah, Commander. Good evening, Miss Harrad—always a pleasure."

"Thank you, Carlos. Would you be so good as to announce us?"

"But of course."

She leaned in close to his ear. "You did want an entrance."

The butler placed his pad on a podium and stepped through the inner doors into a grand ballroom. "Ladies and gentlemen." The music faltered, and heads turned. "Commander Erik Sandoval-Groell of Tikonov and Miss Elsa Harrad."

Erik took Elsa on his arm, and they swept through the door. People looked and whispered. He felt splendid, and he had certainly made his grand entrance. Dignified old men fell over each other to be the first to greet Elsa, and she addressed each and every one by name. She also skillfully disengaged herself from each—shedding them as easily as a duck sheds water, and leading Erik through the crowd to the bar. *Whatever else she is, she's a smooth social operator, and I can use that.*

The bartender walked over, and Erik turned to Elsa. "I had a local dark whiskey a few days ago. A nice smoky bite, but I don't remember the name."

She glanced at the bartender. "He'll have a Malvern Black, on the rocks. I'll have a Firestarter."

Erik chuckled. "Are you sure? That's a MechWarrior's drink."

"I can handle it," she said. "I have a stomach made of armor. It's part of what's kept me from embarrassing myself at these things over the years."

He took a proffered tumbler, with its cubes of ice and deep amber whiskey. He held it under his nose, enjoying the woody aroma, then sipped, feeling it burn smoothly down his throat. Either this whiskey was even better than he remembered, or it was a better brand of the same stuff.

He watched as the bartender mixed two kinds of transparent fluids, followed by a shot of red liquor, and shook the combination before pouring the result into a cocktail glass and garnishing it with a slice of green pepper. He handed it to Elsa, who took a deep sip, licked her upper lip in a way that made him quiver, then smiled. "I will say this for the Hereditaries, they do have the best-stocked bars."

"Commander!"

Erik turned in response to the voice, and spotted Ozark Kinston moving toward him from across the room. "I'm glad you could make it"—he glanced at Elsa and smiled—"and I see you arranged for your own escort."

"A very fortunate and timely encounter," he explained.

"Well," said Kinston, "indeed. You're already being

seen, mingling, that's good. Don't plan on leaving early. I'll come around later and bring you into a few backroom gatherings. That's where much of the real business gets done, you know."

He looked around the room. "Meanwhile, circulate. You couldn't have a better guide than Elsa. I have to go set things up." He took Elsa's hand and bowed. "I hope you'll save me a dance for later, my dear."

She smiled graciously. "I wouldn't miss it, O."

They watched as he walked away.

"So," said Erik, "you're a diplomat, too?"

"Many skills are necessary on this battlefield, Erik."

Well, now there's *an opening.* "Really? I'd like to hear more about that."

The band struck up a slow number. Elsa took his hand. "And I'd like to find out how many left feet you have."

He smiled. *Skillfully dodged.* "I'm told I can make a fifty-ton 'Mech seem light on its feet."

"It's *your* feet I'm more concerned about."

"I rarely get to use them. Shall we see what happens?"

They stepped onto the dance floor and he put his hand around her small waist, feeling the delicate curve of her back through the thin material of the dress. She stepped in close to him, and at the gentle urging of the music, they moved as one.

For Erik, the evening seemed to fly by. They danced until they were too tired to stand, found quiet corners to talk, then danced again. She was intensely curious about him, especially his most recent adventures. He told her of his defeat on Mara, and how he'd redeemed the situation on Achernar, and of his victories on New Aragon.

He was careful not to say anything that a spy—or even an interested citizen—might not pick up from other sources, or to provide any current information of strategic value. Yet he found that he enjoyed talking with her. She showed eager interest in his stories of battle and adventure. Though she didn't say so, he felt she'd lived a safe life—perhaps too safe for her taste.

He imagined her, pampered and coddled, never really tasting the spice that made life worth living— now off on her own for the first time. What lengths might such a person go to in order to experience danger and intrigue? He'd known soldiers like that— lesser nobles, trained by the finest teachers in the martial arts, seasoned from hundreds of hours in a 'Mech simulator, and yet having no comprehension of what real adversity was like—real danger. He knew to watch those soldiers closely, because for each of them would come a moment when they realized they were far too deep in danger, and that it was no simulation, no fantasy, no game. Elsa reminded him of those officers—of someone who was just starting to realize the reality of the situation they'd put themselves in.

Though he told her freely about his own family and background, he seemed to learn very little about her personally, which bothered him. Not that he hadn't expected her to be evasive. Soldiers were about the only people in Erik's day-to-day life who ever spoke the unadulterated truth, and then only because they sometimes couldn't help it. With nobles, politicians, and diplomats, what came out was shades of deception. He was entirely used to that.

It was the nature of her evasiveness that both intrigued and frustrated him. Hers was not the calculated evasion of someone seeking advantage or clouding the truth, it was the withdrawal of someone hiding painful emotions. She was, despite her smooth exterior, very human, very vulnerable. He found himself wanting to protect her, and having no idea how. He wanted to know about her. Everything about her.

Suddenly, he found himself telling her about his troubles with his uncle. It wasn't a calculated effort to draw her out, it just happened. He reproached himself even as he started. His family problems were of strategic and political value—the sort of thing that could, at the very least, give encouragement and comfort to their enemies.

Yet, it was liberating, intoxicating—perhaps not in spite of the danger, but because of it—and all the more so because he knew his uncle would be outraged if he knew. But he wasn't there, wasn't calling the shots, and Erik needed a confidante.

He got little in return. She was still close-mouthed about her family and personal history. Yet there was a connection. They shared something in common, even if it was unspoken. He knew in his heart that they were somehow very much alike.

Later, the tempo of the music picked up, and they danced until they fell, exhausted and laughing, into each other's arms. Her lips found his, and he was lost. When he regained his senses, he was suddenly aware of how many people were around, and he didn't want to share her with anyone.

She seemed to sense his concern. She grabbed his hand. "Come with me. I know someplace where we can be alone."

He had a flash of guilt, and his sense of duty tugged at him. "Kinston said he had people he wanted me to meet."

She leaned close against his chest, and looked up into his eyes. "It's early for one of these things. The real business won't happen until nearly dawn, when half the guests have already left." She stepped back and tugged at his hand.

She led him past the bar, through a servant's passage and down a narrow staircase that led underground. They passed through a heavy iron door at the bottom and into a large room lined with utilitarian bunk beds, and doors leading to other passages.

He looked around. "What is this place?"

"Catacombs. Kind of a defensive shelter. All the older buildings here have them. Shensi hasn't been attacked in a long time, but it's a strong local tradition."

"Cozy," he said.

She reached up with one hand and quickly opened the top button of his uniform. Her fingers brushed his chest, and then hooked into the front of his jacket, pulling him down with her onto one of the beds. "Fully equipped," she said softly, "with everything needed in an emergency."

9

GOFF: "SHENSI SAFE FROM LIAO"—Hereditary House Lord Speaker Goff is quoted as saying that his personal belief is that House Liao is, "no threat to Shensi. I'm confident that their advance will bypass our world. This is no time for a dubious alliance with a rogue Lord Governor who doesn't know his place."

—Shensi NewsNet exclusive

Fairview Tower Hotel
Whitehorse, Shensi
Prefecture V, The Republic
21 November 3134

Erik awoke in an unfamiliar place, and it took him a moment to recognize his hotel room. He was disappointed to discover that Elsa was gone. He rolled over to smell her perfume on the pillow, and spotted a note on the night table. He read it. She had an early class, and promised to meet him for lunch.

Erik had his own appointment with Ozark Kinston, to review the previous evening's events. He smiled. *The official ones, anyway.*

He and Elsa had emerged from their hideaway in time for the appointed meetings. Erik had pleaded his case to several men and women, all of whom Kinston swore were important, and all of whom showed, or at least feigned, some degree of interest in what he had to say.

Erik had expected that Elsa would excuse herself when the meetings started, but she was there till the end—listening, yes, but also working the room quietly to help win people to his cause. In the end, Kinston assured him that they had swayed critical votes, but Erik had only his word to prove it. As was usual with the local politics, he was never sure what he was accomplishing.

Instead, his thoughts flashed back to before the meetings, when he and Elsa had been curled together in the bomb-shelter cot. There had been an exchange. At the time it had seemed like a trifle, casual pillow talk, the sort of random thoughts that sometimes surfaced at such moments.

In retrospect, it was the most candid moment Elsa had allowed him. It had started when she'd asked a simple but unexpected question, "Have you ever been to the circus?"

"There are still circuses? I thought they were only in old books and fairy tales."

"There's at least one, Captain Rose's Traveling Extravaganza. No reason you should have ever seen it, or even heard of it. For all I know, that's the only one left, and it's a big galaxy. For that matter, maybe even it's gone now. It was a long time ago.

"But they used to travel from planet to planet in a couple of ancient *Leopard* DropShips, stripped of their weapons—so old they looked like they'd crumble if you touched them. They were painted in gaudy colors, and had murals and billboards of the acts on the sides.

"My parents took me to the show. I might have been eight or nine years old. The star act was a family of high-wire acrobats, and the ringmaster announced that this was to be the debut of their youngest member as a soloist. I was so excited. She was a girl, and I identified with her at once. She seemed like she wasn't much older than me, though I now suspect she was probably a smallish teenager. She got up on the wire, high over our heads, all alone, with only a pole to help her keep her balance.

"She was so graceful, so beautiful, so confident—and I felt like I was up there with her. Every eye was on her, and I wanted to be just like her: the star of the show."

"You are a star," he'd said, but she had ignored the compliment, as though eager to get on with the story.

"Things were fine, until she got to the middle of the wire. Then something went wrong. I never knew what. Perhaps she just looked down. But she stumbled, staggered—and I remember that she dropped the pole. It fell for a long time, and as it clattered to the arena floor, I realized that there was no net.

"I looked back to the girl. She had fallen—one knee on the wire, arms out, desperately trying to keep her balance. I could see her family on a platform at the end of the wire, wanting to go to her, but afraid they'd just make her fall. And it was so far back. So far to the other side. She looked very small."

"What happened?"

"I don't know. My parents grabbed me, kept me from seeing, and whisked us out the nearest exit. They never spoke of it again. Later, when I was older, I wondered. I knew I could go look it up in the old news databases, see if a girl fell that day. See if she was hurt. See if she was killed."

"Did you?"

"I never had the courage. As long as I don't look it up, she's the way I last saw her: all alone on the wire. But she's okay. Maybe she'll stand up. Maybe she'll find her balance, and walk back to safety. Maybe."

And then the moment was over. They'd dressed and gone back upstairs and to their meetings. She'd returned with him to the hotel, but after that she was guarded.

As he showered and dressed, he phoned his assistant and checked his messages. As he'd instructed, Kinston had been forwarded the latest batch of invitations, which seemed to come in at the rate of two or three a day. Most seemed considerably beneath the power level at which Erik needed to operate, but only Kinston could tell him for sure.

He had breakfast with his aide in the hotel's restaurant. On impulse, he had flowers delivered to Elsa's apartment. Then he called his car around and left for his meeting with Kinston.

Kinston was working the Capitol Building that morning, so they'd arranged to meet in the rotunda there. As they drove up to the diplomatic entrance, Erik was struck by how attractive the building was. There were three golden domes over the central rotunda, and three long wings projecting outward, each pointing toward a different House of Parliament.

The whole compound was set on a triangular tree-dotted lot surrounded by a low granite wall; each side of the building seemed to present a flawless public face to the world. Erik wondered where the mechanicals were located—the inevitable service entrances and loading docks. There were also no obvious connections to the Houses of Parliament. He remembered what Elsa had said about catacombs. He suspected that much of the complex was underground, with tunnels—perhaps even subways—connecting the three Houses, and service-tunnel entrances that might be located blocks away from the actual complex.

He flashed his diplomatic credentials at the entrance, and had the guard direct him to the rotunda. He walked half the length of one wing, passing through only a single security checkpoint before entering the more public rotunda area. The security was amazingly lax to Erik's eyes, but these people had known peace and safety for a long time. That, of course, was part of Erik's problem.

The rotunda was a vast, three-lobed space, symmetrical except for the public entry located at the juncture of the two eastern wings. The three domes overhead were painted with murals of trees and mountains. At the juncture of each wing, a five-story glass wall admitted natural light, and the grand entrance to each wing was marked with a three-story marble arch, carved in beautiful relief, depicting the heroes of some unfamiliar 'Mech battle. The floor was a mosaic inlay of many kinds of stone, representing a somewhat dated star map of the Inner Sphere.

He spotted Kinston sitting on a bench near the entrance, reading a newspaper. Kinston stood as Erik approached, and greeted him with a handshake. "I've got maybe half an hour, then I need to get over to the Hereditary House." He looked up nervously. "Sound plays tricks under these domes," he said. "Someone across the room could be listening in on us. Come on, I know somewhere safer."

He followed Kinston through one of the archways, past another low-security checkpoint, and into a side corridor. They entered a glass-walled room full of neatly packed bookshelves and small tables. Gold letters on the door said, LAW LIBRARY 1-B. Kinston glanced back into the stacks to make sure they were alone.

He returned and beckoned Erik to sit across from him at a small reading table. "You did well last night. I've scheduled a follow-up meeting tomorrow with Senator Prescott based on the groundwork our little midnight meeting established. If we can revise your accord to his satisfaction, we'll be a long way toward getting a favorable result next time it's before the Hereditary House. Who knows? We might even come up with something the Legate likes and shortcut the whole process." He smiled apologetically. "But probably not."

Erik sighed. His initial feeling that he might be able to ram things through and sign Shensi to the coalition was fading. He seemed as mired in the local politics as ever.

"Chin up, Commander. This is going nearly as well as it could, under the circumstances." Kinston put his briefcase on the table and opened it. He pulled out an envelope. "I've got a new draft of the accord for you to examine here. It removes all the Capellan trade restrictions that were in the original draft."

Erik blinked in surprise. "What? No trade restrictions? You expect to go on selling ore to our enemies?"

"Understand, Commander—that's at the heart of the accord's initial failure. This planet has strong historic ties to the Capellans, and they're important trading partners. The actions of House Liao surely don't represent the entirety of the Capellan Confederation, and even they are only trying to recover those worlds, historically theirs, that were ceded to The Republic.

"The conservatives are leery about the current incursion, yes, and might be willing to lend some material support to a stabilizing resistance. But not to the extent of losing a substantial portion of the trade that gives them their power."

"That's unacceptable."

"But it may be inevitable, if you want to get this accord accepted."

He looked faintly embarrassed. "There's also one other matter—a technicality, really. The original document never explicitly mentions The Republic. The agreement is worded so that it's a pact directly with the Duke and 'his allies, present, and future.' One might assume that such language refers to him as a representative of The Republic, but it's not explicit."

Despite the many things already troubling him, Erik was able to maintain a proper poker face. The omission of Aaron's role as a Lord Governor of The Republic had been intentional and carefully calculated. In a way, Erik was surprised it hadn't been noticed before, but negotiation of treaties usually comes down to small details. Politicians were often so quick to focus on those details that it was possible to miss the big, obvious things. The SwordSworn had gambled that it might work.

An agreement with the Duke that included The Republic would muddy the waters considerably when they openly pledged themselves to House Davion. It might hold if they were too far down the road to turn back, but it would make it easier for the alliance to be broken. "The Republic," Erik said, "is implied here. It's a given. I don't see why we need to make changes just for the sake of making changes."

Kinston frowned. "I don't know how extensive your diplomatic experience actually is, Commander, but nothing is a given in these matters."

Erik looked straight ahead, saying nothing.

Kinston studied Erik's face, looking for some sign of capitulation. "Look, you have both versions of the agreement here for comparison. Underline where you have problems, cross out what's totally unacceptable, and we'll discuss it tomorrow morning." He pushed the envelope over to Erik's side of the table.

He seemed to shake off the previous difficulty almost immediately, and his smile returned. "Now, we need to review last night's meetings so that I have a better idea of where we stand, and what needs follow-up on my part."

"You were there for most of it, other than the mingling and casual introductions. Chitchat, mostly."

"Nonsense. You were gone for quite some time early in the evening. I assume you were pulled aside by one of our Senators or senior staffers for a conference. I need to know the details."

Erik was silent.

"You were in a private conference?"

Despite everything, Erik found himself grinning. He felt like a teenager again, but not in a bad way this time.

Kinston's mouth opened, and hung that way for a moment. "Oh." His eyes widened. "Oh! You were alone with Miss Harrad."

Erik felt his grin spread.

Kinston took a deep breath, and let it out slowly. "Commander, excuse me for prying into a client's private affairs, but you have the look about you of a man who is smitten."

"Smitten?" He sighed. "I suppose that's possible."

Kinston pinched the bridge of his nose and closed his eyes. "Oh, this is awkward. I assumed you knew. I assumed that this was all part of one of those espionage intrigues that you House Davion types always have in your holovids, that you were just—playing her."

He frowned. "Kinston, what the devil are you talking about?" He said it, and yet he knew. At some level, all along, he'd known.

"Miss Harrad is a Capellan spy."

The restaurant where Elsa had arranged to meet him was located just across the street from the Hereditary House. Once he and Kinston had finished their business, he offered the facilitator a ride. There was an awkward silence as they stood waiting for the car.

The drive was only about a kilometer, but they were quickly snarled in city traffic.

Erik looked at the thick envelope in his hand, feeling sorry for himself. "You don't have any real evidence, though?"

Kinston looked up from where he was sitting, across from Erik. "About what?"

"Elsa. Being a spy."

"Evidence? No, I suppose not. But it's a well-known fact that she collects information for them. I mean, it's not like she's stealing people's files or breaking into places and photographing our secrets. She really is an art student. She merely has other interests on the side.

"She's . . . tolerated. As I said, Shensi has deep historical ties with the Capellans. In a sense, I suspect many people in the government are glad that they're keeping tabs on us. Perhaps they even consider it their right."

Erik shook his head. How was he supposed to turn these people against the Capellans in any way? It was madness, and he had no one to blame but himself. He should have left as soon as he'd seen the Duke's real intentions regarding this mission. All he wanted to salvage from this now was Elsa, and he couldn't see how that would be possible.

One night. How can one night change so much?

He dropped Kinston near Senator Prescott's office, where he announced he planned to spend the afternoon reviewing a land-use bill with a top aide.

Erik arrived at the restaurant early. With a few whispered words to the maître d' and the exchange of a hundred-C bill, he arranged to change their table to an intimate private dining room in the back. He ordered a bottle of wine, and was already sipping when she arrived.

He stood as she was escorted in. She took his hands and leaned forward to kiss him passionately. She put her arms around his neck and he held her close, smelling her perfume, enjoying the moment despite himself, knowing it could be the last time.

They sat, and she studied his face, seeming to sense something was amiss.

He poured her a glass of wine. She took a deep

drink. "Erik, what's wrong? Is it last night? Are you having regrets?"

He put his hand over hers. "No. It's not that. Last night was— Last night was something I'll always cherish." He licked his lips. "I—I heard some things about you today."

She smiled nervously, eyes wide, head shaking. "What?"

He took a deep breath. *Out with it.* "Are you a spy for the Capellans?"

"Who told you that?"

"Never mind that. It's true, isn't it?"

"I'm not a *spy,* Erik. It's not like that at all."

He stared straight into her eyes, offering no comfort. This was hurting him more than he could have imagined. "What is it like, then?"

She hung her head. Took another big drink of wine. Silence. She tipped the glass back and drained it. "Erik, you know what it's like to depend on others for everything you have, everything you are. I was Daddy's little girl, and Daddy was a rich and powerful man. He sent me here because they have one of the finest art schools in The Republic, and I loved it so much. That was all I wanted. To paint." She looked away at nothing. "To paint."

"What happened?"

Her eyes were moist. "I'd been here six months when they sent word. There'd been a scandal at the mining company, and my father was dead. They said it was suicide. I never believed it. Everything we had was tied up with courts, lawyers, and accountants. The rest of the family disowned mother and me—took control of what was left of the business." She chewed her lip. "I think they were behind it somehow." She looked at him, her eyes full of shame. "I know. How could people in a *family* do such things to one another?"

His resolve was melting. "I know all too well."

"I was all alone here. Mother was having enough trouble taking care of herself. I had tuition bills, and not even enough money for passage home. But Daddy had friends, business contacts in the Capellan Confederation. They came to me with an offer of help for Mother and me. All they wanted was for me to go to some parties, talk with people, let them know what I heard." She smiled through tears. "I'm not a spy. It's just been fun. It's no more than a game, really."

"Was I part of your game?" He recalled his initial suspicions and chided himself for not listening to them.

"No! I mean . . ." She looked away. "It was no coincidence that I ran into you the other day. They told me you'd be here—that they would be very grateful for anything I could tell them about the Duke's intentions and your mission here. But that's all. A chance meeting, and the rest just happened." She looked at him. "Erik, I'm not a prostitute! How could you think that? I go to parties. I flirt, I talk. Men like me, and I like them back. But that's all. I don't sleep with people for information."

He drained his own glass, poured another. "I want to believe you."

"What was between us was real, Erik. Please believe me. It still is."

"This changes everything," he said.

She hung her head. "I know. I'm sorry, Erik. I can't help what I am, any more than you can. People like us, we're never really free. We're always beholden to someone."

The words were especially bitter, because they were true. Yet what could he do? *Uncle Aaron, I'd like you to meet my girlfriend, the Capellan spy.* There would always be lingering doubts.

The Sandovals didn't even trust each other. There

was certainly no reason to trust an outsider, a spy, *a Cappie*.

Part of him wanted to stay in the trap, to let the accord run its long and unnatural course, while he spent his nights in Elsa's arms. But it would only be prolonging the agony.

He was trying to think of something to say, when there was a rumble like thunder, and the room trembled. They both looked around.

Elsa looked at him. "What was that?"

Another rumble, louder this time. Then another sound—a siren of some sort. Though he'd never heard it, he thought he knew what it was. He grabbed Elsa by the hand and pulled her up and out of the room. "We have to get somewhere safe."

The main dining room was in chaos—people scrambling out the door without paying, the staff in confusion. Through the row of windows across the front they could see people running down the street in both directions.

"I don't understand," said Elsa. "What's happening?"

There was a flash in the sky outside, followed moments later by the sound of an explosion.

"My God," she said. "It can't be."

He looked at her. "The Cappies really didn't tell you, did they? Didn't warn you?"

She shook her head.

"War," he said, "has come to Shensi." Another explosion, and the floor shook. "These are the people you're working for," he said.

She seemed genuinely surprised. He felt sorry for her.

A louder explosion, frighteningly close. Then the whole front of the restaurant seemed to light up, and the noise hit them like an invisible hammer, as every window in the building shattered.

10

CONTROLLER: *Attention, unauthorized spacecraft: You have entered the Shensi atmosphere without clearance. You are not cleared to enter the Whitehorse-controlled air zone.*

[Static]

CONTROLLER: *Unidentified spacecraft, you are ordered to turn right on a heading of one-eighty degrees and proceed to the Chung Military Airfield, where you will land and surrender yourself. If you do not turn, air defenses have been activated, and use of deadly force is authorized. [Unintelligible] I don't think they're listening! Do those missile batteries still work?*

—Shensi Planetary Traffic Control transcript

La Cuisine Traditionnelle
Whitehorse, Shensi
Prefecture V, The Republic
21 November 3134

Erik peered out from behind the table he'd overturned as a shield. Through the broken windows he could see people screaming, running—some of them covered with blood. He knelt down to check on Elsa, who cowered next to him—scratches on her face, a cut on her right cheek. "Are you all right?"

She stared at him for a moment, eyes wide, as though he were speaking some alien language. Then it finally seemed to register. "I'm fine." She laughed nervously, almost hysterically. "No, I'm not fine. But I don't think I'm hurt." She brushed the hair out of her face, and was shocked to see blood on her hand.

He took her hand in his. "It's just a scratch. Listen to me. Listen carefully. Unless you seriously believe your friends know not to drop a missile on your head, you have to get off-planet. Now. There will be a rush on the spaceport as foreigners try to leave, but you can find passage on a ship before it's too late."

"What? Why? My apartment—"

"Forget it. If things calm down you can send for your things. Don't even go back there unless you have some cash hidden—and I think you might. If you're really a spy, you'll have a bug-out kit with money and travel papers stashed somewhere. But I'm not sure you're that much of a pro. Just go. This planet isn't safe anymore."

She clutched at him. "Come with me!"

He looked off in the direction of the Capitol Building, already planning. "I can't. Wait here."

He scrambled back to their table and dug through the mess of broken dishes and fallen ceiling tiles to find the envelope that Kinston had given him. He duck-walked back to where Elsa was hiding.

"Erik, where are you going?"

"There may still be something to salvage here. I'm going to try, anyway." He looked at her. "You can tell that to your employers if you talk to them again."

She looked hurt. He wanted to take back the words, but it was too late.

"I'm sorry," he said. "I'm sorry it has to be this way. Maybe this just wasn't meant to be."

More explosions, distant, possibly from across town. The lights flickered and went out. "Come on."

He grabbed her arm, half guiding, half dragging her out of the building. They ran down the street—Erik on the outside, pushing her close to the buildings.

Aerospace fighters flashed overhead, and he saw missile tracks scribbled across the sky. They crossed a street, and he got a clear look at the Capitol Building, the three domes over the rotunda burning and half-collapsed.

An unfamiliar car, dodging rubble in the street, screeched to a halt in front of them, one wheel up on the curb. The door opened. Lieutenant Clayhatchee was driving.

"Commander! Get in! Your driver ran off when the bombing started, but I knew you'd be here."

"Where did you get the car?"

He grinned and held up his side arm. "I charged it to diplomatic immunity, sir!"

"Good work, Lieutenant. There's a medal in this if I have anything to do with it!" He pushed Elsa into the car, but didn't follow her.

Clayhatchee was confused. "Sir, aren't you coming?"

Elsa stared at him. "Erik!"

He leaned in and kissed her hard.

"Get her to the spaceport, and on some kind of transport off-planet. Get yourself on one, too, if you can. Head back to my uncle, and tell him what's happened here." He paused. "Tell him"—he held up the envelope—"that I carried the mission to its logical conclusion."

Clayhatchee hesitated. "That's an order, Lieutenant!"

"Yes, *sir!*" He saluted sharply, then backed the car off the curb, and zoomed away down the street.

Erik looked around. He could just see the roof of the Hereditary House a block over. He had no way of knowing if Kinston was still there, but he needed a guide. He ran toward the building.

He found the entrance unguarded, and a few frightened people cowering in the lobby. Where was everyone? In the catacombs, undoubtedly. But where? Probably these people were outsiders, too. If they knew, they'd already be down there.

He tried to remember the stairs leading into the basement at Senator Prescott's house. There had been a symbol on the wall. At the time, he'd thought it was just a decoration. It had been a chevron over a triangle of small dots. But the chevron might represent a roof, and the three dots might represent people. *Shelter!*

He headed for the building's core, where an entrance to the shelter might more logically be located. It took him five minutes before he spotted the symbol next to an arrow pointing down a dead-end hall. At the end was an unassuming door next to a janitor's closet. The door had the same symbol on it. He turned the knob. By the reddish glow of emergency lighting, he could just make out a stairway leading down. He could hear people below.

He climbed carefully down the stairs. Somebody pointed a flashlight up into his face. He shielded his eyes. "I'm looking for Ozark Kinston. Do you know him?"

Silence.

"He was at Senator Prescott's office when the attack came."

"I saw—" A woman's quavering voice came from behind the flashlight. "I saw some of the staff head down that way." The beam pointed back toward the rear of the building. "Maybe he's down there."

Erik made himself smile. "Thank you."

He pushed on to a central corridor, surrounded by rooms—most with doors open. He glanced in, and by the dim red emergency lights he could see people in almost every room—some waiting quietly, some talking, or sobbing, or huddled together for comfort. With each distant explosion they would tense and pull together.

Erik wondered how Elsa was doing. He hoped she could take care of herself, and if not, Lieutenant Clayhatchee could take care of both of them.

"Kinston," he called to anyone who would listen. "I'm looking for Ozark Kinston."

"Here," he finally heard a voice say. "I'm here."

He found Kinston in one of the side rooms, sitting on a folding cot. He was dirty, and had a bloody handkerchief wrapped around one hand, but otherwise looked in good health. He looked up at Erik, his eyes like those of a whipped dog. "What's happening?"

Erik stood over him, arms crossed. "My guess is that House Liao has come to pay its respects to Shensi." He held out the envelope. "It seems to me that an alliance with Duke Sandoval would be a good thing right about now."

Kinston shook his head. "I know, I know. I did my best, Commander. A few more weeks and I might have had them."

"Not in a few weeks," he said. "*Now*. We're going to sign an accord now."

Kinston's eyes widened. He wiped his face with the flats of his hands. "What?"

"We're going to go get this accord signed by the Governor and the Legate. The original, not that other piece of crap you tried to pass off on me."

"Yes," he stammered, "of course, they'd sign it now."

"Then let's go find them."

Kinston looked pale. Despite the cool of the subbasement, he was sweating profusely. "Find them? Us?"

"Us. You and me. Come on."

"Us? No. No, I can't."

"Look, Kinston. The Governor and the Legate have probably gone to ground. I'm betting there are shelters under the Capitol Building, catacombs, and that you know how to find them."

Kinston blinked; thinking seeming to take enormous

effort. "Yes, I suppose I know the way in. I saw the Situation Room once. The Legate might be there. But I can't—"

"You can, Kinston. I can't find them alone."

Kinston looked like he was about to burst into tears, but he slowly pulled himself to his feet.

Erik handed him the envelope, and he clutched it, almost gratefully. Then Erik took him by the arm and led him out into the hall. "Which way?"

Kinston looked confused. "I don't know."

"Come on, Kinston. There are tunnels running from this building to the Capitol Building, aren't there? Can we get there without going up to street level?"

Kinston nodded. "Yes. There's a tram. A subway. This way." He pointed back toward the middle of the building.

With Erik urging Kinston along, the two of them reached the door to another stairwell, which they took down two more flights. They emerged at a tram station.

Surprisingly, the lights were on here. Perhaps the subway had its own power source, or was powered from the Capitol Building end. They stood on a long platform tiled in white marble, the roof supported by Greek columns. Large potted plants spaced regularly along the platform helped mute the cold sterility of the place.

There were two tracks running through the center of the platform. The side they were on seemed to be for departing cars, the other for arriving cars. The two sides of the platform were connected by a short tunnel running under the tracks. A line of small, open-sided cars, each with ten or so seats, sat lined up at the platform.

"They're not running," said Erik. "Is there a pedestrian tunnel?"

"No," said Kinston, pointing. "See those lights. They have power. They're like elevators. You just get on and push a button."

"Show me."

They climbed into the front row of seats in a little car. In front of each seat was a single button. Kinston pushed his, and it lit up green. "Push yours," he said.

Erik pushed his button, and it turned green as well.

"This car is now departing for the Capitol Building complex," said a recorded voice. "Please hold on to a post or handrail. Keep your head and hands within the vehicle at all times."

Erik couldn't help a slight grin. These recordings were the same, no matter what planet you were on.

The car accelerated smoothly out of the station with only a slight whine. Almost immediately, the track curved thirty or so degrees to the right. Once it was straight again, the car began to speed up.

The tunnel was well lit. Maintenance catwalks ran along either side, and periodically there were metal doors leading to some unknown destination—possibly a machinery room, or even a manhole to the surface.

The tunnel jogged slightly to the left, and suddenly they were plunged into darkness.

"Uh-oh," said Kinston.

"This isn't supposed to happen?"

"No."

"We're still moving. Maybe it's just the lights that have failed."

There were occasional emergency lights still working. Erik could see fresh cracks in the concrete walls. Broken pipes leaked water and foul-smelling fluids. Erik hoped the city didn't have gas mains down here as well.

He squinted into the darkness ahead. He thought he saw something.

Erik yelled something guttural—not a word, just a

sound—as he shoved Kinston out of the moving tram and went tumbling after him. They hit sand. Erik rolled, coming up on his feet just in time to see the tram smash into the stalled car ahead of it.

There was a crash, a shower of sparks that illuminated the collapsed section of tunnel roof, and then they were plunged back into gloom. He looked over, and could just make out Kinston, on his face on the ground, trying to get to his feet.

Something in the wrecked tram burst into flame, and it was suddenly much less gloomy.

Erik picked up the fallen envelope, brushed it off, and helped Kinston to his feet. "The whole tunnel isn't blocked," said Erik. "We can get around the wreck."

Fortunately, they were almost to the Capitol. Only fifty meters past the collapse, Erik spotted the lights of the station ahead. Erik climbed onto the deserted platform, and pulled Kinston up after him.

Erik could smell smoke. A large concrete beam had collapsed at the end of the platform. "Where now? How do we get into the shelters?"

"I don't know from here. I only know from above. We'll have to get up to the building, then back down."

Erik remembered the collapsed domes he'd seen from the street. "Not an option. You sure you don't know how to get there from here?"

Kinston stared at him blankly.

"Okay, what levels are they on? Up or down?"

"I don't know. I took an elevator. Down, I'd think."

Erik nodded. "Makes sense. They'd bury it very deep."

They exited the station into a wide, subterranean concourse. A few people huddled in doorways along the side, but it was largely deserted. Erik scanned every door and side corridor, looking for some sign. Finally, he spotted an unmarked door with an armored guard window next to it. The guard station was empty. The door, fortunately, had been blocked open with a chair.

Erik looked inside. Another stairwell, leading down. The walls were heavily reinforced, and there was no visible damage. "This looks good."

They climbed down the stairs: two flights, three, four. There were no exit doors. Finally they reached the bottom of the shaft, and an enormous vaultlike blast door. Again, it was unguarded, and open just far enough for a person to slip through. Erik shook his head. "You people really have a thing or two to learn about security."

He squeezed through, and Kinston followed. The tunnel beyond was narrow and lined with pipes and conduits of all kinds. They'd traveled a dozen yards when a voice addressed them.

"Halt!"

Somebody slipped out a side passage and Erik felt the barrel of a rifle pushed against the small of his back. Erik slowly put up his hands and turned to see who was confronting them. He found himself looking into the frightened eyes of a young private, whose finger seemed to spasm in the trigger guard of his automatic rifle. "Aren't you supposed to say, 'Who goes there?' "

"I've got orders not to let anyone pass without a staff ID."

"Son, I'm Commander Erik Sandoval-Groell, envoy of Lord Governor Duke Aaron Sandoval. I've got important business with the Governor and the Legate. Are they down here?"

"I can't tell you that, sir."

"That wasn't a no."

The soldier looked even more nervous, if that was possible, as he tried to figure out if he'd been tricked into revealing a secret.

"Look," said Erik, "we just need to talk with them.

Haven't you heard about the accord I've presented?" He glanced up at the ceiling as another missile fell somewhere. "Those are our mutual enemies up there. We need to form an alliance to help defend your world."

"Sir, you are a foreign national—the last person I should be letting in. You could be a spy." He licked his lips. "Maybe I should just shoot you."

Erik held up his index finger. "No! Look, we've got this accord. Show him the accord, Ozark."

Kinston fumbled with the envelope, trying to open it.

"This is Facilitator Ozark Kinston. He's not a foreigner. Homegrown Shensi native. Haven't you seen him around before?"

"I—I don't know. He maybe looks familiar."

Kinston managed to pull the accord out of the envelope. He held it out, and the soldier leaned over to see. For a fraction of a second, he was distracted.

Erik stepped from in front of the rifle barrel and spun, grabbing the barrel and pushing it up, twisting.

The soldier pulled the trigger, and a short burst of shells fired, bouncing around the tunnel and showering Erik with stinging rock chips.

Erik shifted his weight, grabbing the rifle with both hands now, using it as a battering ram to jam the stock into the soldier's kidney. The private doubled over. Erik twisted again, rotating the rifle so that the barrel came up and hit the guard in the chin. By then, he was able to rip the rifle completely from the young soldier's fingers.

The private was already off balance. Erik stepped on the man's foot, pinning it in place, and pushed him over backward. Erik spun the rifle around, and looked down the sights into the kid's face.

"Stop." Kinston tugged at his sleeve. "He's just doing his job."

Erik relaxed slightly. That was true, and he was just a boy. Besides, Erik had the gun now. He considered the value of a hostage and dismissed the idea. But there was one thing he could use.

"Put your hands behind your head, and show me where to find the Situation Room. Now!"

11

It was almost comical. Fifteen people in the Situation Room, twelve of them holding guns. Erik's was pointed at the Legate of Shensi. The others were pointed at Erik.

The three people without weapons in their hands were the soldier Erik had disarmed, Kinston—who cowered behind Erik, envelope clutched to his chest as though it might stop bullets—and Legate Tarr himself, who stood in front of his overturned chair, fists on hips, looking at Erik as though he were an especially unpleasant bug. The man didn't so much as blink.

Neither did Erik. "Can we put all these guns down now? The Duke is offering his forces to fight alongside you, not against you."

The Legate stared at him for a moment, then cracked a smile. He held up his hand, and the guns began to lower. "I'll give you this: You've got nerve, Sandoval. If your soldiers all have your kind of guts, you'll make excellent allies."

Erik pointed the rifle at the ceiling, then handed it to the private.

Kinston looked desperately at the Legate. "I didn't know, Legate, I swear I didn't know there would be guns. I just brought this for you to sign."

Erik snatched the envelope, and was careful to extract his original document, not the adulterated version. He spotted a document shredder at a nearby communications console. He tossed the envelope in and watched it turn into confetti, then handed the original to the Legate. "I assume you have a pen here somewhere?"

The Legate looked at the shredder. "What was that?"

Erik grinned. "Something I might have been willing to agree to a few hours ago. Now it appears the situation has changed."

The Legate looked at the document. "I can't sign this without reading it."

"You've already read it. It's the one you rejected previously. I assume you have no problem with that." A distant explosion made the room shudder, and the lights flickered momentarily. "Those are your 'friends' blasting your capital into rubble. Your Prefecture is in shambles and you count on them for help. Do you wish to face House Liao all by yourselves?"

The Legate looked at him and blinked. "The Governor still has to sign."

"The Governor will sign. *You* have always been the problem." He glanced up at the ceiling as another distant explosion made the light fixtures sway. "This is on your head."

The Legate grunted. He bent over the table, flipped to the last page and signed.

"Where's the Governor?"

"A secure room, one level down. I'll have someone escort you. Someone with a pass."

Erik shook his head. He handed the document to Kinston. "It's a milk run, Ozark. Go be important, and then bring it back here to me."

Kinston nodded, and followed a staffer out of the room.

"One of the first things we should do for you as an ally is teach you how to set up an emergency perimeter. I only had to get past five guard posts: one unmanned, two that I overpowered, one that I talked my way through, and one where the guard appeared to be so busy calling his wife that he didn't see Kinston and me slip past."

The Legate sighed. "We're a bit rusty."

"I predict many opportunities to practice, very soon. What's your situation?"

The Legate turned to a holotable, which currently showed a world situation map. Red triangles seemed to indicate attacks on all three continents. "We had six ships come in undetected. They must have used a pirate point, so we didn't spot them. We've had sporadic hit-and-run attacks all over the planet. All aerospace fighters; no ground forces that we've been able to detect."

"What kinds of targets?"

"The Capitol, of course. Power plants, some major bridges, important monuments."

That last caught Erik's attention. "I don't think there's an invasion force behind this—at least not immediately. You'd be seeing ground forces, scouts, and probes at the minimum. And the choice of attacks implies that they're going for psychological, not tactical advantage. No military targets. It's a warning shot."

The Legate nodded. "I agree—and one we can't

afford to ignore. We either turn over our world to them, or we prepare to fight. I've already made my decision. I assure you, Commander, historic ties or not, the people of Shensi value our independence. It may seem that we've forgotten how to fight, but we are eager to relearn the old ways, and we are not without weapons."

Erik grinned. "So rumor has it—or resources to make more."

"Legate, this just came in." A pretty blond officer handed over several fax pages.

The Legate flipped through them, then handed one—a photograph—to Erik. "One of our Militia-Mechs on Klondike managed to bring down a fighter."

Erik looked at the photo. It showed a burned scar amid frozen tundra, scattered with blackened wreckage. A nearly intact wing jutted up out of a snowbank, emblazoned with the shield of the St. Cyr Armored Grenadiers. "This confirms it, then. The Grenadiers have been Liao's hired muscle on this campaign from the beginning. I need to get word of this, and our accord, back to the Duke."

The Legate ducked away and conferred with a technician working a tactical console. He returned a moment later. "There's a Sandoval-flagged courier ship in orbit right now. We'll give them priority landing clearance to the Capital Spaceport, and I'll have an armored car waiting to take you there when they arrive. We can have you off the planet in less than two hours."

He smiled and extended his hand to the Legate, who shook it firmly. "Thank you, Legate. You're doing the right thing."

Kinston returned, looking calmer now. He handed the document, now emblazoned with the Governor's seal, back to Erik.

Erik took the agreement triumphantly. *This would*

show Aaron! "Thank you, Ozark. It's been a pleasure doing business with you. You'll send us a bill?"

"Oh," said Kinston, wiping his brow, "you can bet on it."

Erik had to hand it to the Shensi. Though they'd reacted poorly to the surprise attack, they were pulling their forces, and their security, together. Not only was he taken to the spaceport in an armored personnel carrier, it was part of a motorcade escorted by four hoverbikes, and after they'd left the inner city, a pair of combat-modified MiningMechs.

He felt better having some kind of 'Mech cover, but according to the latest reports from the Legate, their telescopes showed multiple plasma burns on a trajectory away from Shensi, probably heading back to the pirate point from which they'd arrived.

Erik had advised against sending ships after them. It could only be a ruse to lead the planetary defenses away while a main assault force came in from another direction.

In any case, he didn't want the military forces of Shensi getting themselves in over their heads in a solo effort, when his real objective was to tap their forces as part of a coordinated counteroffensive.

At the spaceport, the motorcade drove directly out to the end of one of the huge runways, where a delta-winged *Buccaneer*-class cargo-hauler waited. It was comforting to see the symbol of the Sandoval family painted on its T-shaped vertical tail. As they approached, a vehicle ramp lowered from the belly of the big craft, and the APC drove directly inside for unloading.

The captain, a muscular woman with silver-blond hair, was waiting next to the base of a bridge-type cargo crane. She walked up as the APC door opened. "Commander, welcome to the *Mercury.* I'm Captain

Yung, at your disposal. I'm glad we were in the neighborhood for you. We've got a full load of rare metals and mail bound for Tikonov, but we'll get you back to the Duke first. Latest word we have is that he's on his way to Ningpo."

Erik nodded. "That was his plan. How are our connections at the jump point?"

"There's a SwordSworn JumpShip charging right now. They'll hold off their jump till we arrive." She looked at the APC, which was already backing down the ramp. "No baggage, Commander?"

He held up the signed accord. "This is all I really need." He smiled sheepishly. "However, if one of your crewmembers is close to my size, I could stand to borrow a few things."

She smiled and nodded. "I'll have someone show you to your quarters later, Commander; right now, we're ready to take off. Would you care to join me on the bridge?"

"I'd like that. Show the way."

Captain Yung strode down the length of the ship's central corridor. The *Mercury* was an aerodyne DropShip, with her engines in the back. That meant that while "down" pointed at the belly of the ship now, while they were still on a planet, once they were in space and under power, the apparent "down" would be in the direction of the tail. As such, the central corridor had a switchback stairway built sideways along its ceiling. It was a bizarre sight, but once they were under way, this corridor would look like a fairly standard stairwell.

Side corridors branched off the main corridor at regular intervals. No fun-house stairways were necessary in these, as people would simply walk on what was now the sternward wall of the corridor. The only unusual feature of the hall was that all the hatchways to individual compartments—apparently crew quarters in this section—were in the floor and ceiling, currently accessible only by ladders.

The ship was already rolling when they reached the bridge, which was fairly cramped for an otherwise spacious ship. Erik wedged himself into an observer's seat near the back, where he had a good view of the crew stations in front of him, and the big expanse of ferroglass looking out the front. The captain slipped into a seat up front, next to the pilot, quickly strapped herself in, and donned a headset.

The big ship turned sharply, lining up on the runway. The captain flipped a switch activating a warning Klaxon, and announced the launch. "All hands, beginning liftoff roll now."

There was a shudder as the pilot pushed the throttles forward. Erik felt a gentle push against his back as they started to roll. They were picking up speed, and the pilot shoved the throttles some more.

Erik felt himself pushed back into the seat more strongly. They were moving very fast now. The captain continued to talk into the microphone. "V-one." A pause. "V-two. Rotate."

The nose of the ship lifted, and a change in the vibration told Erik that they were off the ground. Immediately there was a rumbling growl in the deck under his feet as the gear retracted, followed by a series of bangs and clunks as it seated itself and the doors in the hull closed.

"Crew, we're airborne. Stand by for ballistic climb-out."

The pilot pushed the throttles full forward, even as he pulled back on the control yoke. The nose climbed higher, higher, till Erik found himself lying on his back, squeezed back into the padding of his seat by acceleration. The *Mercury* had stopped pretending to be an airplane. They were a rocket now, and headed rapidly for space.

Erik watched, fascinated, as the sky darkened from blue to indigo, purple, and finally black. The pilot began to throttle back, and the acceleration eased.

Captain Yung glanced back at him. "We're about to do a rollover, then burn a direct trajectory to the jump point. No wasting time in orbit."

True to her word, the ship began to roll over on its back. As they rolled, the curved surface of Shensi came into view. He looked down at the green continents floating in dark blue oceans. The terminator between day and night was below them now. Beyond it, he could see the glowing stars of cities, and the spidery webs of light connecting them.

He wondered where Elsa was—if she'd gotten off-planet safely. He'd asked the Legate to look into it, but there had been such confusion at the spaceport right after the attacks, he doubted he'd hear anything more. He hoped she was in a DropShip somewhere, maybe looking down at those same, twinkling stars.

12

Buccaneer-class **DropShip Mercury**
Outbound to Shensi jump point
Prefecture V, The Republic
21 November 3134

Erik climbed the many dozens of stairs between his quarters and the bridge. His borrowed uniform was too long in the legs, so he kept tripping over his own cuffs, and his too-tight collar chafed. They were only a few hours out from Shensi, and he wasn't sure why he'd been called to the bridge. He hoped it didn't mean another attack force had appeared.

He reached the ladder at the top of the stairs. The hatch to the bridge was above the landing, and he climbed up to reach it. What had before takeoff been a flat triangle of a room was now vertical, with the captain's chair and pilot's station at the top. Metal-grid catwalks and ladders had been unfolded after launch to allow access to the higher stations.

The captain, however, was currently on the lowest level, leaning over a navigation-radar station. The navigator kept pointing out things to her on the screen. Through the windows ahead, he could see a lumpy, potato-shaped rock, which he assumed must be Shensi's small moon, Kung Pao.

"What's the situation, Captain?"

She frowned at him. "About twenty minutes ago, we started picking up a distress call. Low-power transmitter, and tight beam—definitely intended for our ears only."

"So?"

"It comes from a small ship hiding behind the moon. We think it's a fighter—one of the ones that attacked Shensi. It must have missed the hookup with its carrier DropShip."

"Could it be a trap?"

"Possibly, Commander, but I don't think so."

"This could be good intelligence, then. Can we bring it aboard?"

"It will delay our arrival at the jump point by a few hours, but it can be done. But I'm troubled."

"How so?"

"They signaled *us*, Commander. It wasn't an all-points distress call, and they're obviously trying not to be detected by the planet. Why would they send the call to us?"

Erik shrugged. "Because we're such swell and fair-minded folk? How should I know?"

"Just the same, it strikes me as curious. All the readings we're getting say this ship is really damaged, and there's an injured pilot onboard. It doesn't seem to be a trap, and yet it has all the makings of one."

"Still, I don't see how we can let this opportunity pass us by."

"Your call, Commander. We'll pick it up and see what happens." She picked up her microphone. "All hands, free fall in thirty seconds. Turnover and deceleration burn in five minutes. Be prepared for unexpected acceleration as we rendezvous." She called up to the pilot. "Shut her down on my mark, then prepare for rollover."

"Aye, sir."

She turned her attention back to Erik. "You'd better hold onto something, Commander."

"I've been on a DropShip a time or two before, Captain."

"Of course; sorry. Should we call Shensi about this?"

He considered, then shook his head. "Let's find out what intelligence we've got before we decide who to share it with. Doubtless, somebody is going to wonder what we're doing poking around their moon, so come up with a cover story and stick to it. We'll have rounded up any survivors, and will be on our way to the jump point before they get overly suspicious."

"Throttling down," said the pilot, as he slowly reduced thrust.

Erik supposed doing it that way was safer than cutting the thrust instantaneously, but he had the feeling that he was in an elevator where the cable had snapped, and he was just beginning to fall.

It took several hours for the *Mercury* to kill its velocity and park itself in a close orbit above the little moon. It could have been done in less time with a high-G burn, but that would have attracted even more attention than their current activities. Erik considered using the time to have his long-delayed lunch, but decided that testing his stomach under the current erratic acceleration wouldn't be a good idea, even with anti-space-sickness pills.

Instead, he nibbled a few crackers, and caught a nap in a hammock someone had hung in an equipment room behind the bridge. It was the sleeping-bag type, with a zip-up cover to keep the occupant from floating out in zero-G, or being thrown out by the maneuvering thrusters. As a MechWarrior, he prided himself on his ability to sleep anywhere, but he still woke several times after dreams of falling.

The captain didn't wake him until they'd already dispatched an S7A Bus to the surface. Though Erik protested that he would have preferred to go along, the captain wasn't having any of it. "No offense, Commander, but working in microgravity like this is a lot harder than it looks. You could almost jump into orbit, but if you found a crevasse, you could still fall far enough to kill yourself. My guys have been doing this half their lives, so you'd only slow them down."

They returned to the bridge to supervise the mission. "The distress call is just automatic now. There are actually two fighters down there. Our instruments show one of them as registering a temperature of about 120 degrees below zero. It's dead, and so is whoever was inside. We're showing residue of reactor plasma and life-support gases that probably vented from one or both vehicles. There's another one plowed in next to it, but we're getting energy readings that tell us it has a barely functioning reactor. Of course, that just may mean we'll find a warm corpse instead of a frozen one."

These weren't just lost ships that were hiding. They'd obviously taken severe battle damage, and had barely made it away from the planet. "Well," said Erik, "looks like the Shensi did manage to get a few licks in, even if I didn't see it."

There was a crackle from the radio. "Captain, Brinks here. We've got one survivor, but he's unconscious and in bad shape. I think a missile peeled most of his radiation shielding off, and solar flare activity is high right now. Poor bastards were limping back to their ship while the flare was cooking them from the inside out. They must have tried to land here and use the moon as a radiation shelter, but by then it was too late."

The captain looked a little pale. Radiation: one of a spacer's greatest enemies. "Get him back as soon as you can, Brinks. You know the drill."

"Yes, sir. Strip the ships of any intelligence materials, pull the computer cores for analysis, plant a thermal charge and melt the rest to slag." There was a pause. "And sir?"

"Yes, Brinks."

"Should we bring back the other body?"

She glanced at Erik. Then her jaw clenched and she shook her head. "Burn it."

As soon as the shuttle was aboard and secure, the *Mercury* went to a one-G thrust. Not only did it get them away from the prying eyes of the Shensi, it made handling the survivor easier.

The *Mercury* was a large ship, but nominally had a crew of only twelve. She had a well-equipped infirmary, but no doctor. Sergeant Brinks had the most medical training of anyone aboard, but the survivor, if he could properly be called that, needed far better care.

Erik and Captain Yung stood outside the plastic bubble that had been inflated around the pilot's bed. A drip IV depended on the reliability of a planet's gravity; therefore, Brinks hooked the patient up to a number of electronic IV pumps. The man's eyes were clouded white, his gums bled profusely, and his skin was turning a mulberry color. Exposure to heavy radiation was a horrible way to die.

Brinks emerged through a simple airlock that closed with zippers. He was wearing a full surgical garment and mask. His face was gray. This was every spacer's nightmare, and he was getting to see it closer than anyone. "I've done what I could. I'm pumping him full of the antiradiation cocktail they supply us with, and loads of painkillers, but he's way beyond my help."

Yung looked at Erik. "We could turn back to Shensi."

Brinks shook his head. "No point. He'll be dead before we get there. We might make it to the jump point, and possibly one of the ships there has a real doctor. But—" He shook his head again.

Erik looked at the man in the bubble. "Can he talk?"

"He's in and out of consciousness. Keeps talking about Sergi. I think that's the pilot of the other fighter. Maybe his wingman."

"I want to talk to him."

Brinks shrugged. "Put on a mask and gloves. He's got no immune system left to speak of—not that I think he'll live long enough for infection to be an issue. And don't expect much."

The captain patted the sergeant's shoulder. "If there's nothing else you can do here, take a break." She turned back to Erik. "Commander, I've got my engineer poking around those computer cores we salvaged. The radiation didn't do them any good, either, but he thinks he can extract some data. I'm going to go see how he's doing." She looked into the bubble and shuddered. It was obvious that she had her own reasons for leaving.

Erik nodded. "I'll stay here till Brinks comes back. I'll call for help if I need it."

Reluctantly he put on the mask and gloves, and zipped himself inside the bubble. The air had the nasty smell of stale vomit and decay. If the man wasn't a corpse already, he was starting to smell like one. His cracked lips were moving, like he was trying to talk, but he made no sound other than his raspy breathing.

Erik glanced at the IV pumps. The drug canister

on one apparently was the all-purpose antiradiation cocktail Brinks had mentioned. The other was Morpidine, a powerful painkiller that was in every combat medical kit. Every soldier knew about it. It was the stuff you administered to comfort the dying, or, through overdose, to end their suffering. There were dozens of oft-circulated jokes about Morpidine, and yet the sight of the stuff made anyone in uniform squirm.

Erik forced himself to lean closer to the doomed pilot. "Can you hear me?"

The man flinched, his blind eyes turned toward Erik's voice. "Who? Sergi?"

"My name is Erik Sandoval."

To Erik's surprise, the man managed a little smile. "Sandoval. I told Sergi you would come. Help us." He swallowed. "Didn't believe me. Told him."

Erik frowned. "Why did you think the Sandovals would help you?"

He smiled, showing his blood-reddened teeth, and Erik averted his eyes. "Wasn't supposed to know. Lady, hired us to attack. Didn't say who she worked for, but I knew. Lady . . ." He seemed to lose focus. He coughed wetly.

"What lady?"

"I—used to be Republic—army. Guarded Duke Sandoval once at—meeting. This lady was with him— all the time. Pretty—Hired us—Told Sergi was Sandoval hired us—Didn't believe—"

Erik straightened. His gut knotted. Could it be true? The man had no reason to lie, and his description, crude though it was, fit Deena Onan. He remembered their encounter as they'd met at the *Tyrannos Rex* vehicle bay, and now it all seemed clear. He didn't know whose betrayal stung him more, the Duke's or hers.

What now? This information was like a grenade

with the pin pulled. One radio call back to Shensi would break the accord, derail the Duke's plans for a coalition, and perhaps bring his quest for power right down on top of his head. Was that what Erik wanted?

No. Not yet. But if this information was to be of any value to him, he had to control it. Exclusively. This pilot would die, certainly, but perhaps not soon enough.

Erik glanced up at the IV pump. Simple buttons with UP-DOWN arrows controlled the flow rate.

It would be a mercy.

He stared at the pump for what seemed like hours. This man was an enemy. In combat, he would have killed him without hesitation or remorse. Why was this so different?

It just was.

Erik reached up to where the pump hung next to the bag, held it in his hand, and started pressing the UP arrow. He kept pressing, until the numbers reached maximum and stopped.

He looked at the pilot, and realized he'd never learned the man's name. There was only one name he did know. "Say hello to Sergi for me."

13

Rampant speculation continues concerning the symbols seen painted in Duke Aaron Sandoval's flagship as it departed Azha—symbols that are rumored to be associated with the splinter group known as the SwordSworn, a militant faction reportedly loyal to House Davion. Duke Sandoval is Lord Governor of Prefecture IV, and his presence, along with a sizable military force, in Prefecture V is as yet unexplained.

Reports indicate that the symbols were painted on the ship at the Cushman Coating Works facility in Casella shortly before the ship's departure. Officials at Cushman have declined to comment. The Duke's forces have had several skirmishes with advancing House Liao forces, and dealt them a major setback on New Aragon. One Senator, who asked not to be identified, is quoted as saying, "I don't care who he's loyal to, if he stands between us and the Cappies, he's a friend of mine."

—FreeNews Azha

Capital Spaceport, Ningbo
Liampo continent, Ningpo
Prefecture V, The Republic
28 November 3134

It was a landing like Ningpo's Capital Spaceport had never seen. The huge *Excalibur* DropShip came out of a north-south polar orbit, rather than the normal west-east orbit. This brought it down across the landmass of the Liampo continent, and nearly over the capital city of Ningbo, rather than across the ocean.

This was not only unusual, it was a violation of half a dozen flight rules.

The ship came in steeply, necessitating a hard burn directly over the city that rattled windows well out into the suburbs. Those who came outside to see what the noise was looked up to see a blue sky, dappled with wispy white clouds. Moving from north to south was a huge silver egg, gleaming in the sun, with the blue glare of four mighty fusion thrusters shining from its base.

A diplomatic vessel arriving at the spaceport could be counted on to land in one of the more isolated landing pads, far from prying eyes, but this ship was different. It came in over the pad closest to the crowded terminal so that thousands of eyes were drawn to its glittering, freshly painted beauty.

The ship lined up over the pad and began to lower, tail first. Three hundred meters above the reinforced thermocrete of the pad, it once again did something extraordinary. The ship *stopped,* and hovered motionless—not only a violation of regulations, but an enormous waste of fuel.

There it paused just long enough for everyone's attention to focus on the ship. Four thrusters around its midsection began to fire, and the DropShip began to turn gracefully on its axis, like a 16,000-ton ballet dancer. In the terminal, there was a collective gasp, an intake of breath, as they watched the silver egg slowly revolve in front of them, displaying the seventy-meter SwordSworn symbols painted on two sides—an amber disk surrounded by a white circle, representing a dark planet with the burst of a rising sun around it, and in front of it all an upward-pointing sword, its blade overlaid with some mirrorlike material that flashed in the sunlight as the ship turned.

Then, one final flourish. Two of the main thrusters

in the base of the great ship, an opposing pair, throttled up. As they did, the two other opposing thrusters throttled down to almost nothing so that there was no net change in thrust and the ship remained perfectly suspended. Then, after a moment, the first two thrusters throttled down, and the other two throttled up to compensate. This continued, back and forth, perfectly timed so that it happened twice per revolution. It was a breathtaking display of piloting skill, which turned the ship into an inverted fountain of dancing fire.

Then, and only then, did the ship settle to the apron, which was now glowing from the sustained heat. Just short of the ground, the mighty landing legs unfolded from its base, just in time to gently kiss the ground.

Those who were there would still talk about it years later, and the holovids would be shown again and again. No one would ever forget they were there the day *Tyrannos Rex* arrived on Ningpo.

On the bridge, Captain Clancy took his hands off the controls and clapped them together with childish glee. "I always wanted to do that, Duck! Always!" He looked up at Duke Aaron Sandoval, who stood behind him. "Now, you're sure I'm not gonna get my license yanked for this?"

Aaron smiled. "One way or the other, I assure you, it will all be taken care of. Any bribes or fines I have to pay will be well worth it. But actually, I don't think it will come to that." He grinned slightly. "A Republic-issued Master's license may be of limited value to you after this, anyway." He glanced over at Maxton, the first officer, and noticed that she was still clutching the arms of her chair, and looking a little ashen. "Is there a problem, Mate?"

"Low-altitude hover is the most dangerous thing a

spherical DropShip can do. If we'd had a thruster problem at that altitude, there would have been no time to recover."

Clancy made a hissing sound. "Those engines are solid as rock. Anyways, it was worth the risk. If our numbers got called up—well—what a way to go!"

Aaron raised an eyebrow. This wasn't the first reference that Clancy had made to wanting a suitably spectacular death. He wasn't sure if it was anything to be concerned about. Probably it was just gallows humor, but Clancy was getting on in years. There was some cause to worry that, if an opportunity presented itself, Clancy might be tempted to go out in a blaze of glory, and take anyone else on the ship along for the ride. Still, Aaron would trade this small worry for more typical political duplicity any day.

Clancy unbuckled his straps and climbed out of his seat. He slapped Maxton on her shoulder as he went past. "Relax, Mate. This is one you can tell your grandkids about."

"Aye, Captain." She grinned at him weakly. "Just don't make a habit of it, or you'll make a landlubber out of me."

Aaron had left instructions for a call to be put through to the Governor as soon as they landed. The operator looked up, nodded, and pointed to a nearby communications screen. Aaron stepped up to the screen.

In a moment, the Governor's face appeared. He looked slightly flustered. "Duke Sandoval, was that air show truly necessary?"

Aaron smiled. "I apologize, Governor. But, as you may have heard, an attempt was made on my life mere weeks ago. The unorthodox approach was part of my security precautions. I would have secured advance authorization, but announcing one's plans does tend to defeat the purpose."

The Governor frowned. "Well, I suppose that's justifiable."

"I hope this doesn't get us off on the wrong foot, Governor. I'm here to make a very important proposal to your government—one that will affect the safety and independence of your world. I'd like to discuss it as soon as possible. Perhaps over dinner?"

"I've got a dinner meeting scheduled with key members of the Congress."

"I've got no problem including them in our meeting, Governor, if you don't. In fact, the more the merrier."

The Governor hesitated. "Well, it's short notice, but I suppose I can have the chef make room for one more at the table—"

Aaron chuckled and shook his head. "No, Governor, you don't understand. I wasn't trying to crash your dinner. I was inviting you to mine. I'd like you and your guests to dine with me here tonight. Have them bring their spouses as well, if you wish. We can slip aside and discuss our business after dessert."

The Governor was puzzled. "Dinner there? Where? At the spaceport?"

"On my ship, Governor. I'd like you to accept my hospitality on the *Tyrannos Rex*."

The Governor blinked back his surprise. "Really, Lord Governor. If you think I'm going to trade my palace chef for some . . . mess hall, then—"

"It's not like that at all, Governor. Let's see." He pulled a sheet of paper from his pocket and unfolded it. "Chef Bellwood has given me a menu. We'll begin with a *Foie Gras Sauté au Framboises* and a *Tarte d'Escargots de Tomate et l'Estragon*. The main course will be *Thai Saumon Oriental* in a sweet cream ginger sauce—"

The Governor's eyes widened, and he waved for Aaron to stop. "I apologize, Lord Governor. I would be . . . fascinated to see what you have to offer."

Aaron smiled broadly. "Very well, Governor. Would seven, local time, be agreeable?"

"But of course. I look forward to it. Until tonight."

The screen blanked, and Aaron's smile became even broader, and perceptibly more genuine. "The opening salvo of our campaign has landed squarely on target." He turned to Clancy. "I'm headed below. Call Ulysses and tell him I'm ready to meet the press at any time."

The press conference had been ordered up, catalog-style, by downlink as they were approaching Ningpo. A semicircle of modular risers and seats had been set up near the base of *Tyrannos Rex.* In the middle of the seating was a raised dais with a podium, positioned so that the speaker would be just, and only just, above the eye level of most of the reporters. A silk Sword-Sworn banner was draped over the front of the podium, and a larger one was draped from a backdrop behind the speaker. Both were dwarfed by the *Tyrannos Rex,* with its gigantic version of the symbol looming over everything. Any symbols of The Republic were conspicuously absent.

The orientation of the seating was such that the reporters would be near, but not in, the shadow of the ship. It would be back-lit in a spectacular way that would show off its silver paint to best effect. It was what the press people like to call "good holo." Aaron fully expected the image to be on almost every home Tri-Vid screen on the planet that night.

Even the reporters had been "ordered" after a fashion, press releases going out to all those news sources likely to be most favorable to the SwordSworns' proposal, and to only a few who wouldn't be friendly at all. A few hostile questions would place the Duke in a sympathetic light, while giving the whole thing a stamp of legitimacy.

Aaron stood just inside the *Tyrannos Rex,* looking

through a small window of one-way glass at the jammed seats, and at the podium, which was surrounded by holocams and microphones. The window was located in a small security room off the grand lobby that was the formal entrance to the ship.

To his left was the "hole" Captain Clancy had complained so mightily about—a Greek revival entrance framed by two columns. A stairway and a red carpet led from the door to the podium. Some of the architectural elements were now permanently fixed to the ship's hull. Others were built in the temporary shops that now filled much of the hold in bay number three, and had been attached after landing.

Aaron stepped into the entrance lobby, inspecting the grand stairway leading up to his quarters in bay number one, the wildly impractical crystal chandelier that hung from the ceiling (and retracted into a padded garage for flight), the paintings on the walls. The effect, he hoped, was not one of hopeless luxury, but rather of classical elegance. The air was perfumed to hide the ever-present mechanical smells of the ship, and soft music issued from hidden speakers.

Aaron smiled. He felt confident, ready to face his public. He turned to Ulysses Paxton, who struck an imposing figure in his gray pin-striped suit and dark shades. "You did an excellent job preparing the news conference, Ulysses."

Paxton frowned. "You realize this is a security nightmare, don't you? As for the rest, you really need a press secretary."

Deena Onan rushed down the stairs, took Aaron by the shoulders, and turned him so she could look. She straightened his collar, ran her fingers down the creases in his pants, and finally produced a handkerchief to polish a spot on his boots. Aaron looked at himself in the mirror, turning his head to inspect his topknot. "You've both done an outstanding job, you know—taking roles you were never hired for and doing them well. It will be rewarded."

Deena glanced up at his face for a moment, and then went back to her preening. "I expect so," was all she said.

"Ulysses, see what you can do about lining up some press-secretary candidates while we're here. Quietly and discreetly, as always."

"Certainly, Lord Governor. Assuming you survive the press conference." He gestured at the door. "Shall we get this over with?"

Aaron grinned and they stepped out through the incongruously conventional-looking wood-paneled door, Paxton leading the way. Cameras turned toward him like fame-seeking missiles.

In the near distance, he could see the glass walls of the terminal building filled with curious onlookers. He waved. Amazingly, people surged forward. Children waved back. Most of them probably had not a clue who he was, *but they wanted to know!*

This is going to work. In my hand, this sword will win my war.

Paxton stepped up to the podium. "I present to you Duke Aaron Sandoval, Lord Governor of Prefecture IV."

Aaron made a show of surveying the assembled crowd. He worked on projecting the impression that he cared about *them,* each and every one, as individuals. He had to reach them so that, by the time he brought his proposal to the Governor, to refuse it would seem like a betrayal to his people.

"People of Ningpo, I bring you greetings from Tikonov, the SwordSworn, and House Davion." There was a murmur among the assembled as he said "Sword-Sworn," which became much louder as he said "House Davion." "I have come to your world with important matters to discuss with your Governor. I should not

detail those matters until he and I have had time to
discuss them privately.

"I will say, however, that I stand before you today
to extend a hand of friendship and cooperation in a
time of confusion and fear. The universe has been
plunged into darkness, and there is much disorder and
uncertainty. But I have come to tell you that there is
still strength and stability in the stars—that there is
still a sword that stands against aggression and
tyranny.

"I have said we are SwordSworn, and this may puz-
zle some of you, anger you, even frighten you. You
may wonder why I invoke the name of House Davion
rather than that of The Republic. I remind you that I
have served The Republic loyally for many years, and
in many capacities, most recently as Lord Governor
of Prefecture IV. I do not renounce this, nor do I
regard those years with anything but pride.

"But our universe has changed, and—as the incursion of House Liao has shown us—without the HPG
network, The Republic no longer serves us, no longer
can keep us safe or free. In the current situation, the
universe is too vast to maintain order. Terra is too
distant to aid us. Even the regional governments are
failing. My Prefecture remains strong, but to my great
sadness, Prefecture VI has bowed to the Capellan ag-
gressors, and sold out their people to the enemy. Your
own Prefecture has known war, border raids, and up-
risings at the best of times, and now stands on the
brink of disaster.

"I have spoken with your current Lord Governor,
and he has confessed his inability to keep the peace
or to protect his worlds." There was much whispering
among the reporters. "You have heard the rumors,
and they are true. Your leaders are weak. They have
not betrayed you, but they have certainly, by their
own admission, failed you. You know it to be so.

"During this emergency, we must seek present and immediate solutions for order and protection; for those solutions to have strength and longevity, we must turn back to the Great Houses.

"This is not betrayal. This is not treason. The Republic that I served, that we all served, has failed. It may succeed again someday, but first we must have order, we must have peace, we must have freedom from tyranny. I remind you that The Republic was built from worlds ceded by the Great Houses, and if order and communications are restored, that may happen again.

"But for now, we must *choose* what banner we follow, and we must not let history choose for us. I have chosen to pledge my SwordSworn to House Davion, not merely because it is the house of my forefathers, but because of its traditions of honor, integrity, and justice.

"The SwordSworn are strong, and we stand against the aggression of our common enemies. We stand between you and the tyranny and harsh rule you know you would suffer under the Capellans.

"We are strong. But together with your freely given aid, we could be stronger. I extend the hand of friendship, and the pledge to join you in our common defense. I pray that you will see the wisdom in taking that hand, before the freedom to choose is lost to House Liao aggression."

He paused, again scanning the assembled press. "I will now take a few questions." Hands rose, reporters called to him. He picked a woman whom his intelligence report told him worked for a major Tri-Vid network—one likely to value the appearance of objectivity. She might ask a difficult question, but she was unlikely to go on the offensive immediately.

She stood. "Lord Governor. Nina Wu, Interworld. What do you say to the recent rumors of your death?"

He tried to look mildly shocked. "Well, Nina, first just let me say that, to the best of my knowledge . . . those rumors are false."

There was laughter, and the mood suddenly seemed to relax a bit.

Aaron allowed himself a smile—not at the joke, but at the question. That it hadn't been about The Republic or the possibility of treason was telling. These people already had fundamental doubts about The Republic and their own Prefecture. He was only addressing their preexisting concerns.

Once the laughter died, he suppressed the smile, replacing it with a look of concern. He continued. "But in all seriousness, an attempt *was* made on my life—a cowardly act of sabotage, done in the name of House Liao. I survived only through the heroic actions of Captain Gus Clancy of the DropShip *Tyrannos Rex,* and especially those of my bodyguard and security chief, Mr. Ulysses Paxton." Aaron turned and bowed his head toward Paxton.

Paxton smiled slightly, and Aaron held his bow for several beats. *Let the cameras linger on Ulysses. Everyone loves a hero.*

Then Aaron turned back to the crowd. "I speak from personal experience when I say that safety is an illusion. Peace is fragile and easily broken by men and women of ill will. Kiss your spouses, hug your children as though it were your last day, because you never know if it might be."

He called on a young male reporter from a computer news service. "Lord Governor; Paul Yi of UniPage. There are rumors that you've changed your ship into some sort of luxurious flying palace. Comments?"

"Thank you for asking, Paul. I have indeed turned this fine ship into a flying home for myself and my staff. And if you mean 'palace' as in 'seat of government,' then yes, that's what it is. With the fall of the

HPG network, it is no longer practical to govern from a fixed capital. Not on far Terra, not even on Tikonov or Liao or New Canton.

"Tikonov is my place of birth, and my heart will always live there, but it would be both foolish and selfish for me to insist on living there. I have responsibilities to a growing family of worlds, not just one. So I have given up my home there to live in this home among the stars, to go where there is trouble. I want those under my protection to know that their home soil is also *my* home soil—that I care as deeply for their worlds as they do. With this great ship, I can go where the people need me, and do for them what must be done."

He scanned the faces of the reporters. *Time to take a hard one.*

He recognized a face from his intelligence photos, and pointed at a balding man sitting near the back. "Duke Sandoval, Van Harding of *Truth Magazine*. You ask us to take the drastic step of abandoning The Republic, to trust you, and you suggest that you are only a servant of the people. Yet your ship is named *Tyrannos Rex*. Are you our friend, or just a would-be tyrant king?"

Aaron smiled. Exactly as Clancy had predicted. Smart man. "As you can tell from our arrival, I have been lucky enough to secure one of the finest ships, and the finest captains, in the Inner Sphere. This came to me ready-made, and for that, I am most fortunate.

"But the ship came with a name as well, and Captain Clancy informs me that it is highly unlucky to change a ship's name. I owe the captain my life, and he has never steered me wrong in such matters. Therefore this ship is called what it is called, though the name is ironic. I come not to enforce tyranny, but to stand side by side with you against it!" He shook his fist in the air. "Death to tyrants! Long live House Davion!"

The guests arrived by limousine, motorcade, and, in one case, VTOL executive plane. Altogether, there were about twenty-five for dinner. The politicians were perhaps surprised to see some of the planet's hottest holo and music stars in their midst, but the mysterious invitations, along with lavish gifts, had been arranged and sent to those celebrities as soon as *Tyrannos Rex* arrived in the Ningpo system.

Two by two they came, up the red carpet into the entrance hall, and there they waited under the light of the crystal chandelier. And waited.

Crisply uniformed waiters served fine champagne, and a string ensemble in the corner played selections from Bartow's *Symphony for Davion*. There was adequate room for all to mingle and talk, though even a few more people might have crowded things a bit.

Aaron watched them on his security monitors and smiled. "Anticipation," he said to Paxton, "is as powerful an intoxicant as the fruit of the vine."

The little room, the nerve center of Paxton's security network, was located in what had come to be called "backstage"—the more functional part of the complex-within-a-ship that Aaron was building. This area included the kitchens, storage areas, some of the servants' quarters, and a war room where Aaron could work with his senior advisors to oversee his three interlocking empires: political, business, and military.

Per Paxton's suggestion, the plans had also just been amended to include a press room, where his staff could both monitor and feed the press of any planet they were visiting. It would include a small holostudio where Aaron could record or broadcast his own speeches and announcements.

Paxton nodded. "And it gives the workers a few more frantic minutes in which to tie up loose ends."

"Well, that, too." While the transformation of *Tyrannos Rex* was remarkable, it was far from complete. The carpenters, craftsmen, decorators, and shipwrights he had hired had labored through the journey—and quietly since their landing—to get as much ready as possible.

Yet a great deal of what would be seen was just for show. Many rooms were represented only as rough metal frameworks into which walls and ceilings would later be built. There were doors that opened to nowhere, and Aaron had instructed that the locks be double-checked, lest some curiosity-seeker accidentally plunge into a darkened cargo bay.

He hoped that what his guests *did* see would be perfect, and would provide the illusion that the rest of his quarters were finished as well. As with a Tri-Vid set, the object was to show what needed to be shown, and allow the mind to fill in the rest.

The door opened and Deena Onan entered, looking lovely in an emerald gown that shimmered when it moved, and which provocatively bared one shoulder. Her auburn hair was braided and piled on top of her head.

Paxton looked at her and raised an eyebrow.

She shrugged. "How often do I actually get to dress *myself* up? It's a treat."

Aaron ignored their banter. "The progress report, Deena?"

"The workers have cleared out of the finished areas. I'm having the maids make a last sweep to be sure everything is clean and that the workers haven't missed any details. The parlor off the main ballroom is ready to use, and I'm even told that you should be able to sleep in your new bedroom tonight."

Aaron frowned. "That wasn't supposed to be a priority. None of the guests are going to see my bedroom."

Deena grinned slightly. "Really, my Lord, you should be more optimistic. Anyway," she continued, "the chef is complaining that the kitchen is a kludge—inadequate—and dinner is ruined. Never mind what he says. I've tasted the soup, and I've now found something better than sex."

"Well, then," said Aaron, "I will at least have that to look forward to." He looked back at the screens. "I suppose it's time, then." He turned to Deena and came to attention. "I present myself for inspection."

She scanned him from the shoes up. "I can't improve upon perfection, Lord Governor."

"Well, then, let's go win ourselves a world."

He made a dramatic entrance at the top of the stairs, gave a little speech of welcome, and then led his guests up and into the main part of his quarters.

The grand hall was wide and opulently furnished with antiques, tapestries, and paintings by modern masters. Many of these furnishings were recognizable from the Chipley Arms. He'd liked the hotel's style so much, he'd ultimately decided to strip three suites and a mezzanine before leaving.

The grand hall was an important part of the illusion. It allowed a clear view from the top of the stairs to the far wall of the ballroom—nearly the whole length of the cargo bay—making the quarters seem vast. In fact, it was little more than a hallway at this point, with most of the doors leading to unfinished space, or to rooms too unfinished or not yet fine enough for public viewing.

A few doors were simply façades, nearly flush against hidden bulkheads or the outside hull. A door suggested a space beyond, even if it was permanently screwed shut. One of the designers Aaron had hired had a background in amusement-park attractions, and had proved to be an excellent asset.

As they arrived in the ballroom, the formal dining room could be seen through sliding pocket doors to one side, the long table set with fine silver and china. The centerpiece was a three-dimensional version of the SwordSworn shield, carved from ice, and surrounded by fresh flowers.

Before dinner there was more champagne, and hors d'oeuvres on silver platters. A soloist played the viola while the rest of the musicians were moved upstairs. A blond, waifish Tri-Vid starlet abandoned her companion and began flirting with Aaron, who found himself flirting back.

Aaron spoke with the Governor, of course, but merely to greet him and his wife, and to exchange a few social pleasantries. He made a point of paying no more attention to him than any other guest. For now, he wanted to draw the focus away from business, and make the Governor forget Aaron had arrived not just with a ship, but with an agenda.

The meal, as Deena had predicted, was excellent and well received. The finishing touch was a flaming ice dessert made with sweet cream, native Ningpo fruits, and eggs, in a crisp pastry shell.

It was over coffee afterward that the first discussion of the SwordSworn coalition took place. As Aaron had hoped, Governor Xiao was the one to bring it up. "Lord Governor, as charming and impressive as this evening has been, I'm afraid I can't offer you what you want in return."

"A gracious host expects nothing of his guests but the pleasure of their company, Governor. Whatever could you be talking about?"

"I know you've come hoping I'll commit the Ningpo military to some sort of joint action against the House

Liao incursions. I don't see how I can justify such a thing to my people. We're already allowing your forces to use our jump points, and I have reservations about that.

"Frankly, it's the only reason I can imagine House Liao would even bother us. I'm not sure we can afford the risk any longer. It's quite true what you've said about our Lord Governor. I don't think we can depend on him for protection from House Liao, but that assumes we *need* protection. There are many people here tonight who believe—and I'm inclined to agree— that expelling you from our system and seeking a non-aggression pact with them would be our best course of action."

Aaron sipped his coffee thoughtfully. In truth, Ningpo's military might was minimal, the planet poor in strategic resources. The only really useful thing about it was its location.

"Governor, I do understand your position, and I appreciate your being so forthright about your opinions. I think, however, you should consider all the facts.

"First, no matter what these fine people here tonight may believe, I think the majority of your people are quite concerned about the possibility of living under Capellan rule. Ultimately, you are only valuable to House Liao so long as you have the backing of your people. If you do not, you'll be of no use to them, and you will be replaced.

"Second, I'm not seeking military assistance, though it is always welcome. I would like to continue our current agreements for the use of your jump points and, in addition, I would like to use your system as an advance staging area for my forces. As such, Ningpo would enjoy our full military protection, and reap indirect economic benefits as well: My troops will need R and R, and, I assure you, they're well paid and would be eager to spend their money on such a beautiful world."

The Governor shook his head and smiled. "Really, what you're proposing is to turn us into an irresistible target for Liao."

Aaron suddenly turned to the starlet. "My dear, what do you think?"

She seemed shocked to be drawn into such a serious discussion, and Aaron wondered for a moment if she'd even been listening. She blinked. "Well," she finally said, "I think war is bad."

Aaron nodded appreciatively. "As do we all. And yet war is a fact; it's already happening."

Her wide blue eyes looked at Aaron. "Not on Ningpo."

Aaron held his hand out toward her. "Exactly! The people of Ningpo do not want war to come to their world. And I'm sure you'd agree, my dear, this is exactly what the Governor has in mind."

She looked at the Governor as though she'd just noticed he was there. "I suppose."

"But the question everyone will be asking themselves tomorrow will be: Is this the best way to go about it? What do you think?"

She shrugged. "If they'll agree to leave us alone, that would be good."

Aaron nodded. "I'm rather certain they will. So that settles it." He leaned back in his chair, arms crossed over his chest.

The starlet beamed.

"There's just one thing," said Aaron. "Can you trust them?"

The starlet's smile faded, and she looked questioningly at the Governor.

The Governor looked slightly annoyed, yet Aaron

was sure the man was imagining millions of his constit-
uents asking just the same question.

He turned back to Aaron. "As I said, unless they
have some reason to attack us, I just can't see why
they would lie."

Aaron uncrossed his arms and leaned forward wearing his best poker face. "If the Ningpo system would
make a good staging area for my forces, it would be
just as useful for Liao's forces moving in the other
direction. And if they should realize this as well, do
you suppose they'll ask permission, as I have?"

"I think they would."

"You trust them then?"

"Yes!"

"What about Shensi?"

"What about it?"

"You knew the Shensi government was negotiating
a pact with House Liao?"

The Governor looked uncomfortable, obviously
wondering if this was a verbal trap. Aaron knew there
was political backchatter between the two governors,
and Xiao had likely known of the negotiations long
before the SwordSworn had. "I'd heard something of
the sort might be in the works."

"*I'd* heard things had progressed well beyond that.
Which leaves one wondering how to explain the Liao
attack on Shensi."

This caught the Governor totally off guard.

Aaron was secretly pleased. With the HPG network
down, it was difficult to predict how rapidly news
could travel from one system to another. Aaron's intelligence people could only provide a "latest possible" time, when a scheduled freight shipment from
Shensi was to arrive in the system. He had hoped the
news would wait till then, and apparently it had.

"Attack? What attack?"

"Just before our jump here, we received word that an unprovoked aerospace attack was made on the capital city and various strategic targets around the planet. The news was sketchy, but we assumed your intelligence people had already heard."

Now the Governor looked flustered; his face reddened. "Is this a joke, Lord Governor? We've heard no such thing. If this is a cheap deception to secure my cooperation, I'm neither impressed nor amused!"

"I assure you, Governor, it's no joke. Frankly, I was hoping you might have additional news, as a member of my family, Commander Erik Sandoval-Groell, was last known to be at the Shensi capital, trying to salvage the political situation there. I've had no word from him." He looked down, chewed his lip for a pregnant moment. "I fear the worst."

The starlet gave him a sympathetic look and he felt the soft skin of her hand as it rubbed the top of his. He gave her an appreciative glance, then looked back at the Governor.

Actually, he was looking *past* the Governor, at a strategically placed clock on the wall behind him. By his estimate, the scheduled ship should have jumped into the Ningpo system approximately seventy minutes before. It was an event that the entire evening's festivities had been timed around. The light-speed delay for a radio message traveling from the jump point to Ningpo was about fifty-three minutes. Assuming the attack had gone as planned, and Aaron was only assuming that it had, word should have reached the planet by now. The question was how long it would take to filter through channels to the president's ear.

Aaron sat silently for perhaps thirty seconds.

The Governor leaned over and whispered something to his wife.

The starlet leaned closer, putting her other hand on Aaron's shoulder.

One of the Governor's aides slipped into the room, a grave expression on his face. He leaned over the Governor and whispered in his ear.

As he watched the Governor's reaction, it took all of Aaron's self-control and acting skills to keep from breaking into a broad smile of victory.

"Lord Governor, I regret to inform you that I've just received confirmation of the surprise attack on Shensi. Mercenary forces employed by House Liao have been implicated. I'm afraid we don't have any specific word about Commander Sandoval, but the Capitol Building itself was a target, and there are many casualties. My sympathies."

Aaron nodded. "Of course, Governor. Thank you. For now, I must hope for the best."

The Governor nodded. "Perhaps it would be better if we discussed your proposal tomorrow. This is a stressful time."

"No, Governor. If family blood has been spilled in this matter, I will feel better knowing it was not spilled in vain. I have the papers in my drawing room, if you'd care to accompany me."

Aaron stood at the top of the entry stairs, watching the final guests depart. The Governor had signed his agreement. It would need to be ratified by the planetary council, but an emergency session had been scheduled for first thing the following morning. Debate was expected to be minimal.

He was only a little surprised when he felt a soft, small body press against his back. "Lord Governor?"

He turned and looked into the starlet's eyes. "What about your companion?"

She smiled. "He was just some flavor-of-the-week the production company sent along. It was supposed to help his career. Maybe it did, but he left early."

"How unfortunate. Will you be needing a ride?"

She leaned into him. "Maybe later."

He carried her through the door, paused, and looked around to find the big oval canopy bed against the wall to his left. He dropped her on the bed playfully and fell down next to her. He glanced at the open window and wondered if they should close the drapes. Then he realized sheepishly that it was only a holoprojection—the skyline view taken from a camera outside the ship.

She laughed and touched his face. "Aaron, you'd think you'd never seen your own bedroom before."

He smiled. "You'd think."

The starlet snored softly, though pleasantly. It reminded Aaron of a cat he'd once had.

He felt good, and why shouldn't he? Diplomatic victory, and its rewards, were his. Yet he couldn't sleep.

Why? Not the snoring; even the sounds of battle had never kept Aaron awake when he determined it was time to rest. He had no worries about tomorrow's council session. What then?

The bed seemed very large, even with two people in it. The sheets were satin and gently perfumed. The room was lovely—everything he had hoped for.

He thought of Shensi.

He slipped quietly out of bed, careful not to wake his sleeping companion. He checked the closet, and found that Deena had already moved his clothing in— both the small amount that had fit in his old quarters, and the rest, which had been stored in an adjacent cabin. He selected a silk robe, embroidered above the pocket with the SwordSworn shield, and a pair of leather slippers.

He left the room quietly and wandered down the hall, through a butler's pantry, and out through a rear door that took him into the ship proper. He felt better, seeing the gray metal walls and exposed pipes. The show was over now. It was good to be backstage.

He startled a maintenance crewman working the late shift, as he shuffled past and found the door to his old quarters. Gratefully, he found it hadn't been reassigned. His name was still on the placard above the number. He punched in the lock code and slipped inside.

The bunk had been made with standard ship's-issue sheets, coarse and common. There was a single foam pillow; the mattress was hard. He took off his robe, hung it on the hook on the wall. He slipped under the sheets and put his head on the pillow.

Almost immediately, he was asleep.

14

Actress Ginger Li's career took a stunning leap today as she was signed to headline Ningchow Studios' big-budget holoproduction of The MechWarrior's Mistress. *The holo is the first major 'Mecher to be produced on Ningpo since the genre fell out of favor two decades ago—but, given the current rumblings of war, it's sure not to be the last.*

Insiders report that executives first considered Li for the role only after reports connected her romantically with Duke Aaron Sandoval during his just-concluded diplomatic visit. Li's agent reports that she and the Duke are just "dear friends," and that she "supports him in his epic battle for freedom, not unlike the one to be portrayed in the upcoming production."

—*Showbiz Ningpo*

SwordSworn Flagship, Tyrannos Rex
Outbound to Ningpo jump point
Prefecture V, The Republic
5 December 3134

Aaron sat in his newly completed office on the *Tyrannos Rex,* enjoying the last hour or so of normal gravity. They had already arranged passage to Poznan on a *Merchant* JumpShip currently recharging at the star's zenith jump point, but the ship would not be fully charged for another seventy hours.

Until then, the ship would float there, its unfurled sail absorbing solar energy for the trip. The *Tyrannos Rex* would have to wait in free fall. It was then that the practicality—or lack thereof—of his new quarters would be revealed.

Already the servants and workers swarmed over the place, double-checking the bolts that held the furniture to the floor, securing loose objects, retracting the chandeliers into their storage nooks. Even then, the space would be largely useless—devoid of handholds where they were needed, sharp corners everywhere waiting to catch the unwary, the furnishings largely useless. Aaron expected to retreat to his original quarters until after the jump, when they were again under one-G acceleration for the nine-day journey from the jump point to Poznan.

There was a knock at the open door. Paxton leaned in. "Lord Governor, do you have time to brief the new press secretary?"

"Now's as good a time as any, I suppose."

He'd only met Joan Cisco briefly after she'd come aboard. He hadn't even read her credentials, and was simply trusting Ulysses' judgment. In any case, her hiring was probationary.

If she didn't work out, he'd simply write her a termination check and try again. He didn't think it would be necessary, though.

According to Ulysses, she had been working in the Ningpo branch of a Tikonov farm machinery company. She'd been remarkably successful in selling unwanted tractors and AgroMechs to skeptical Ningpo farmers.

To Aaron's mind one product—and he did consider himself a product—was much the same as another. Moreover, as a Tikonov native, she would be likely to understand his politics and methods better than any off-worlder.

Cisco walked in. She was a tall, graceful woman, who carried herself with a poise and confidence that he admired. Though her crisply tailored business suit was tasteful, she had long legs that she obviously enjoyed showing, as the skirt was cut accordingly. Her blond hair was worn pinned high on her head, and black, horn-rimmed glasses took the edge off a face that was almost too beautiful. Her tan suggested that she spent a great deal of time outdoors, and her muscular calves and thighs supported this assumption.

"Lord Governor, thank you for making time for me. I'm running to catch up here, and I understand our next jump is less than three days away. I'd like to leave the jump point with a steady stream of press and publicity material traveling in front of us."

Aaron smiled. *Send in the advance forces to soften them up and feel them out, before the main assault begins.* The woman's way of thinking was to his liking. "There's time to talk about Poznan later. First, I assume Ulysses and Deena have brought you up to speed with what we've been doing?"

"I've been given copies of everything that was sent out, and all the local press coverage you were able to record or acquire on your previous stops."

"And?"

She took a deep breath. "How frank would you like me to be, Lord Governor?"

"I need an honest assessment. That is what I will always require from you. You need not coddle my ego, nor those of any of my staff."

She nodded. "Very well." She licked her lips, thinking. "First, to some extent, results speak for themselves. Ningpo was a huge victory for you, and that creates a momentum that will greatly assist your future endeavors. Your handling of the press arrangements was very good. Considering their lack of experience in such matters, Mr. Paxton showed outstanding organizational skills, and Ms. Onan wrote some surprisingly good releases. In fact, if she ever wants to consider an alternate line of work, I could introduce her to some people."

Aaron smiled, but without much humor. "Deena is an educated woman, with quite a few hidden talents. I warn you, however, that I very much wish to keep my valued employees in my employ." The smile was gone. "Don't ever talk about such matters, even in jest. I won't look kindly on it."

Her eyes widened, as she saw how serious he was. "Of course, my Lord. It was only a joke, and it won't happen again."

"Good, then." He let the matter pass as though it had never happened. "Go on with your analysis."

"This ship itself is a stroke of genius. With The Republic fragmented, worlds isolated from distant authorities will rally to a tangible symbol of power, especially one as benign as this. It seems your intent was to make yourself into a kind of royal celebrity, and in that, you're well on your way." She lowered her voice conspiratorially. "Your liaison with Ginger Li was an especially masterful touch."

Aaron frowned. "Who?"

"Ginger Li, the Tri-Vid actress."

"Oh," said Aaron, leaning back in his chair. "So that was her name."

Cisco raised an eyebrow, but made no comment. "Moving on, Lord Governor; with as much good as you've done, you've taken huge risks, and have been incredibly lucky. I don't believe in leaving things to chance. It's just as easy to generate negative spin as it is to generate positive. If we're going to work together, you have to trust me to know the best way to project the image you wish to create."

Aaron rubbed his chin and smiled slightly. He wasn't ready to tell her the true story of Shensi, and might never be. On the other hand, she had to know on some level how he worked, and the lengths to which he was willing to go to in order to achieve his goals. "Ms. Cisco, I believe that there is no such thing as luck. You're right about not wanting to leave things to chance. I believe that successful people make their own luck, and that even adversity—such as the attempt on my life—can be used as opportunity.

"Know that you will not—at first, anyway—always be privy to all my dealings. Those aren't your concern. My public face is. Know, too, that if you need something—anything, no matter how outrageous or impossible it may seem—to shape that public face, then you must tell me."

"Anything?"

He looked her squarely in the eye. "Anything. I have remarkable resources at my disposal. Don't assume I can do 'anything,' but don't assume that I can't."

He smoothed his hair with his fingers. "Which brings us back to Poznan. It's going to be a difficult world to win: a nest of ethnic tensions, dissidents, and malcontents. There are many there who would welcome Liao forces with open arms."

She nodded. "And just as many who would start a civil war to resist them, which isn't in our interests, either.

"We have to convince all the ethnic groups that you are offering them something they've never seen before—something that addresses all their desires. I have some suggestions—"

The intercom built into the desktop chimed gently. "Excuse me." He pushed a control. "Duke Sandoval."

It was Clancy's voice. "Duck, just thought you'd like to know. A ship just jumped into the point ahead of us. Got a DropShip called the *Mercury* on it, and they've got your boy, Erik."

* * *

Erik leaned his face against the cool ferro-glass of the shuttle's viewport to get a better look at the *Tyrannos Rex*. He hardly recognized the ship now, its silver hull gleaming in the light of the nearby star over whose north pole the ship was currently floating. As the shuttle moved around the egg-shaped hull, the huge SwordSworn seal came into view.

The sight of it caused a tightness in his chest that he couldn't identify, a strange mixture of pride, anger, and revulsion. Nor could he identify the source of the negative feelings. Was it because of the symbol itself, or the fact that it was on Aaron Sandoval's ship? There was a great deal to sort out yet, and he'd hoped for more time.

It was an unfortunate accident for them to arrive at the Ningpo jump point just as the Duke was about to leave the system. If things had gone a little differently, he might have had additional days, or weeks, to untangle that knot in his chest. Now he was going in, wounds still fresh, the sting of betrayal coloring his every thought.

He was shocked, as they approached the bay, to see an archway flanked by Greek columns grafted to the side of the ship. Perhaps Aaron really had gone mad. Perhaps the man who had come back from New Canton was not at all the uncle he had once known.

The shuttle slipped into the bay, the door slid closed, and the bay began to pressurize. Erik was the only passenger in the little ship, which was otherwise jammed with cargo, military equipment, and parts requisitioned from the *Mercury* to help complete the Duke's irrational plans for the *Tyrannos Rex*.

The hissing of air outside became louder and finally stopped. The shuttle's doors opened with a slight whoosh, and Erik's ears popped. Apparently the pressure regulator on the shuttle was out of adjustment.

He climbed down the line to the inner airlock, and was surprised to find Deena Onan waiting just inside the door.

She smiled as she saw him, and it seemed genuine. But the smile quickly faded as she saw his face, and she looked away. "I'm glad to see you're well, Commander."

"Amazingly, I escaped death several times over during my little visit to Shensi. Who knew it would be such an exciting place?" He waited for her answer.

She didn't shift her gaze. "For what it's worth, Erik, I thought you knew—that you were in on the plan. I wasn't trying to deceive you that day; I just didn't know how to tell you."

He looked at her. His face felt still and dead. He had been attracted to this woman once—even gladly endured the hidden laughter and taunts of those who claimed she was unapproachable. Now he felt nothing, and wondered why it had ever been different. "Perhaps—" He swallowed. "Perhaps you were deceived yourself. I'd like to think so, anyway. But you're still here."

"I have my loyalties, Commander," she said stiffly. "I will not apologize for them."

"Your loyalties have been bought, you mean. The Duke is your meal ticket, your shortcut to wealth and power well above your station. I've always known this. I simply didn't understand, until now, exactly what it meant."

She did not bend, but he could see that his words had stung her. *Good.*

"I'm sorry," she said, "that you feel that way."

"I have to see the Duke. Where is he?"

"The gymnasium on the crew deck. He's expecting you."

Erik brushed past her. "I imagine he is."

*   *   *

Aaron slipped his feet into the stirrups at the base of the resistance machine, and slid his shoulders under the bar, placing his hands around the grips. The gymnasium, and as many of its facilities as possible, was designed to function either in free fall or normal gravity.

Since weights wouldn't work without gravity, the resistance machine allowed the user to work against computer-controlled bands of myomer, the synthetic muscle used in 'Mech limbs. The myomer could be programmed to provide any amount and pattern of resistance. Aaron currently had the machine programmed for 130 kilograms.

Working out in free fall was an old habit of his. In theory, a simple pill taken every day prevented the loss of muscle and bone density that had plagued early space travelers, but he didn't want to take chances with his body.

Captain Clancy watched him skeptically. It was clear that what muscle the little man had came solely through honest toil. Clancy could often be seen down in the engine rooms or in the cargo bays, working right along with his men. "Don't bust a gut there, Duck. I still got some use for you."

Aaron tensed, pushed the bar to its stop, slowly lowered it back down. The rep-counter clicked to one.

"So you do, Captain. That's what I wanted to talk to you about. We haven't had time yet, given the current emergency, but I wanted to assure you that, at the earliest opportunity, the *Tyrannos Rex* will get the finest upgrades available, to all its systems. With a special emphasis on the armor, engines, and weapons."

Clancy squinted with one eye. "I'm wondering if my ship has just been insulted?"

"Not at all, Captain. She's a fine ship, and I know you've made many improvements over the standard

Excalibur specifications. Despite your ingenuity, however, I know cost has *always* been an object. That will
no longer be the case. I want you and your engineers
to draw up a wish list. Anything that can be made
better, do it. For the major things, we'll have it done
in dry dock when the time comes."

"Fair enough, Duck."

Aaron grunted. The rep-counter read ten.

"I've also arranged for a team of naval architects
to work on the weapons problem. *Excalibur*s are notoriously ill armed."

"I've made some improvements, but that's a tricky
proposition."

"I know there have been previous efforts to upgrade *Excalibur* weaponry, with mixed success. But in
every case, it was done while trying to retain the ship's
original capabilities as a military transport. Given our
somewhat different mission, we might just have
enough flexibility to turn her into a formidable fighter.

"You have a problem with that?"

"If you can make it work, Duck, be my guest."

The door opened, and someone cleared his throat.

Clancy turned and his eyes narrowed. "Well, Duck.
Looks like the pup has come home."

Erik glared at Clancy. "I've got no patience with
you today, Clancy. Shut up, and get out. I need to
talk to the Duke."

The little man slid in close and looked Erik in the
eye. "Nobody tells me where to go on my ship, *pup!*"

Aaron made eye contact with Clancy and shook his
head. "Please, Captain, humor him. Or if not, humor
me."

Clancy glared at Erik. "I'll do it for you, Duck. Me
and the pup can settle this later." He pushed off from
a bulkhead and sailed effortlessly out through the
doorway.

Erik reached over and closed the hatch.

"Erik, I'm glad to see you safe."

"I hear a lot of that," said Erik dryly.

"What news from Shensi?"

Erik tossed an envelope at Aaron, who snatched it out of the air. "A signed agreement, our original draft, without a word changed."

"Excellent! Well done!" Aaron wedged the envelope between the frame of the resistance machine and the wall, then went back to lifting.

Erik watched him silently for a minute. "Is that all you have to say?"

"What else is there? You were given a mission that you fulfilled completely. . . . Did I ever tell you the story about the sword of the First Knight?"

"A million times!"

"Well then, what more do I have to say? Good job."

Erik felt his face getting warm. "You tried to *kill* me!"

Aaron stopped lifting, half-turning in the stirrups to face Erik. "I did no such thing."

"Then you deny hiring Liao's mercenaries to attack Shensi while I was there?"

"Of course not. That's exactly what I did. But clearly the intent was not to kill you. There would be a million easier and more certain ways of doing that."

"Of course you had other reasons, but you might have had the decency to tell me what I was walking into."

"If I'd told you, would you have gone?"

"If you'd ordered it, of course, without question. I'm shocked that you even have to ask that."

Aaron's face was unreadable. "I did not order Erik the soldier, I sent Erik the Sandoval."

"What is that supposed to mean?"

"Erik the soldier would have gone, but his responses to the situation would not have been useful to me. Having a Sandoval in harm's way is what sold the attack as a genuine act of the Liao incursion. I had no idea where you'd be when the attacks began, or who you'd be with. Your reaction, your shock and surprise, had to be genuine. I'm afraid those acting lessons I arranged for you as a teen never seemed to take at all."

"You placed me, your own kin, in mortal danger simply as a bit of window dressing?"

"And when I order you into combat, are you in less danger?"

"That's different. I go into combat with my eyes open. I know the risks, and I have the tools to fight them. You sent me on this mission without telling me that I'd be attacked. Attacked by mercenaries that *you* hired!" Erik was disappointed that Aaron didn't seem the least bit defensive or apologetic. He just looked . . . puzzled.

"So? What if Liao really did attack while you were there? What if the Shensi had turned on you, or arrested you? What if there had been another assassination attempt? *Any* diplomatic mission can turn deadly. I know that better than anybody."

"That's not the point—"

"That's *exactly* the point, Erik. When I put you in danger's way, it is with the trust that you have the cunning and warrior skills to extricate yourself from *whatever* happens. It doesn't matter who arranged the attack. What matters is that you *did* survive it, and you returned victorious. You've vindicated yourself, Erik."

"Vindicated? What?"

"You've disappointed the family and me repeatedly, Erik. On Mara, losing your 'Mech, failing to secure the HPG station on Achernar. New Aragon was an opportunity to prove you deserved another chance to distinguish yourself. Your performance there was adequate, so I sent you to Shensi, where you availed yourself well."

"I fought for my life and survived."

"And if you hadn't found a way to do that, then you wouldn't deserve to be called a MechWarrior, or a Sandoval."

Erik was finally speechless. Aaron clearly had no remorse—saw nothing at all wrong with his actions—and nothing Erik could say would change that in the least.

"You've proven yourself worthy, Erik. Therefore, I'm giving you command of our forces on St. Andre until I arrive. You're to inspect the troops there and prepare them for a defensive action against House Liao. I want you to proceed there immediately, while I continue my mission to Poznan. Then I'll rally the coalition forces, and we'll see if we can turn that defense into a counterattack."

Erik was silent.

"Erik, you should be honored!"

Honored? Under other circumstances, he would have been. Some time ago, they'd identified St. Andre as a key to stemming the House Liao incursion. Now their intelligence showed the world directly in the path of the Capellan advance, with leading forces already having flanked it on their way to Terra. A significant portion of the SwordSworn might have been allocated to the planet's defense.

If Erik couldn't hold the world, the surviving SwordSworn would have little hope of standing against House Liao, with or without coalition forces. Now that they had cut ties with The Republic, there was no turning back. The defense of St. Andre was either a bold venture or a desperate gamble, depending on how you looked at it. In any case, Erik was literally being entrusted with the survival of the SwordSworn.

"Mark my words. St. Andre *will not* fall."

Then, disgusted at even being in the same room as the Duke, Erik left. The curse of free fall is that it doesn't allow one to stomp out of a room. He floated down the hallway to a junction, then grabbed a handrail and just hung there. What was he going to do next?

Go to St. Andre, obviously. Organize the defense. Act like nothing had happened.

But it had. Now Erik carried in his head knowledge of the Duke's deception. If that information were conveyed to the right people, it could ruin Aaron's reputation and derail his coalition before it even began. Erik clung desperately to that thought.

Despite the authority of his new command, that information seemed the only real power he had. Yet, the problem with it was in how absolute that power was. Right now, he wanted to hurt his uncle, strike back at him. But was he really ready to destroy him?

Part of Erik said yes, but a calmer, more rational part told him to wait. If he lashed out now, he'd destroy himself right along with Aaron Sandoval. *Take care of yourself first!*

Ironically, it was his uncle who had taught him that. That was one lesson, at least, that Erik had learned well.

15

This is Sword [garbled] *JumpShip* Marty *off* [static]
incoming House Liao JumpShip [static] [garbled]
pirate point! [static] *Five—no, six* [static] *May be
jamming my* [static]. *Advise Command* [unintelligi-
ble] *immediately!* [static] *Mayday!* [garbled]—
opened fire [static; transmission ends].
   —Radio transmission, intercepted off St. Andre, 12
      December 3134

Monarch-*class liner* **Boiler Bay**
Ningpo jump point, en route to St. Andre
Prefecture V, The Republic
12 December 3134

Lieutenant Clayhatchee, having traveled by a more
indirect route from Shensi, arrived at the Ningpo jump
point eleven hours after Erik, in time to rejoin him
for the trip to St. Andre.

Erik inquired after Elsa Harrad, but Clayhatchee
reported she'd kept to herself after they managed to
secure passage on a hurriedly departing cargo ship.
He knew only that she'd remained on the JumpShip
that had taken them out of the Shensi system, and
seemed intent on finding passage elsewhere. Clayhatchee wasn't privy to her destination.

Erik was disappointed, but unsure what he'd been
expecting. A love letter? Coordinates for a secret rendezvous? He couldn't blame Clayhatchee for failing
to be more diligent in collecting information. He'd
simply told him to get her off-planet, not spy on her
movements or grill her for information.

In fact, he'd failed to tell anyone that she was, at the very least, a House Liao informant. There was a certain seductive danger that he was coming to appreciate in keeping secrets. As with the knowledge of the Duke's treachery, this secret pleased him, made him feel more secure and powerful. He found himself wanting more.

Not wishing to stay on his uncle's ship any longer than was absolutely necessary, Erik and his aide took a freighter back to New Aragon.

At the jump point there, Erik and Lieutenant Clayhatchee managed to secure passage on a *Monarch*-class liner, the *Boiler Bay,* bound directly for St. Andre. He took some small pleasure in charging their first-class accommodations to the Duke, but was slightly disappointed when the charges came to a relative pittance.

According to the ship's steward, while passenger ships leaving the threatened planet were jammed, returning ships ran nearly empty. The *Boiler Bay* had two hundred and sixty-six staterooms. Fewer than fifty were currently booked, all in first class, all sold at cutrate prices. The second-class deck had been turned over to the ship's crew, who enjoyed the relative luxury.

The ship loitered for days, waiting for its JumpShip to finish charging, and for the remaining booked passengers to arrive on other vessels. Erik spent most of that time alone in his suite, watching Tri-Vids, reading outdated status reports from the forces on St. Andre, and trying not to think about Elsa or the Duke.

Finally, it got to be too much. He didn't crave human company, but he needed something to distract him from the uncomfortable thoughts filling his head. He wandered over to the ship's nearly deserted casino. Other than a handful of people playing slots, the only activity was in the poker pit, where a handful of people sat around a table engaged in Texas Hold-'em.

Like everything else on the ship, the poker table was designed to work even without gravity. The chips were magnetic, the tabletop covered with thousands of tiny holes and equipped with a suction fan that kept the cards on the table. Dealing without gravity was, of course, a specialized skill, but the croupier running the table handled things expertly.

The buy-in limit was five hundred C-Bills—just large enough to be interesting, but not so big that the game wouldn't stay friendly. Erik bought his chips and was dealt in. He looked at his cards. Three-seven offsuit. He sat the hand out, and the next several, as well. Meanwhile, he learned a little about the other players.

Two—a man and a woman—were businesspeople from St. Andre, rushing home so that a Liao takeover didn't strand them away from home and family. Another fellow was a would-be mercenary, headed into the war zone hoping to fight for the highest bidder. Erik decided if the man didn't fight any better than he played poker he was going to have a hard time selling his services, especially to the SwordSworn. The last, a younger man with dimples and too-perfect hair, was an Interstellar News Network stringer, hoping to send back some dispatches from the front.

Next hand, Erik turned up an ace and a two. The dealer turned over another pair of twos and a king at the flop, which was good for Erik, but which spooked most of the rest of the players out of the game. The mercenary hung on for the distance, finally going all-in. Erik cleaned him out when he proved to have only a king, making two pairs against Erik's three of a kind.

The frustrated mercenary unfastened his seatbelt and stood up too quickly, helplessly flailing toward the ceiling. Even the dealer laughed, and the red-faced wanna-be merc managed to reach a handrail and beat a hasty retreat.

Erik raked in the pot, and began stacking his chips in a rack.

The male business traveler seemed to be working up his courage to ask something. "So, Commander, is war really coming to St. Andre?"

Erik glanced warily at the reporter. "Is this on or off the record?"

The reporter grinned. "Off, if that's the way you want it, Commander Sandoval. With the HPG network gone, it isn't likely to be an issue, anyway. By the time I can file a story, it will have happened—or not, as the case may be."

Erik shrugged. "My crystal ball is no better than anyone else's. House Liao is moving around past the planet on either flank, and could bypass St. Andre completely. But I doubt it."

"But you—the SwordSworn"—the name rolled off his tongue awkwardly, like an unfamiliar word in a foreign language—"you're going to fight for us, right?"

"That's the plan; hopefully we won't be alone."

"But," asked the man, "can you win?"

"We've beaten them once already, on New Aragon, and the situation is better here. It's always better to fight a defensive action. House Liao is spreading itself pretty thin, and hiring excellent mercenaries—like our departed friend." That generated chuckles around the table. "They're vulnerable."

Erik heard another person buying chips, and so wasn't surprised when someone slid into the empty seat across the table from him. But he was surprised when he looked up to see Elsa Harrad. "Can somebody deal a lady in?" She looked over, made eye contact, and smiled coyly. "Good evening, Commander."

He looked at her, but said nothing.

The cards were dealt. Erik glanced at his; jack-ten of diamonds. He checked, and Elsa opened with a fifty-C bet.

The dealer turned over the flop: a five, a six, and a three. No diamonds. The businesswoman and the reporter folded. Erik saw Elsa's fifty, as did the businessman. Elsa raised another fifty.

The next card over was a jack of clubs, giving Erik a pair—not bad, but very beatable. He looked at Elsa. Did she have a straight? A pocket pair that could beat his jacks? Two pairs? Three of a kind?

The businessman was out.

Next card was a ten of spades.

What did she have? Well, one way to find out. "All in," Erik said. He'd just bet his entire pile on this hand.

Elsa stared at him.

He stared back.

She grimaced. "Fold."

"So," he said, "what did you have?"

She tossed her cards back to the dealer, facedown. "You'll never know," she said.

Erik took his pot, and pushed it to the dealer. "Cash me out. I think I'll call it an evening."

He signed off as the winnings were credited to his account, then headed away from the table without looking back. He was almost out of the casino when Elsa, still struggling to stuff chips into her purse, caught up with him. "Quitting just when things were getting interesting?"

"No action at that table," he said without slowing down.

"Looking for some action, are you?"

He stopped, turned, and glared at her. "I don't have time for games, Elsa. That was an INN reporter at the table."

"Did I say anything? Do anything? I knew who he

was before you did, Erik. While you've been hiding in your cabin, I've been circulating around the ship."

"Looking for me?"

"As a matter of a fact, yes. You'll notice I was discreet enough not to come to your cabin."

"How good of you," he said sarcastically. He looked around nervously. "We can't talk out in the open."

She moved to a nearby door marked Sauna 2. A movable sign indicated that it was unoccupied—hardly surprising considering how empty the ship was. She poked her head inside. "It's not even on," she said.

He followed her inside and locked the door. The room was lined with cedar planks, and benches lined the lower and rear walls.

"So," he said, "you *are* a spy."

She laughed. "I told you what I am. My friends knew that the Duke's forces were massing on St. Andre, and I'd hoped you'd be heading there. I used some of my connections to put myself along one possible path and waited at the jump point. I was on the lookout, and checked the passenger manifest of every other ship through."

"And if that hadn't worked?"

She shrugged. "I'd have gone to St. Andre and tried to contact you there, but that would have made it much more difficult to be discreet. I wanted a chance to talk to you alone, before you got stuck neck-deep in command responsibilities."

"So you can pump me for information on our defenses?"

"Erik, I could give a dead moon about your defenses. I want *you*."

"You want me, or Liao does?"

"Both, Erik." She licked her lips. "I helped you before, and I'm going to help you again. Erik, I'm betraying my friends by telling you this, but St. Andre is going to fall."

"You know this for a fact? If you like playing spy so much, tell me their plans. We can pay you as much as they do—maybe more."

She laughed. "You don't think they trust me with their battle plans, do you? They just told me that St. Andre was going to be theirs, and I believe them. They told me I could make you an offer."

Klaxons sounded, warning that the ship would shortly be making the hyperspace jump to St. Andre. Never having been troubled by jump-sickness, he paid only passing attention. He looked at Elsa. "An offer?"

"Switch sides, Erik. Convince St. Andre to surrender. We don't know how many of your forces are committed there, but it must be significant. At the very least, it would wound the Duke's reputation, and demoralize the SwordSworn.

"You could do well with House Liao. Certainly, it would be no worse than being the Duke's errand boy, and probably better. You could be an important person in your own right."

It was actually tempting in a way. To be free of Aaron once and for all, to answer the Duke's betrayal with one of his own. To abandon everything and seek his own destiny.

"How important? Important enough to be given my own army?"

She laughed. "Erik, you just don't understand, do you? To be blunt, other than your name, you just aren't considered that important. Until a few months ago, even your uncle was beneath their notice, though he's managed to change that somewhat.

"Don't you see, Erik? People like us, we don't really matter much. We don't have many choices. We have to know our place in the world, know our limitations, and make the best of it."

Erik wiped his face with his hands. *Know your place. Know your limitations.* He'd heard it all before.

Yet this time, he had one last chip to bargain with, and the only way to use it was to play all-in. House Liao didn't seem to have figured out the Duke's deception at Shensi yet, and that had value.

If Liao could make the SwordSworn coalition fall apart without landing a single 'Mech or firing a single shot, what would that be worth? If that happened, perhaps they could be persuaded to bypass St. Andre for now, saving SwordSworn lives.

Yet, when it all was said and done, once the deal was made, he would be no more important than he'd ever been. It was the information that was valuable, not Erik Sandoval-Groell. Here or with Liao, he wasn't much—a little fish in a very big sea. But as long as he was with Aaron, he was at least swimming with a shark, and there was something to be said for that.

"I'm sorry, Elsa. I can't do that." He considered. "I'll make you the same offer. Come over to our side."

She smiled sadly. "And I can't do that, Erik, for a lot of reasons. But most of all, what have I really got to offer? My services as your concubine? I care for you Erik, but I can't be beholden to you that way. It would poison everything, and I'd end up hating you." She shook her head. "No, I've set my course, and I'm staying with it."

"Well then," he said.

"Well," she said.

He unlocked the door. "When we get to St. Andre, just stay on the ship. If you go down to the planet, I can't be responsible for what happens."

He considered returning to his quarters, but instead went back to the casino to ride out the jump.

He was still there, sitting at an empty poker table, half an hour later when Clayhatchee appeared. "Commander! I've been looking for you everywhere!

"The ship was contacted by St. Andre as soon as we jumped into the system. There isn't going to be any defensive action, Commander. Liao forces started landing three days ago, and they've dug themselves in good."

=== 16 ===

Aaron managed not to flinch as a bottle smashed against the limousine's ferro-glass window, a few inches from his face. He glanced at Joan Cisco, who sat on the other side of the car taking notes on a computer pad. "Well, it's at least good to know that the cost of armor-plating this car was money well spent."

Outside, blue-uniformed police tried to shove throngs of protesters back onto the sidewalk, and out of the motorcade's path, with limited success. Aaron looked out dispassionately at the screaming, contorted faces—the waved signs and banners reading things like DEATH TO SANDOVAL, and LIBERATE US, LIAO! There were people spitting on his car.

He shook his head sadly. "Don't they understand that *I'm* here to liberate them? Give me six months and I'd have this place cleaned up—end all this unrest."

Cisco looked at him sideways and lifted an eyebrow. "By crushing it under your iron heel, Lord Governor?"

Aaron grinned. He *had* given the woman license to be frank. "If necessary. Order has its price. But my heel would fall equally on the oppressed ethnic groups and the people who oppress them. To do otherwise is to simply allow the groups to switch places, or to drag on the conflict for generations." He saw his own reflection in the window glass. "I could restore order and purpose to the crumbling remains of The Republic," he said in a low voice. *Two hundred fifty worlds for House Davion, delivered by my hand.*

"Excuse me, Lord Governor? I didn't hear."

"Nothing. Nothing."

A small man dressed all in black jumped down from a traffic signal he had climbed and landed sprawled on the roof. He pounded on the skylight with his fist, yelling something that Aaron couldn't hear through the soundproofing. Aaron's hand strayed down to the armrest. He flipped it open, revealing a hidden control panel. His finger hovered over the controls. He turned to Cisco. "Can I push the button?"

The button was connected to one of the car's defensive options. If pressed, fifty thousand volts of electricity, at very low amperage, would be transmitted through the car's exterior rails and trim, guaranteed to turn anyone touching them into a twitching heap on the ground.

She sighed. "No, Lord Governor. You must demonstrate tolerance."

"I don't feel tolerance. I feel an intense desire to push the button."

"I wouldn't advise it. We must keep up appearances."

"I suppose so." He reluctantly snapped the armrest back down over the panel.

There was a pause. Cisco studied him. "You were just joking, Lord Governor?"

He grinned slightly. "About the button? I suppose. About the urge? Not at all." He looked out the window at the angry crowds. "All people have urges, impulses, and it's no less true of the very powerful. But when most people slip and let one of those impulses loose, perhaps a window gets broken, or a car fender gets bent, or at worst a nose gets broken. At the very, very worst, the body counts can be tallied on the fingers of your hands.

"But when people like me slip, wars start, planets fall in ruin, thousands or millions die. I have to be very careful about those urges, and so when one comes along like that, where death is unlikely, where the victim is certainly deserving, it is very, very tempting."

Cisco nodded. "But you still resist."

"Mostly. But just in case, I depend on my people to remind me of my station. Consider that a test. You passed." He looked around. The crowds had thinned, and they could at least drive freely, without concern about running someone over. "Where are we going, anyway?"

"Nowhere, Lord Governor. We're simply out so you can be seen."

He watched a group of children raiding a trash can, and throwing garbage at them. "And this is helping me how, exactly?"

She raised an eyebrow. "I sent you an executive summary. I'd assumed you'd read it."

"A month ago, I'd have known everything there is to know about this planet; I hired you so I didn't have to think about such details. I have a war to win. I need to be able to trust you to take care of everything under your purview, and I don't want to have to oversee everything you do. So tell me what we're doing here."

"Poznan is a former member of the Duchy of Liao. Under the Duchy's control, immigrants of Chinese descent turned the ruling descendants of the original Spanish colonists into an oppressed minority—a fine tradition of hatred that continued for centuries under the rule of the Capellan Confederation. Though this oppression was moderated when The Republic assumed control, it lingers." She gestured at the windows. "These are members of the Spanish minority, by the way, who are throwing rotten fruit at us."

"Good to know. And I suppose the people with the 'LIBERATE US, LIAO!' signs were Chinese?"

"Exactly, but that was a block ago; the Chinese never cross Xu Avenue west of 110th Street."

Aaron shook his head. "This is barbaric."

"I won't even discuss the other original colonists, who were of Polish descent. They lost a civil war with the Spanish, and still hate them with a seething passion. I'm sure if we drove across town to their neighborhood, they would throw fruit at us, as well."

"Delightful. I can hardly wait. Let's go." He rubbed his chin. "You still haven't explained how this helps me."

"The people throwing fruit at you are secretly glad that you're here listening to them without fighting back, without"—she pointed at the armrest where the button was hidden—"and the people who oppress them are pleased that you've seen, up close and personal, what their 'problem' is, and aren't afraid of it. Or at least, they all will be, after you give some speeches I write, and sign off on some statements I'll fabricate. If we play this right, we can make them all hate each other even more, and love you at least a little bit." She went back to her writing.

She looked back up at him. "You've read the executive summary, haven't you?"

"I skimmed it. Frankly, there wasn't much I didn't already know from my own research, but I found it to be concise and well written."

"That was another test, wasn't it?"

"It was."

"I don't like secret tests, Lord Governor. If you want to test my competency, you have only to ask."

Aaron studied her for a minute. "You don't like me very much, do you, Cisco?"

She glanced up at him. "Is that a job requirement?"

"No. I insist on competence and loyalty. 'Like' I can live without."

"Good, because you're not liable to get 'like.' But I'm not going to pass judgment either.

"I'm a professional liar. I sold my soul to the farm-machinery devil a long time ago. I've spent half my life convincing people to mortgage farms that have been in their family for a hundred years, to buy Agro-Mechs that will only drag them into bankruptcy.

"I make truth seem like lies, and lies look like truth. I run black and white through a blender every day, and make it come out gray."

"You don't paint a very flattering portrait of yourself."

She shrugged. "People pay me to manipulate the truth for them. I've got nothing like that left for myself."

"So what is bothering you, then? Are we going to win this planet to our cause or not? Because"—he gestured at the screaming mob outside—"it doesn't look good to me."

She half-smiled. "When you started this, did you think they'd all be easy? Like I said, you were lucky, and you hired me just in time. It's just"—she paused in her writing—"that if they sign on to your coalition, my polls and surveys show it's going to aggravate an already bad situation. If Liao doesn't take this world, they'll have a civil revolt within a year, and it will likely spiral into a full-blown war."

"I don't need them for longer than a year. If we haven't stemmed the tide of Liao in six months, it won't matter."

"I know, which is why I'm just here doing my job. It's just—" She put down the pad and stared out the window. "What then?"

"Then, when this is done, I will return, and I will give them order. I promise this."

The crowd ahead of them suddenly surged to the left side of the street, people trampling each other in panic. From behind a building to the right, a Riot-Mech appeared, the little black-and-white machine wading through the crowd, red and blue lights flashing from the bar above its cockpit. Tiny for a 'Mech, it was still a terrifying presence among the mostly unarmed mob, which scattered from it like a school of fish facing a shark. A rotary launcher on the Riot-Mech's right arm swiveled down and began to pelt the crowd with rubber bullets. Even in the car he could hear the screaming.

"It's about time," he said.

Ulysses Paxton kept his cool reserve as he drove the limousine past the two SwordSworn 'Mechs standing guard, and up the ramp into the *Tyrannos Rex*'s abbreviated vehicle bay. He watched in the rearview cameras as four members of his recently hired security force opened the door, and ushered the Duke into the relative safety of the ship's living quarters.

His eyes missed nothing, not where it concerned the Lord Governor's safety, or the performance of his new team. To his satisfaction, as he watched them disappear, he detected not a single flaw in their procedures.

Maybe, in six months or so, they'd be as good as the people he'd lost on New Canton.

He watched the inner hatch seal shut. Only then did he let his body go a little slack, leaning forward to place his forehead on the steering wheel. They'd spent four hours driving around the city. It seemed like a lifetime, without a single moment where threats, or potential threats, to the Duke's safety weren't all around.

Even now, his job wasn't done. He still had to make sure the car was screened for bombs or other booby traps that might have been planted during their close contact with the protestors. It also needed to be scanned for bugs.

He climbed out of the car, put his fists on his hips, and stared at it. He felt he *should* personally supervise the security sweep on the car, but he had to start trusting the new people at some point. Maybe today was the day. He touched the plug in his ear. "Timms. I need a full security sweep on limo two."

"I'm on it, Mr. Paxton," said the voice in his ear. "Long-sword"—that was their radio code for the Duke—"is in a planning session with Ms. Cisco, and says to tell you he won't be needing you for the rest of the day. He seems to think you could use a break."

Ulysses grinned. "The Duke is a perceptive man. Call me if anything comes up. Otherwise I'll see you at eight."

"Sure thing, sir."

He tapped the earpiece, breaking the connection. He reached up and took it from his ear, then held the device in his open palm, looking at it for a while. Then he slipped it back in. "No rest for the watchers," he said.

"Hard day at the office, Paxton?"

Ulysses turned to see Captain Clancy leaning just

inside the airlock door. He frowned, wondering what the captain wanted with him.

Clancy grinned at him. "Don't be like that. We're on the same team now. Buy you a drink?"

Ulysses studied the captain's grizzled face, and didn't detect any subterfuge there. "Sure."

He followed Clancy to one of the three main elevators and they rode up to officers' country. They went to the officers' mess, which was nearly deserted at this hour.

Like most of the ship's workspaces, the mess was more functional than luxurious. There were a few amenities, though: folding wooden tables and chairs here, rather than the metal-and-plastic ones in the crew's mess; real china and silver—at least when they weren't in free fall; and the serve-yourself drink and snack-food areas were generally better stocked. But it wasn't much.

Clancy walked over to the drink area and bent down to reach a small refrigerator built in under the counter. The door was protected by a coded lock. Ulysses had seen it before and wondered about it. Clancy tapped in the code, opened the door, and took out a tall amber bottle. It was a very expensive brand of ale that Ulysses recognized as coming from the Duke's private stock. He decided it would be better not to speculate how the captain got his.

Clancy held out the bottle to him.

Ulysses shook his head. "I'll take some herbal tea. I don't drink."

Clancy raised an eyebrow. "Do tell?" He closed the fridge and unscrewed the top on the bottle. He took a swig, and looked over at the hot-water dispenser. "I'll buy"—he grinned—"but you got to make it."

Ulysses walked over and punched the button on the hot-water dispenser, put a cup under the spigot, and rummaged through the wooden box where the tea bags were kept.

Clancy watched him. "Don't drink, huh?"

"Corrupts the body, and the mind." He glanced at the captain. "No offense."

"None taken. I'm pretty durned corrupted all right." He raised the bottle to Ulysses, then took another swig.

Ulysses dropped a tea bag into his cup, and then looked back at Clancy. "What's this all about, Captain?"

Clancy turned two chairs around to face each other, then sat down in one and put his feet up, legs crossed, in another. "Shop talk, I guess. You and me are pretty much in the same business now. Different ways of doing it is all. Both of us moving the Duke around, trying to keep his hide in one piece."

Ulysses watched as the cup filled with steaming water. The scents of orange and cinnamon filled his nose. He took the cup and sat down at one of the empty tables near Clancy. "You just called him 'Duke.'"

"So? He is one, ain't he?"

"Yeah. But you called him, 'Duke.'"

Clancy grinned. "You mean, instead of 'Duck'?"

"Yeah."

Clancy's grin got even bigger. He made a show of looking around the empty room. "Well, he ain't here, is he?"

Ulysses smiled and shook his head. "You should really show him more respect."

"If I didn't respect who he was, and what he could do, he wouldn't still be on this ship."

"Then why not—?"

"Kowtow to the big man, like the rest of you? Because he's a giant walking ego who needs somebody to keep him in line. He knows that—part of him, anyway. That's why he puts up with me."

Ulysses sipped his tea. He was too discreet to say that Clancy was right.

"So," said Clancy, "as one fellow in the same business to another, what do you think our chances are?"

"Of keeping the Duke safe?"

"Yeah, I reckon."

He took a deep breath and considered. Finally he said, "My professional opinion is that the Duke is a dead man. It isn't a question of if, but of when."

The captain nodded. "That's what I figured."

"You? Same opinion? As a professional, of course."

The captain held his bottle up to the light, and studied the little drops running through the condensation on the sides. "My brain says that, but my gut says different. Duke Sandoval, he's harder to kill than a Chichibu cockroach. He won't go down easy."

"No," agreed Ulysses, "he won't."

"But this big plan of his, I don't see it ending pretty. Things are going to get messy."

Ulysses nodded slowly. "Agreed. It all ends badly." He took another sip of tea.

Clancy took two big swallows of his ale.

"So," said Ulysses, "if that's the way you feel, why are you letting us stay on this ship?"

Clancy shrugged. "Nobody lives forever. My worst nightmare is to die old and in bed—that the day will come when me"—he glanced upward—"and this ship have to part company—by hook, or by crook—or I just can't handle her no more. Whatever happens with the Duke, I reckon it's going to be interesting."

"I'd say so."

"What about you? Man with your skills, he could find some rich guy who only *thinks* everybody is out to get him. Get set up real sweet."

Ulysses grinned. "Well, I *do* want to live forever. . . ."

Clancy held up the bottle. "Drink some of this; you won't live forever, but you won't care."

Ulysses chuckled. "It's like you said. It's going to be interesting. Maybe I'll come out on the other side, maybe not. If I'm as good as I think I am, I'll survive. Can you understand that?"

"You ever see a rodeo, Paxton?"

"As a matter of a fact, I have."

"Cowboy doesn't prove nothing riding on a broke-down nag. Man wants to ride a bronco breathing fire, with blood in his eye and murder in his heart. Anything else just don't count."

"Well. I guess we'll see who gets bucked off first."

"We will at that." He raised his bottle to Ulysses. "Toast."

Ulysses raised his glass in return.

"To the ride," said Clancy.

"And," added Ulysses, "the inevitable fall at the end."

Clancy laughed as bottle clinked against teacup. "I'll drink to that."

Just then the intership link on Clancy's belt activated. "Bridge to Captain. The Duke wishes to speak with you."

Clancy held the device to his ear. "Well then, put him through."

"Clancy, we've run out of time. An incoming ship has just reported that Liao is in place on St. Andre. Get ready for immediate takeoff—and I need all the Gs you can muster getting us back to the JumpShip. It may already be too late."

17

REFUGEES, MILITARY ACTION DISRUPT SHIPPING—*Correspondents throughout Prefecture V are reporting disruptions in both passenger and cargo runs as refugees flee the advancing House Liao forces, and JumpShips are appropriated for military use by both sides in the conflict.*

Yet JumpShip and DropShip captains aren't complaining. "If there's an invasion coming to a planet and you're the only way out, you can pretty much name your own fare," says freighter DropShip captain Kristen Witchey. JumpShip captains have also reaped enormous profits. "I've been paid to bump other ships for military transports," reports JumpShip captain Lance Lake. "I've been paid to wait at a jump point for a priority vessel. If you're willing to take risks—hauling into a combat zone, or jumping into pirate points—the rewards are almost unlimited."

Responding to charges that ship owners are profiteering from the war, Lake just shrugs. "Business is business," he says. "If you can't pay, nobody says you have to go."

—Stellar Associated News Services

St. Michael Station, St. Michael
St. Andre system
Prefecture V, The Republic
17 December 3134

For Erik, it was four days of agony as the liner made its way from the jump point to St. Andre. Along the way, he could do little except read faxed battle reports—all of them bad.

The liner didn't have the kind of facilities he would have needed to assume proper command of the SwordSworn forces on the planet. He did have limited ability to confer with Campaign Commander Justin Sortek and offer advice, but even Erik had to question its value, given his limited access to current intelligence.

Liao forces had appeared at the zenith jump point days earlier. Their DropShips immediately began high-G burns toward St. Andre. While SwordSworn forces had landed near the old Star League base on the polar continent of Ravensglade, House Liao had put down on the more populated desert continent of Georama and attacked the capital city of Jerome.

Fearing the attack was only a distraction, Sortek had been afraid to commit significant forces to the fight. The city fell in only two days. Now they were moving their forces to cut off ports of supply to Ravensglade. The freshly landed SwordSworn were short on fuel and food, having counted on the ready availability of local supply.

Erik's pleas to the liner's captain to shorten the trip, by increasing the acceleration beyond the standard one G, were ignored. In fact, only repeated insistence by Erik and other passengers kept him headed to the embattled planet at all. The captain was prepared to turn back, and still refused to land on the planet itself.

Instead, the passengers would be unloaded at a station on St. Michael, the planet's only moon, and left to find their own transportation to the planet's surface.

For Erik and Clayhatchee, at least, that shouldn't be a problem. The SwordSworn had a shuttle available, and promised that it would be waiting.

St. Michael Station was little more than an outpost on the moon's airless surface, with no more than a few thousand permanent inhabitants at the best of times. Now it was a ghost town, with most of the inhabitants having retreated to the greater security of the planet's surface. The harbormaster at the little spaceport was one of the diehards who simply refused to leave.

He met the arriving passengers at the end of the airlock tunnel. He was a small man, round-faced, bearded, and balding on top. "Welcome to St. Michael," he said, his hand out. "Ten-C-Bill landing fee from each of you, please."

Erik looked around the terminal, which was deserted except for half a dozen cats stalking the corners, or napping on the empty waiting-room chairs—probably somebody's solution to the rodent problems stations like this sometimes suffered. "You've got to be kidding."

"Not kidding," said the harbormaster. "Business is slow, and I have to pay my salary somehow. I'd hate to have to lay myself off."

Erik stepped forward. The floors had strips of a sticky material that made it easier to walk in the reduced gravity. He pulled out his wallet, and produced a five-hundred-C-Bill note—enough to cover everyone. He kept his voice low. "I'm supposed to be meeting a SwordSworn shuttle. Are they here?"

He shook his head. "You're the only arriving ship today, other than some suborbital hoppers. Helium-3 miners coming in from the boonies for supplies, you know."

Erik sighed and looked at Clayhatchee.

Clayhatchee shrugged. "I'll go see if I can get a call through to our headquarters, and find out what's happening." He headed off to find a vidphone booth.

"Look," one of the passengers said, stepping forward. It was the businessman Erik had played poker with only a few days before. "We need to get down to the surface. Are there any shuttles running?"

The harbormaster shook his head. "All the scheduled service to the surface was through the spaceport in Jerome. When the capital fell, the shuttles stopped coming. There's one on the pad out there that came in last week and needed minor repairs. But there's no crew to fly it. The flight crew rotated home on another flight, and, obviously, they aren't sending anybody to pick it up."

The businessman's eyes were wide with concern. "So what are we supposed to do?"

The harbormaster shrugged. "You could stay here. Lots of rooms here at fifty Cs per night. Or you could hope that there's an unscheduled ship through. Or you could get back on that pretty liner of yours and leave. Me, I'd go for the last choice. Not much left here, not much chance of getting to St. Andre anytime soon, and, from what I hear, the ugly is just starting down there."

The businessman scowled. "That 'ugly' is home for a lot of us, sir."

The harbormaster shrugged. "What do I know? I'm from Tybalt myself. Do what you want to. I just know we're tracking a bunch of incoming plasma flares that look like Liao reinforcements."

Erik grimaced at this bit of news. Intelligence already had SwordSworn forces slightly outnumbered.

Clayhatchee returned, leaned in, and whispered to Erik. "Commander, our transport should be here within twenty minutes. They're sending a landing craft for us. Plenty of room for all these people, if you want to be generous."

He glanced at Elsa, standing among the assembled passengers in the terminal. She was talking with the would-be merc from the poker table, and he felt a little pang of jealousy. *Damn it, why isn't she back on the liner?*

He turned his back to the group and whispered to Clayhatchee. "We're not running a spaceline, Lieutenant, so I'd like to keep that quiet. Anyway, most of them are going to be from Georama. We'd be taking them into a combat zone, on the wrong side of the lines. Better they sit this one out here, or, better yet, on some other planet."

"Yes sir."

One by one, the passengers began to return to the ship, until finally about half of them were gone. The rest were determined to stick it out on St. Michael in hopes of getting home. He noticed the two businesspeople among those who stayed, but at some point, Elsa had disappeared. So had the merc, which ordinarily would have amused Erik. But he remembered the two of them talking, and looking a little too friendly.

Shake it off. You've got no claim, no prospects, and, ultimately, no interest. His heart, however, didn't respond well to logic. *At least she's safe.*

The military landing craft arrived as promised. By that time, Erik had bribed a maintenance woman to take them out to meet it in a pressurized buggy. Halfway there, the buggy stopped. The woman driving the little vehicle activated controls extending a manipulator arm, which reached down and grabbed a recessed tie-down lug in the pavement. "Ship taking off," she explained, pointing at the liner. "Back blast could blow us away like a leaf if we aren't careful."

Erik watched, curious. The landing had been more than a shade terrifying, but, with the pitching and odd acceleration, he wasn't sure how it had been done. The liner was a winged aerodyne—not normally capable of vertical takeoff or landing. Evidently, St. Michael's low gravity and lack of atmosphere made some unorthodox maneuvering possible.

The ship lifted off on maneuvering thrusters alone, its full power only slightly more than was necessary to get the ship off the apron. Then the nose began to pitch up; as it did, the ship started sliding forward. He tried to imagine the ship doing something like this in reverse, and was just as happy he'd been blissfully unaware of the landing procedure.

As the ship picked up speed, the main drive ignited. True to the maintenance woman's prediction, the buggy shuddered violently, and actually seemed to slide sideways on its wire-mesh wheels.

The liner shot upward. Even at low throttle, the local gravity could do little to impede the ship's fusion drive. Erik watched the ship grow smaller against the black sky. "Bye, Elsa," he said quietly. "It's been interesting."

The continent of Ravensglade was located entirely above St. Andre's arctic circle. It was relentlessly flat, frozen for six months of the year, plagued with gnats for at least four of the rest. Except for gnat season, the wind ripped constantly across the land like an unseen demon, tearing at anything not tied down.

Though the land was flat, it wasn't level. The whole continent seemed to tilt, almost imperceptibly, like a table with one leg slightly longer than the others. Near sea level, and occasionally lower in the south, the land rose slowly in the north until it met the ocean in a nearly unbroken line of hundred-and-fifty-meter cliffs. It was along the inlets, bays, and narrow beaches below these cliffs that most of the permanent settlements on the continent were located.

The inland wastes were temporary home to miners, prospectors, and oil workers, who scratched what wealth they could out of the land, hurriedly returned to Georama to spend it, then trudged back to Ravensglade to make more. The towns along the coast offered them a few mild vices, a place to pick up supplies, and were ports for the ships and hovercraft that connected the continent with civilization's more respectable outposts.

It was also above these cliffs where the old Star League had elected to build a base that still stood, a monument to the quality of its engineering, and a magnet for any power attempting to establish military dominion over the region. The Capellan Confederation, the Blakists, House Davion, Devlin Stone—all had fought over it, or occupied it.

The complex was vast, and distributed in a radially symmetrical arrangement of hardened barracks, hangars, landing pads, shops, command centers, and a hospital. All were connected underground by a network of tunnels—some of them big enough to accommodate armor and 'Mechs. Along the east and north sides, vast runways for aerodyne DropShips bordered the grounds.

In the last fifty years, the base had fallen into disuse. It now stood on the plains like a ghost city—a training center for some of St. Andre's few remaining elite military units, and home to oil companies and miners who appropriated some of the shops and barracks along its north edge.

It seemed, thought Erik Sandoval-Groell as he strode along the perimeter in a newly requisitioned *Hatchetman*, that battle was to come to the base once again. The place was empty and desolate—the low, fortified buildings as ugly as they were sturdy. In the distance, clusters of oil derricks jutted, and flames emitted from their tops, making them look like black candles as they burned off waste gases. It didn't look like anything worth fighting for. It didn't look like anything worth dying for.

Justin Sortek's smaller *Arbalest* trotted into his field of vision on the right. "Not much to look at, is it, Commander?"

"No," he admitted, "it isn't."

"See, that's the problem. Morale is really low right now. We're on short rations. Plenty of ammo—we brought that with us—but not even enough spare fuel for training maneuvers. So the troops hang around the barracks all day, looking out at this lovely base, and wondering when House Liao is going to drop in with an overwhelming force. To top it all off, the Duke's sudden departure has started talk among the men that he's forsaken us, or he's secretly negotiating a deal with the enemy."

Erik again felt a knot in his chest, both at the mention of his uncle, and at the memory of his own brush with betrayal.

"It's especially hard on my men and women in the Davion Guard. Our entire ethos is built on the idea of the worthy prince—great leaders who can in turn inspire us to greatness. Many of us believed Duke Sandoval could be such a leader, that he could help us fight for the greater glory of Davion."

"Do you still believe that?"

"From what you've told me, the Duke has not forsaken us. I find it interesting, however, that I had to infer that from your reports. You've never explicitly said so."

Erik was quiet for a moment. He steered his 'Mech onto a taxiway running parallel to the north-south runway, and opened up the throttle. There weren't many places to enjoy the simple pleasure of taking a 'Mech for an all-out sprint. The *Hatchetman* wasn't a fast 'Mech, but it could still do well over sixty kilometers an hour in a dead run.

The *Arbalest* was faster—this was barely above its cruising speed. Sortek had no trouble keeping up, and Erik certainly couldn't run away from his inquiries.

The smaller 'Mech easily sprinted in front of him. "Look, Commander. People think the Davion Guard is fanatical, but we're not delusional. The Duke is far from a perfect leader, but he has potential. You know, I'll let you in on a secret about the nobility. People talk about 'the divine right of kings.' That suggests that the nobles are somehow touched by divinity, and therefore are better than the rest of us."

Erik thought about Aaron's story about the sword of the First Knight. "Do you believe that?"

He laughed. "Not for a minute. Yet I don't entirely disbelieve it, either. I know that sounds contradictory, but let's put it this way: I believe in the divinity part of things—that some people act as conduits to a higher power. It isn't the frail humans, noble or otherwise, who possess that divine spark. They only carry it, channel it. And being only human, sometimes they lose their way—betray the divinity they carry.

"But that doesn't mean the light of divinity is gone. It always exists, and we are simply seekers of that light. It's possible that Duke Sandoval carries it. I think he might."

"But if he doesn't?"

"Our allegiances could change, as they did when my father declared his loyalty to Devlin Stone. But our *loyalty* never changes, Commander. It's the men and women we follow who sometimes lose their way—or find it.

"You're a Sandoval, Commander, of noble blood, with your roots deep in House Davion. That means something to these troops. They know, as do I, that the light is always there. It is exclusive to no man, certainly not the Duke. It might flow through you as well. Know that if you are worthy, we will follow."

"What are you saying?"

"The Duke may return, but he isn't here today. You are. Liao forces are massing on the north coast of Georama. We know they're coming. We need you to lead us to victory—or at least to glorious death."

He laughed. "Don't flatter me with your optimism, Justin."

"Things don't look good, Commander."

They moved past one of the air-defense emplacements that surrounded the base. They were still largely intact, and at least protected the base from easy air attack. There were nine of them, and, in theory, any three could protect the base against anything but the most massive air assault.

They did nothing to protect from an attack by land or sea, however. With so many troops historically garrisoned here, the base depended on conventional forces for ground defense. But the SwordSworn were far short of that strength—the current troops rattling around in the base like peas in a beer keg.

With morale poor, and fuel for their tanks and IndustrialMechs in short supply, they were ill equipped to resist the inevitable invasion, much less mount an offensive against House Liao's increasingly entrenched forces on Georama.

Erik looked again at the oil wells. They represented an almost unlimited supply of potential fuel, but there were no refineries on Ravensglade. The crude oil was shipped, by pipeline or tanker via nearby Port Archangel, to Georama for processing.

They were passing the corner of the base used by oil companies and miners. It seemed nothing was ever discarded here. Decades worth of old machinery and equipment were scattered around, some of it parked in neat rows, as though ready to be used tomorrow, more discarded in huge scrap heaps, and still more cannibalized for parts until little more than metal skeletons remained.

Erik's eye was drawn to a row of IndustrialMechs towering above the rest. They were covered with a dark red crust, a mixture of local red dust, crude oil, and ice. But so was the machinery in current use. Appearances could be deceptive.

He trotted toward them. "What are those?"

"Specialized MiningMechs used by the oil companies. The ones with the big claws and the welding torches are PipelineMechs. The others, with the drills and the arms for handling drill pipe, those are DrillingMechs. There aren't any new pipelines being built right now, and the fields are all well established, so most of them are mothballed."

"Have you considered appropriating them for combat use?"

"Sure, but they're IndustrialMechs. Internal combustion engines. If we had a surplus of fuel, they'd be a great addition to our force. But right now, I think we're better off putting the fuel into the IndustrialMech Mods already in our inventory, and into our tanks and other combat vehicles."

"I was hoping that the oil company had some fuel store for these things that we could exploit, but they probably haven't been used in years—maybe decades. No reason the fuel would still be around."

Erik could almost hear Sortek shaking his head. "We've scrounged all the fuel we can off this side of the continent. Some of the outlying mines and distant oil fields may have stockpiles, but they're too far out to be worth looking at."

Erik kept his eyes on the old 'Mechs. They were funny-looking, even beyond the specialized arms and tools. He trotted closer, stopped, and magnified his forward view. In several places, the crusty coating had been scraped off at least partially, usually over access covers or hatches. He spotted one on a bulge below and to the side of the cockpit. He spotted the word FUEL and a fitting of some sort. He zoomed closer. A placard read: NATURAL GAS.

He laughed out loud. "Those oil companies know how to squeeze a C-Bill, Lord bless them!"

"Sir?"

"These 'Mechs are set up to run on the waste gas from the wells! We're swimming in 'Mech fuel! Get your mechanics out here and see how many of these they can get running. And get some engineers out to the wells to see what we need to do to tap ourselves a gas supply. We may even be able to scavenge enough parts from the dead ones to convert some of our current IndustrialMechs as well."

"Yes, sir! But what about pilots? We don't have nearly enough."

"Canvass your men. Find anyone who's ever sat in a 'Mech of any kind, BattleMech, IndustrialMech—even if they have some simulator time, I don't care. Tell them, if they ever wanted to be a MechWarrior, here's their chance."

"Yes, sir!"

Sortek seemed genuinely excited. Erik hoped the feeling would spread to the troops. Certainly, it was the first good news in quite a while.

"And Commander."

"Yes, Justin?"

"I think you just channeled some of that light for us, sir."

For the first time in weeks, Erik smiled the smile of a truly happy man.

18

Fort Ravensglade
Ravensglade continent, St. Andre
Prefecture V, The Republic
23 December 3134

Erik looked at the paper, reading it for perhaps the tenth time, still confused. He looked around the command blockhouse, a nest of computers, cables, and makeshift communications gear. Several dozen staffers circulated around the nerve center of their operation, manning various workstations, monitoring communications, or tracking reported Liao troop movements.

Lieutenant Clayhatchee looked up at him from the watch desk.

"How did this come in again?" asked Eric.

"A civilian courier brought it up through the west tunnel from Port Archangel."

The stationery was from Port Archangel's finest hotel, which Erik had heard was none too fine. It was a waterfront place called, imaginatively enough, the Edgewater. The sealed envelope had his name written on the outside, and there was no return address. Written by hand and in large letters, on the single sheet of letterhead tucked inside, were three words: "The Devil's Punchbowl." It was signed, simply, "E."

Erik read it yet again, and sighed.

Clayhatchee looked at him. "Problem, sir?"

"A nagging pain, Lieutenant. Does 'The Devil's Punchbowl' mean anything to you?"

"I think I've heard some of the officers mention it. A tavern in Port Archangel some of them used to go to, before the Liao forces landed and the base went on high alert."

"Where?"

Clayhatchee turned to a woman manning a logistics workstation. "Astrad, where's The Devil's Punchbowl?"

"Eleventh and Dock, sir, right on the wharf."

Erik looked at her. "Close to the Edgewater Hotel?"

"Right next door, sir. It used to be a popular spot for, you know, *recreation.* Back before—"

"In the good old days—two weeks ago."

She reddened just a little. "Yes, sir."

"Clayhatchee, what's the latest on Liao activity?"

"Still massing on the coast, sir. No sign of an imminent attack."

"I'm going to need a car."

"Sir?"

"I'm going into town. Probably no more than an hour or two."

"Is that wise?"

"Unless there are undetected Liao forces in Port Archangel, I don't see a problem." He sighed again. There were times he thought Lieutenant Clayhatchee would have made a good mother hen. "I'll check with security before I head down."

*   *   *

As the car left the base, Erik was pleased to see their new IndustrialMechs running close-order drills just outside the base. He noticed that the roofs of nearby structures were covered with off-duty soldiers, watching. The training of their ersatz MechWarriors had become a spectator sport, and a major morale booster. That alone made them worth the trouble.

Of course, he knew that in combat, it would be a different matter. They'd added as much armor as they could to the units—especially around those exposed natural gas tanks. But none of them would last long against ranged weapons, and their own attack capabilities, limited as they were, could be used only in close combat. In a conventional military sense, they were almost useless—though Erik had some ideas . . .

As the car left the base, he had yet another opportunity to assess their defensive situation. There were no natural breaks in the steep cliffs that a vehicle could use, or even a 'Mech. The only way over the cliffs would be by air, precluded by their defenses, or in a 'Mech equipped with jump jets.

Two tunnels angled down from just outside the base to the foot of the cliffs below. The west tunnel connected the base directly with the wharves; the east, roughly four kilometers away, led to a barge terminal. These tunnels were sized for bringing up heavy construction, mining, and oil-drilling machinery, and were large enough for almost any conventional armor, though too small for BattleMechs. A similar, though smaller tunnel also existed in Boiler Bay, fifteen kilometers to the east.

All of these were heavily guarded by SwordSworn forces, but any attack would logically focus on opening them to the enemy, and on taking out the air defenses, making them vulnerable to an air assault.

Erik found himself shuddering. The intelligence reports indicated they were outnumbered. Liao could leave adequate forces to hold the capital and other mainland strongholds, while mounting an overwhelming attack.

The tunnel curved slightly as it burrowed down through the cliffs to the town below. The car emerged on Dock Street, which served as the town's main thoroughfare. It was nearly deserted. Many storefronts and homes were boarded up—however both the Edgewater Hotel and The Devil's Punchbowl appeared to be open for business.

The Edgewater was an ugly, gray, three-story structure that appeared to have been constructed from stacked and interconnected modular units. Exposed piping and ductwork crawled up the sides and twisted at seemingly random angles over the roof.

The Devil's Punchbowl at least appeared to have been built on-site, and for something like its current use, though it was old and run-down. It was a two-story frame building. Erik thought the paint on the outside was dark green, though it was so streaked and weathered it was hard to be sure. Perhaps, he speculated, it was just a coating of moss. An animated neon sign over the door featured a cartoon demon stirring a cauldron. Jutting from one side of the cauldron was what appeared to be a cocktail umbrella; the other side was garnished with a slice of lime.

He left both car and driver on the street and wandered in. The place was dark—most of the illumination coming from various neon signs, the lights suspended over an eight-pocket pool table, a few spotlights on the back-bar, and the glow of a holovid screen showing a soccer game. The bar had a dozen stools, and half a dozen tables were scattered around the room; all of them were empty. The bartender watched the soccer game, while a lone man in what was probably a merchant marine uniform played alone at the pool table.

The bartender looked up as Erik slid onto a bar

stool. He walked over and dumped a basket of whole, salted peanuts on the bar top. "What'll it be?"

Erik looked at the peanuts, then noticed that the floor around the bar and a few of the tables was liberally scattered with shells. It was that kind of place. "Beer—whatever passes for your best around here."

The bartender grinned. "Ran out of that almost two weeks ago. Ran out of second best a couple days after that, and third best later that evening. Now I'm down to 'what I've got left' and peanuts, and not that much of either. Of course, business isn't exactly booming."

"I'll take some of that, then."

The bartender produced a long-necked, clear bottle filled with amber fluid, which he opened and set down in front of Erik. The only label was the letter "A" on the side of the bottle. He took a sip. It was awful—bitter and acidic. He looked around. "Town looks pretty deserted."

"The invasion route comes right through here. Folks know that. Town's been rebuilt four times now. Sometimes, I wonder why we even bother."

"You're still here."

"My house backs onto the cliff. I've got an old mine shaft there, converted to a shelter. I'll sit things out, then see what, if anything, is left of this place after you military guys are through."

"What about the hotel?"

"My ex-wife runs it. She's gonna come stay in my shelter." He grinned and poked at Erik's arm with his finger. "I think we're gonna get back together. Third time's the charm."

"Good luck on that."

His smile faded. "We'll probably just kill each other, but I figure it's worth a try."

"At least something good could come out of this."

The bartender squinted at Erik's uniform. "Hey, you're somebody important, aren't you?"

"You might say that."

The bartender squinted at Erik's nameplate and whistled. "A Sandoval, in my bar. That's one to tell the grandchildren. Assuming me and the ex get back together, anyhow. So what brings you down here?"

"Came to meet someone."

The bartender nodded. "Lonely at the top. Well, 'fraid you're out of luck. Not much of anybody left here to meet. Even the hookers took a boat headed south."

"I'm here to meet somebody specific. They sent me a note to meet them here."

Erik looked around. The guy at the pool table had disappeared; the rest of the bar was still empty.

The bartender made a little "O" with his mouth. "What do they look like?"

"I'm not sure. Seen anyone strange hanging around? A woman, maybe?"

"A woman? No, nobody like that." He paused, looking past Erik at the door. "But here's somebody who seems to be looking for you."

Erik turned and stood, expecting to see Elsa Harrad.

Instead, he was shocked to see the would-be mercenary from the liner. An evil grin crossed the man's face. "Sit back down, poker boy. You aren't going anywhere."

Erik sat on the edge of the stool, keeping his feet planted firmly on the floor. The merc looked serious, and if Erik was reading the bulge under the man's coat properly, he was carrying a handgun of some kind. Better to just settle down and see what he wanted. Probably just money. Erik could deal with that.

The merc grinned. "Bet you never thought you'd see me again, poker boy. Least of all here."

"No," he said, "I'll admit, the thought never crossed my mind."

"Man, you don't know how good it feels finally getting the upper hand on you."

"It was just a game."

"I hate to lose."

"You realize, of course, that I have enough forces just over that cliff back of town to turn you into a puddle about five million times over."

"Yeah, well, I have enough just across the big water to come over and clean your guys' clocks."

"You're saying you work for Liao?"

He grinned. "I'm saying I work for *her*." He jerked his thumb toward the door.

Erik looked over to see Elsa, dressed in a trim maroon jumpsuit, walking toward him. She smiled. "Erik, you remember Paul, don't you?"

"I'm afraid so."

"Oh, he's not so bad once you get to know him. Did you know, for instance, that he knows how to fly a shuttle? Not only did he get me off St. Michael, we even made a tidy profit hauling the rest of the passengers down to the planet."

"Does that include whatever you're paying the spaceline when they notice their shuttle is missing?"

She laughed softly. "The way things are going, that could be some time, if ever."

Erik frowned at her. "What do you want, Elsa? I warned you about coming down here."

"It's a free planet, Erik. For the moment, anyway. I came to confer with my employers, and lo, they sent me to talk to you."

"Talk to me? About what?"

She looked at the bartender, who was hovering nearby. "There's a table in the back corner. It would be more private."

"Yeah," agreed Erik, "good idea."

They moved back to the table. Erik was relieved when the merc stayed at the bar. He looked at Elsa. It infuriated him that he was so glad to see her. "What do you want, Elsa? More spy games?"

Her smile faded, and she looked ill at ease. "Erik, I've come to offer you a surrender."

"What?"

"The local commanders have sent me to offer you terms of surrender."

He laughed. "That's absurd."

She reached over and put her hand on his. "It's not in the least bit absurd, Erik. You're vastly outnumbered. You can't win. Your people will die, which isn't exactly breaking my friends up. But I told you before, there will be losses on their side as well. Not as many, but it will cost them, in casualties, time, resources. That's still worth it to them to avoid."

She studied his face. "Erik, they've upped the ante. They're offering you an officer's commission and a command in their military. Sang-shao, that's like a colonel."

"I know what it is."

"Or—" She looked into his eyes. "Or, you could just go somewhere deep inside the Confederation. They'd give you a nice country house, a generous stipend." She paused. "We could be together."

"So now you're part of the package, too? I thought you weren't a prostitute."

She glared at him. "It's not like that. I'm not part of any package, Erik. I go where I want to go. I'm tired of this cloak-and-dagger thing. It was fun at first. In a way, it still is. But it's getting old, getting too personal. And . . . I finally found something worth quitting for."

"I suppose I should be flattered."

She suddenly looked angry. "You *should* be! You're an idiot, Erik, if you don't see that."

"I suppose I do."

"Then come with me. Let's leave this war behind."

"I'd like to. There's just one problem."

She frowned.

"I found something worth going on for."

"I don't understand."

He smiled grimly. "No, you don't. But it's still not too late to change sides. Come with me. Less safe, less certain, but you'd die of boredom after six months in that country house, anyway. For that matter, so would I."

"Or we can die in a few days when the Liao forces flatten your base? Do what you want, but I don't think so. I'm sorry, Erik, but," she glanced at her watch, "the invasion force has left Georama by now. They're on their way."

"That's good information; thanks." He stood up and grabbed her wrist. "Come with me."

She was so surprised that she followed him the first dozen steps toward the door. Then, next to the pool table, she dug in her heels. "Stop! Let me go!"

Erik kept pulling, but out of the corner of his eye, he spotted the merc, Paul, moving rapidly for them. He hadn't gone for the gun. Yet.

Erik's hand fell casually onto the pool table.

Paul stormed up. "Let go of her, or I'll—"

Erik's hand found the end of the pool cue that he was looking for. He snapped the cue up and swung it as hard as he could. The heavy end landed across the bridge of Paul's nose. There was a crunch, and he fell backward clutching his face, gushing blood.

Erik leaned down, reached under the merc's coat, and fished out the Blazer pistol. He hefted the gun, and looked up to see Elsa running for the door. She ran straight into the arms of four SwordSworn security officers. "Take her back to the base," he said. "Don't talk to her, don't listen to her. Put her in isolated custody. She is a suspected spy. Assume that anything she tells you is a lie. I'll personally question her later."

He looked back at the merc, still writhing on the floor, mixing a puddle of his own blood in with the discarded peanut shells. Erik hauled back and kicked him in the groin. "As for you," he said to the cringing heap, "you go back the way you came. And if House Liao doesn't kill you when you try to cross their lines, you tell them Erik Sandoval says he'll see them in hell. You got that?"

The merc nodded desperately.

Erik reached into his pocket and pulled out a radio. "Clayhatchee, we've got an invasion force incoming."

Clayhatchee sounded breathless. "Damn, sir, you're good! The intelligence reports are just coming in. How did you know?"

He frowned. "Bad news travels fast, Clayhatchee. Tell everyone to get ready. The siege of Ravensglade is about to begin."

19

St. Michael Station, St. Michael
St. Andre system
Prefecture V, The Republic
24 December 3134

Word of the impending invasion traveled fast in Port Archangel. Small boats could be seen leaving the harbor, heading along the coast, or out to sea. A few stragglers appeared at each of the lower tunnel entrances, looking for sanctuary at the base. That was one of the first decisions awaiting Erik when he arrived back at the command bunker.

"Send them up. Put them in one of the unused barracks, under guard just in case Liao tries to send spies or saboteurs that way." He had a thought. "Also, canvass them and see if you can find one or two who know the local waters and the shipping trade. If Liao is coming by water, some local knowledge might prove valuable."

The number of personnel in the command bunker had tripled since the last time he was there. The place buzzed with activity, with people literally bouncing off each other as they rushed from place to place. Computers chirped, phones rang, printers whirred. Large holodisplays swirled with colorful patterns that might have passed for somebody's art project. The room smelled of ozone, hot metal, sweat, and a slight but noticeable stink of fear.

They had, at most, hours. Hovervehicles could arrive at almost any time, and surface shipping would take six to ten hours. Erik's guess was that, other than probes and scouting by hovervehicles, the big assault would arrive more in that six-to-ten-hour window. Probably shortly before or after dawn.

Intelligence reported several large surface vessels. Unless they had illusions they could take the heavily defended tunnels from below, the 'Mechs would have to come over the cliffs first and try to open the way for either a sea assault, an air assault, or both.

"They've got multiple DropShips in low polar orbit," reported Clayhatchee. "There's a formation of four in line for a coordinated drop, and five others spread out evenly around the planet. If they keep making orbit-correction burns, reentry opportunities for the formation come about every sixty-eight minutes, and there's an opportunity for at least one ship to drop in on us about every eleven and a half minutes."

"Meaning," said Erik grimly, "that if they take out our air defenses, we won't have to wait long for company. Are the natural gas 'Mechs deployed according to plan?"

"Yes, sir," said Clayhatchee. "Standing by."

The bunker's thick outer door swung open just enough for one man to enter. Justin Sortek, turning sideways to fit his wide shoulders through, entered the room. There was an air of urgency about him. "Commander Sandoval, you sent for me? I really should be in my 'Mech."

Erik shook his head. "Sorry, Justin. You're going to spend this one in command."

He frowned. "Commander?"

"I need somebody here I can trust to tell me what I need to know, not what I want to hear."

"Sir, with respect, I'd be more use out there with my MechWarriors."

Erik nodded. "Possibly you would, Justin, but this time, it's going to be me in the 'Mech. You've got to stay here as my eyes and ears—focus on the big picture, so I can lead these people into battle."

Sortek said nothing.

"You know it's true. Without the Duke here, they need a tangible demonstration that the noble line is with them. Without that, your men can't do what needs to be done."

"It's a terrible personal risk for you, Commander."

"I know that. I won't claim I'm half the MechWarrior you are, Justin, but there's more than one way to fight a battle. I can't win this by playing it safe. Ever play Texas Hold-'em, Justin?"

"Yes, sir."

"Then you know what 'all in' means."

He nodded. "I do."

"If I go down in battle, then this fight is yours to finish. You know what we've set up. You know where we're vulnerable, and you know what their objectives are. Your family has been tied to the noble line for generations. If you have to find some of that divine light, do it."

He smiled grimly. "Yes, sir."

He patted Sortek on the shoulder. "I'm headed for my 'Mech. I'll radio as soon as I'm in."

For Erik, however, there was one stop to be made on the way. The stockade was located one level below the command bunker.

Even more so than most of the base, it had a dank, abandoned feel to it. The area had been unheated for years, and lichen grew in patches on the concrete walls. Though it was relatively free of rust, paint peeled from the metal fixtures and bars. The bare concrete floors were damp, and a leaking overhead pipe in the hallway had a full-blown puddle forming under it.

Erik found a lone guard leaning against a wall—the brim of his hat over his eyes—dozing or close to it. He walked up to him and stood there for a moment unnoticed, then said loudly, "Private!"

The soldier's eyes snapped open. He looked at Erik with horror, then came to attention. "That's *Corporal*, sir!"

"It was until a minute ago," he said dryly. Then he smiled just a little. At least he wasn't talking with the prisoner, which would have been of greater concern. "At ease, Corporal. Be more attentive next time. For now, I'm going to speak with the prisoner. Take a break."

"Sir?"

"Ten minutes. Go wash up, find some coffee."

The soldier looked almost pathetically grateful. "Yes, sir! Thank you, Commander!"

Erik glanced down the hall toward the cells. "Has she said anything to you?"

The young corporal looked suddenly uneasy. "Not really, sir. She . . . babbles."

"Good. She's either a spy or a lunatic. I'm still not sure which. She latched onto me when I was on Shensi, and she's stalked me across half The Republic."

The corporal looked relieved. "Insane? That would explain things, sir. You sure you don't need me here, in case—" He held up his rifle.

"No, I think she's harmless. Back in ten. *Sharp!*"

"Yes, sir!" He dashed off down the hall.

Yet, even after he was gone, his face haunted Erik. The pale, hollow cheeks, the bags under the too-young eyes. He had to keep remembering that face. It reminded him of what he was fighting for. Not the Duke. Not House Davion. These men, who believed in something bigger than all of them. He might have weakened, might have considered betraying those other things, but not these men and women, these soldiers.

He walked down the line of barred cells to the one occupied by Elsa. He found her sitting on the cot, wrapped in blankets, her knees pulled up to her chest, her back against the wall. Her appearance somehow startled him. She'd washed off her makeup, tied back her hair. The sophisticated society woman was gone. She looked young, vulnerable, lost. She looked up at him, and her eyes flared with anger. "Well, this is a fine pesthole you've put me in, Erik."

He shrugged. "It's the best cell we've got. I don't have the troops to spare to put you under house arrest in a barrack, and it's easier to keep you from talking to people this way." He looked at the ceiling. "Besides, this is probably safer."

"As safe as anywhere at ground zero. Erik, they're going to walk over you. You don't have a chance." To his surprise, she seemed as concerned for him as for herself.

"There's always a chance."

"Let me go."

"No."

She stood, the blanket still draped over her shoulders like a shawl. She held onto the bars and looked at him with desperate eyes. "Erik, I don't want to die here. *Please.* This isn't my fight."

He shook his head sadly. "It was your fight as soon as you started working for House Liao. Like you said: People like us, we don't have many choices—and you can't opt out this late in the game. Neither can I.

"What you were doing—it may have seemed like a game, but it wasn't. *This* is what it was about. You made me forget that for a while, but I remember now."

"Is that what this is? You're punishing me for your moment of weakness?"

"You know too much to be let go. I never should have let you go last time, but I honestly thought you might get out. Instead, you undoubtedly went back to your controllers and told them how weak Erik Sandoval-Groell was. This attack might not even be happening if I'd done what I should have done with you in the first place."

"Which would be?"

"You're a spy, Elsa. An agent of the enemy. What do you think?" He turned and walked away.

The 'Mech bays were underground, along the 'Mech-sized tunnels that ringed the base. Erik trotted his *Hatchetman* out of one of those tunnels and up the ramp to the surface. The brightest stars still shone in the purple predawn sky, but at this time of year in St. Andre's arctic, the sun only went down for a few hours each night, and even then, not far below the horizon. Erik could see a glow near the horizon that promised the sun would be back soon.

He switched his viewscreen to NIGHT VISION, and watched the line of armor and artillery along the cliff edge, ready to bring their ranged weaponry to bear against any ship that tried to land. There were sporadic reports of hover scouting vehicles up and down the coast, but they always withdrew as soon as they were fired upon.

Down below the cliffs, there were clusters of armored units guarding each of the tunnel entrances, and squadrons of armored troops inside each tunnel.

Armor and 'Mechs were clustered around each upper entrance as well, since any 'Mechs that made it over the cliff would likely make those a target. Beyond that, he had scattered armor, artillery, and infantry units—dug into the abandoned streets of Port Archangel, or hidden close to the cliffs.

He'd kept most of his 'Mechs up above, some out of necessity, since they lacked the necessary jump jets to transverse the cliffs. But in general, he thought they would be more effective on the flats, where they had room to maneuver.

"Commander." It was Sortek. "We've got one of the locals, who says she knows the ins and outs of shipping here."

"Put her on."

There was a delay as someone probably scrambled to find the woman a headset. "Commander Sandoval, this is Mary Neskowin."

"Mary, thank you for aiding us."

"It's my planet, too, Commander. What can I do for you?"

"I don't quite know yet. It would help to know something about your background."

"Well, I served on a tanker for six years, and I work for the Harbor Authority on dredging and channel maintenance. I've seen every kind of ship that operates in these waters."

"Very good, Mary. If you can stand by there, I'll consult with you if I need you."

He trotted the *Hatchetman* along in front of the line of armor, making sure that every pilot and tank commander got a good look at him.

"Sir." It was Clayhatchee this time. "We've got ships on radar, big and slow-moving. Could be hauling 'Mechs."

"Mary, are you there?"

"Yes, Commander."

"If you can give me any kind of information on those ships, it might be useful."

"I can't tell you much without visual. Based on the speed and size of returns, they're probably tankers or cargo-haulers of some kind, but I can't be more specific."

"Let me know if that changes."

"Commander." It was Clayhatchee again. "We've also got some ghosts about thirty klicks offshore. We can't seem to get past their electronic countermeasures—they could be attack helicopters."

Erik muttered a curse. Intelligence had reported increased use of attack helicopters and VTOLs by the Cappies. The cliffs would offer no defense against them, and the air-defense towers were designed primarily for aerospace fighters and larger spacecraft attacking from above. They'd be of little use against the nimble and low-flying helicopters. On the other hand, helicopters were vulnerable to ground fire, if anyone was lucky enough to get a hit.

Most of the defenders had shut down their engines to conserve fuel. The time for that was ending. Now there were exhaust plumes coming from many of the vehicles.

The light was red, and the sun was beginning to show itself. It would climb slowly, and not very far, casting long shadows over the battlefield. The fighting would all be over before it dropped from sight again.

Erik moved closer to the cliffs. He zoomed his viewscreen in on the big boats on the horizon. They were curious-looking things, boxy, slab-sided, with low, peaked roofs broken by huge hatches. They looked more like floating buildings. Each was big enough to hold half a dozen 'Mechs, but there was no way of knowing what, if anything, they contained. They were lingering just outside missile range, and appeared to have dropped anchor.

Then something else moving on the horizon caught his eye. He panned the camera, and saw dozens of bumps on the horizon. Hovervehicles, tanks, missile carriers, scout cars, APCs—almost anything that could hover. Following them were bigger vehicles—hoverferries that probably had been pressed into service to haul troops and armor that moved on tracks or wheels. The attack was finally here. But where were the 'Mechs? They should be landing ahead of the main force.

He looked back at the big boats.

"Commander." It was Sortek. "It may not do us any good now but Mary Neskowin says she knows what those ships are."

"They're what we call 'bulkers,' Commander. They haul heavy bulk cargo: rock fill, demolition rubble. We use them to haul away material that we dredge out of the channels so we can dump it at sea."

"Dump it? How?"

"There are chutes in the bottoms of the hulls."

Erik suddenly felt his stomach knot. "How deep is the water out there?"

"The bottom is flat out to about twenty miles, and there it's no more than fifty meters deep."

Erik switched quickly to the command channel. "This is Commander Sandoval. All units, we've got massed 'Mechs in the water! They're coming up the beach!"

Just then something like a giant metal frog broke the surface a hundred meters off shore, two metal boxes on its shoulders belching fire. It was the upper torso of a *Catapult*, missile launchers blazing.

It was quickly joined by another, and another, then a *Mad Cat III*, laying down a rain of fire on the shore defenses.

The fire was quickly answered from above. Missiles exploded around the 'Mechs, as Long Toms, Snipers, and Thumper artillery units found their range. Direct fire came from units on the beach, and hoverunits that raced out into the surf to attack the 'Mechs from behind.

For a moment, and only a moment, the advance seemed to stall.

Then, another pair of 'Mechs appeared, breaking the surface even farther offshore than the first wave. They were tall, red-and-black giants, stubby fins on their backs like a hornet's wings.

Tian-zongs. Heavily armored, overwhelming in firepower. In many situations, they were limited by their poor speed.

Not here.

They opposed a force that had nowhere to run. They moved in until they were chest-deep in the water, then set up an overlapping sweep of the beach, firing their lasers almost continuously, hammering larger targets with their Gauss rifles.

Erik watched helplessly as their forces were shredded, the *Catapults* and *Mad Cats* using the *Tian-zongs'* cover to advance toward the cliffs. His fists clenched inside the *Hatchetman*'s cockpit. He ached to be down there with them. But he knew that, soon enough, the battle was coming to them.

The artillery and missiles screaming down from the cliffs were finally getting results. One of the *Catapults* waded back into the water, armor in tatters, plasma leaking from its damaged reactor.

A SwordSworn SM1 Tank Destroyer slid up the beach from behind one of the *Mad Cats*, firing as it skittered sideways on its hoverskirts right in front of the 'Mech, at what must have been its minimum range. It was a gutsy move, Erik thought, and a risky one.

The big gun on the Tank Destroyer fired, and the

Mad Cat was momentarily engulfed in flame—the right arm flying loose in the conflagration, the right missile pod left hanging by a few cables and scraps of metal. But the lasers on the remaining arm and torso fired, cutting into the lightly armored SM1. The Tank Destroyer's hoverskirts collapsed, the vehicle's right side bit into the sand, and it rolled, turning into a flaming pinwheel that smashed into a dune and exploded.

The *Tian-zong* units were moving now, separating, each headed for a different tunnel entrance.

Erik knew what was coming next. "East Tunnel, West Tunnel, expect a direct attack soon. Artillery and missile units, reposition to defend those tunnels."

But he also knew this left the center of the beach more lightly defended, and that the Liao forces would be quick to exploit that. "Everybody on top-side defense, stay awake. The fight is coming to us soon enough."

More 'Mechs were wading out of the water now; lighter, faster 'Mechs like *Spiders* and *Koshis*, as well as more mobile heavy hitters like *Black Hawks* and *Ryoken II*s. All of them, Erik noted, were models equipped with jump jets.

The Liao hoverunits were becoming bolder as well, spending more time on the beach in their sweeps, some of them moving past the docks and through the deserted streets of Port Archangel. Erik watched these latter units carefully, but it wasn't yet time—

"Commander." It was Sortek. "Those hoverferries are coming in closer."

"Try to target them with missiles. They can't be armored."

"Yes, sir, they're almost in range."

Then it happened.

All along the beach, dozens of jump jets fired, and in an artificial sandstorm, a dozen 'Mechs began to rise up along the red cliffs of Ravensglade. "Armor, fall back from the cliff! 'Mechs incoming! 'Mechs incoming!"

And they came, rising over the lip of the cliff like fifty-ton hornets balanced on tails of fire, lasers blazing. A *Black Hawk* slammed down on a Thumper artillery unit, an accidental "death from above" attack that was no less deadly as the vehicle's magazine detonated in a fountain of secondary explosions.

A *Pack Hunter* landed on the lip of the cliff, grabbed the smoking barrel of a *Long Tom* in its hands, and twisted the nearly red-hot metal into a slight curve. Unaware, the crew tried to fire at the incoming hoverferries, and the mighty cannon exploded, showering the surrounding vehicles with shrapnel.

Erik was momentarily awestruck as a *Catapult* seemed to rise out of the ground in front of him and loomed above. The much larger 'Mech landed no more than five meters in front of Erik, but the advantage was all his. Powerful though the *Catapult* was, it was all long-range punch. It had no short-range weapons, and no arms to defend itself.

Erik's *Hatchetman*, on the other hand, was all about close-in fighting.

He swung his 'Mech's namesake hatchet up then down, shredding the big 'Mech's belly armor. It reared back, staggering off-balance, giving him a clear shot. He swung the hatchet again, faster this time, gutting the 'Mech like a trout.

In slow motion, the *Catapult* toppled backward over the cliff. He watched as it fell, and had the added satisfaction of seeing the sixty-five-ton 'Mech land headfirst on top of an attacking *Tian-zong*. Already having weathered countless rounds of defensive fire, the big 'Mech's armor cracked, and it began to hemorrhage fluids through the opening.

The surviving SwordSworn units below the cliff were quick to target the weakness, hammering away at the breach. The *Tian-zong* turned, slowly lumbering back toward the sea. It was a move of desperation. If seawater flooded through the hole into a critical system, the 'Mech would be disabled. In the end, it didn't matter. The concentrated attacks continued until the mortally wounded colossus tumbled face-first into the surf and lay, half exposed, like an artificial island.

Erik heard cheering in his headset, but the fighting had only begun.

A glint of light caused him to look out to sea, just in time to spot a line of flitting insect shapes flying in low over the water. The flash was a reflection from the windscreen of a Donar Assault Helicopter. The nimble aircraft fanned out to cover the landing of the hoverferries: two on the beach below, others beyond at the docks in Port Archangel.

Troops and armor began rolling off. The armor would be trapped below until the tunnels were cleared. But with defenses scattered, troops in powered armor would begin scaling the cliff with jump jets.

Erik heard a shrill voice on the command channel. "This is lower East Tunnel! They're coming through! We're falling—" There was an explosion just inside the tunnel mouth, and the transmission was silenced. Erik grimaced, but it wasn't unexpected.

He could see the streets of Port Archangel filling with fighting vehicles and massed infantry coming from the docks and headed for the East Tunnel. If they thought they had clear passage, they were wrong. Each of the tunnels had a surprise in the middle: back-to-back pairs of DI Schmitt Tanks, deadly "stoppers" that could resist incursions from above or below, and would be protected from 'Mechs and long-range weaponry. If the Liao forces were going to use the tunnels, they were going to have to pay the toll.

Erik had planned one other surprise, too, though

timing was critical. He waited until the helicopters—
with the landing essentially complete—dashed up over
the cliffs to engage the forces above. As the Liao
forces cleared the far side of Port Archangel, he issued
a radioed command. "Force Archangel, attack!"

In the hours before dawn, Erik had deployed powered armor, and many of his heavier and less mobile
tanks, to Port Archangel. They had carefully sheared
off the hidden sides of warehouses—mostly those with
metal sides or roofs, driving the tanks inside the building shells to wait. The buildings would confuse the
enemy and give the SwordSworn an advantage. Likewise, the powered infantry had been hidden around
the city.

Now the city behind the advancing Liao forces literally exploded, buildings bursting apart as tanks
crashed out, turned onto the streets, and began firing
at the enemy's exposed flank.

Powered infantry spread out on either side, using
the buildings as cover, sniping at the surprised and off-
balance column, which was bunching up at the tunnel
entrance. The first units in were shocked to find themselves greeted with a hellish mix of machine-gun bullets, autocannon shells, lasers, and flamethrowers.

Erik's elation was short-lived, as one of the air-
defense towers exploded under a hail of laser fire from
the swarming Donars, and another was taking heavy
fire from a mass of light 'Mechs. "*Legionnaires,* take
those 'Mechs on AD Tower Six!"

A trio of 'Mechs dashed into view from behind a
hangar. The odd-looking *Legionnaires* were little more
than giant rotary cannons mounted on top of humanoid torsos. Fast, specialized, and deadly accurate, they
began pounding away at the smaller 'Mechs with devastating results. A *Spider* was immediately ripped
apart by the massed fire. A *Koshi* spun and returned
fire, a missile smashing into one of the *Legionnaires*

and jamming its cannon. Then the *Koshi* went down under fire from the surviving units' rotary autocannon.

The surviving enemy 'Mech, a *Panther,* ignored the attack and lobbed off one more salvo of missiles at the tower, which exploded and began to burn.

Erik spotted a pair of big *Ryoken IIs* lining up on another tower. He was outmatched, but he might be able to draw their attention. He charged past them, lasers and autocannon firing. He swung the hatchet and managed to wing one of them. It barely scraped the armor, but it made enough noise to wake them up.

"Now I've done it," he muttered as he zigzagged, trying to throw off their fire. The 'Mechs were bigger, better-armed, and faster than he was. His only advantage now was that he was already moving full speed, and they had to accelerate to catch up.

Autocannon fire streamed past his canopy and began peeling off his rear armor. His damage displays flickered to yellow, and then red. Just ahead he spotted what he'd been looking for, the ramp leading down into one of the big 'Mech tunnels. "This is Sandoval. I'm headed into Portal Five with company! Two, heavy!"

He skidded the *Hatchetman* around the corner and down the ramp into the dark opening below.

The bigger 'Mechs had to slow to take the turn, giving him a greater lead. He switched to infrared, hoping that his pursuers would be slower to do so. In the close quarters, they'd be reluctant to use most of their weaponry, though that wouldn't be a problem if they caught him. Even his hatchet wouldn't be enough to save him.

He raced past a row of deep alcoves in the tunnel walls, then put the brakes on, sliding his 'Mech to a stop and turning. The *Ryoken*s slowed as well, suddenly wary.

As they should have been.

From the alcoves burst a veritable swarm of DrillingMechs and PipelineMechs, welders arcing, claws poised to snap, diamond drills flashing. One of the little 'Mechs was quickly swatted aside, and another blasted apart by point-blank autocannon fire, but the Liao 'Mechs were already taking damage, being dragged down. Erik carefully targeted the closer of the two *Ryoken*s, centering the cockpit in his crosshairs and giving it everything he had.

Weapons flashed with blinding brilliance in the dark tunnel. Erik saw the *Ryoken*'s canopy begin to crack. He charged in and brought his hatchet down with all the force he could. There was a satisfying "crunch" as the blade collapsed the canopy and sank deep into the 'Mech's torso.

He turned to the second enemy 'Mech, just in time to see a diamond drill sink deep into its gyro housing. The resulting explosion ripped the drill arm of the IndustrialMech, but the mortally wounded Goliath collapsed and lay twitching on the tunnel floor.

Erik called his congratulations to the Industrial-Mech pilots, but he was already running for the next ramp to the surface.

"Commander!" Sortek's voice sounded high and stressed. "We've lost Towers One and Three! We're losing ground up here—we've lost three of nine towers."

In theory, any three towers could still protect the base. In theory. In any case, at this rate they wouldn't have three for very long. Even one might offer some protection, but the forces waiting to drop down from orbit were overwhelming. "When's the next reentry window?"

"That cluster of four has a window in three minutes and—"

Erik's *Hatchetman* emerged from the tunnel just in time to see the top of Tower Two explode.

He began running toward Tower Eight. "Concentrate on defending the remaining towers! We've got to hold them for at least three more minutes!"

The fighting was furious, and it seemed to be going on everywhere at once. Though Erik didn't notice anyone targeting him, he was repeatedly splashed by stray fire, ripping at the armor of his already battered 'Mech.

His autocannon were empty, and warning lights indicated his lasers were having problems. He didn't have to look at the indicators to know that heat was building up. He could feel it in the cockpit, in the sweat that soaked his body and dripped down his face.

Three minutes! Less now! They might make it!

To his right, SwordSworn troops in battle armor swarmed over a stricken *Catapult*. To his left, an attacking *Mad Cat III* blasted away at a *Legionnaire,* its gun either jammed or out of ammo. Erik spotted a squad of Liao battle armor ahead, and veered to run through them, trampling at least one in the process.

Then the East Tunnel belched a column of fire that angled up a hundred meters before it darkened and turned into boiling smoke.

"We've lost the East Tunnel," shouted Sortek. "We've got heavy tanks incoming!"

Black smoke was still streaming from the portal as the first tank burst through, guns and lasers blazing. It was followed immediately by another, and another—a solid stream of metal that seemed endless.

Erik turned, charging into the firing guns, bringing his hatchet down again and again, while dodging fire. But he kept taking hits. More and more indicators turned red. The cockpit was like an oven. Warning buzzers screamed in his ears as he struggled to keep the 'Mech from shutting down.

Something different popped from the tunnel mouth. A boxy, wheeled vehicle that bristled with missiles the way a sea urchin is covered with spines, a JESII Strategic Missile Carrier. Immediately, every available SwordSworn weapon targeted the lightly armored vehicle, but not before it launched a devastating volley of a hundred missiles over their heads.

Towers Eight and Nine were knocked out.

Erik screamed into his radio. "How long? Did we lock out their window?"

Sortek's voice sounded hollow. "Sorry, Commander. They didn't wait for the towers to be knocked out. They started their de-orbit burn while all four towers were still up."

That was it, then. They'd lost. Even if the DropShips didn't arrive, they'd eventually lose, but when the 'Mechs began to fall from the sky, they were certainly doomed. *We gave it a good fight, though.* He looked at the destroyed and burning Liao 'Mechs and armor scattered around him. *We made them pay for it.*

"Commander. I don't understand. We still show four incoming DropShips, but we're tracking debris along their old orbital track. We're also tracking two more DropShips vectoring away at high acceleration."

Erik's eyes widened. He scarcely dared to hope. "Are we getting a friendly identification on the incoming ships?"

"Negative, Commander. No signal."

"Do you mean they're sending House Liao codes?"

"No sir, no signal." There was a pause. "Commander, we've got 'Mechs separating from the incoming ships. They look like *Union*-class DropShips. We've got four braces of 'Mechs incoming ahead of them. Still no signal."

Erik could do little but try to keep his wounded 'Mech out of harm's way, ducking behind buildings and steering away from obvious threats. He tried to shed heat, so he could at least move in to use the hatchet, do some damage.

He glanced up, and could see the jump jets of incoming 'Mechs, like a staggered line of dim stars. Further back, toward the horizon, he could see the DropShips themselves, four bright stars in a tight line.

"Commander, I've got incoming IFF signals. SwordSworn! SwordSworn!"

The first wave of 'Mechs was landing: *Black Hawks, Pack Hunters, Catapults, Hatchetmen,* all wearing the sword/planet/sun of the SwordSworn. They formed a circle and began spreading out, clearing the landing zone.

Erik realized that Aaron must have called in virtually every 'Mech in their inventory, stripping their forces elsewhere to the bone. It was a desperate, dangerous move, but it would provide a good show for the Cappies, perhaps giving them an inflated impression of SwordSworn forces. If they decided to test the defenses of other SwordSworn-held worlds, it could backfire, but if they were too intimidated, or at least too uncertain—

The command circuit crackled, then a voice boomed through on such high gain that Erik's ears stung. "This is Duke Aaron Sandoval! I have arrived, joined by reinforcements from many worlds. We have already taken Liao blood, and we will take more. Ravensglade is SwordSworn territory! We will fight until not one soldier of Liao stands on our soil! For Davion!"

As though an electric charge had gone through them, the exhausted defenders showed new energy. They joined in with the new arrivals—armor, 'Mechs, infantry, shoulder-to-shoulder, fighting back the invaders.

Another wave of 'Mechs landed, among them a *Black Hawk* freshly painted sparkling white and trimmed in gold.

The Duke had returned.

"SwordSworn! I am here! For Davion!"

Erik managed to coax his slowly cooling 'Mech into motion. He limped in with the others in the circle, his hatchet rising and falling, doing what he could. The circle widened, even as the four spherical DropShips landed in the middle of the site, each bristling with its own weapons, each carrying more forces, infantry, light armor, and massed IndustrialMechs from the coalition worlds. What they lacked in brute force, they made up for in numbers. Just as importantly, they were fresh to the fight.

Overwhelmed and demoralized, the Liao troops were no longer fighting. They were simply trying to get away.

Erik croaked into his radio. "Block the East Tunnel! Bottle them in! Tear them apart!"

The 'Mechs and armored infantry with jump jets went over the cliff, fleeing back to the sea. The other vehicles and the regular infantry that had made it through the tunnel were trapped.

Some surrendered.

Most died.

In time, the frenzy calmed. The smoke began to clear.

Erik slumped in his cockpit, exhausted, spent. In his headset, he heard the chanting begin.

For Davion! For Davion! For Davion!

And then it changed.

For the Duke! For the Duke! For the Duke!

"Commander." It took Erik several seconds to realize that the voice in his earphones was talking to him, and a few more seconds before he realized who it was.

"Sortek?"

"Yes, sir. Hell of a way to spend Christmas, isn't it?"

20

*POLL SHOWS MANY DOUBT THE REPUB-
LIC'S FUTURE—With the results of the scheduled
Exarchal election still unknown in the outlying
areas of The Republic, an INN poll conducted on
three randomly selected worlds in Prefecture V
shows that just over fifty-one percent doubt The Republic will survive another five years. Only twenty-
seven percent of respondents expressed "complete
confidence" in the future of The Republic. Another
seventeen percent believed that the elections "would
not or should not proceed." Dr. Ozmund Banzai
of Pleione said it this way: "It's the wrong time for
a change of leadership. If The Republic is going to
survive, what we need right now is stability. If we
can't have that, then we might as well look around
and see what the various factions have to offer."*
                                    —AP Courier News Services

St. Michael Station, St. Michael
St. Andre system
Prefecture V, The Republic
25 December 3134

A second wave of DropShips followed the first—
mostly aerodynes, bringing with them not just more
reinforcements, but supplies. The last ship to land was
the *Tyrannos Rex* herself, coming in just before sunset,
gleaming in the last rays of the day.

With practiced efficiency, the blast doors over the
formal entry retracted and the decorative wood doors
dropped into place. Crewmembers immediately
emerged, attaching the rest of the decorative portico,

and the steps leading to the door. A cheer went up as the red carpet was rolled out. The Duke's *Black Hawk* walked up and stopped next to the entrance, turning outward before shutting down, standing like a sentry in front of the ship.

The troops began appearing from every tunnel, barrack, and bunker, cheering as the Duke emerged from the cockpit of his towering 'Mech, waving and smiling. As Erik watched from the shoulder of his *Hatchetman,* it seemed the Duke wasn't even sweating, and not a hair was out of place.

A JI100 Field Recovery Unit pulled up to the Duke's 'Mech. The JI100's boom arm raised up until it was even with the *Black Hawk*'s cockpit, and the Duke hopped across the narrow gap to the arm, waving as it lowered him slowly to the pavement of the landing apron.

The men rushed in, and the Duke was lifted onto their shoulders. They carried him in a circle, completely around the hundred-meter-wide DropShip, chanting:

Hail, Duke Sandoval!
Hail the Flying Duke!
Hail, Duke Sandoval!
Hail the Flying Duke!

Finally, they put him down, and the troops cheered as he climbed the steps to the false porch of the *Tyrannos Rex.* He turned and waved his arm over his head, a final broad gesture before vanishing through the doors.

Even then, the troops rallied, singing and dancing, around the huge SwordSworn shields painted on the sides of the ships. Someone located a stash of beer in the basement of a ruined warehouse in Port Archangel, and it came up through the West Tunnel, which had the advantage of not being filled with the charred hulks of House Liao vehicles and the half-cremated bodies of House Liao troops.

The bottles were passed through the throngs, hand-to-hand, and the singing grew louder. As the sun faded, people started pulling fire-starters from their survival kits, waving the little flames over their heads as they sang and chanted.

Weary of it all, Erik Sandoval-Groell slid back into the cockpit of his 'Mech. As he activated it and coaxed it into reluctant motion, the battered machine seemed to moan in pain. He staggered down the ramp into the tunnels, past ruined hulks of IndustrialMechs and ambushed Liao 'Mechs, until he found his alcove and backed the 'Mech into its support structure.

He shut the machine down, and heard it make a sound somewhere between a sigh and a cry of pain, like a wounded soldier, grateful for the sting of death. He knew it would be a long time before this particular 'Mech saw battle again.

The interior of the base was quiet, as most everyone not engaged in other duties was outside joining the spontaneous celebration.

Erik staggered into the mess hall, where crates of supplies were being broken open. There was no hot food yet, but Erik got a cup of fresh coffee and a bologna sandwich—a refreshing change from the meager B-level field rations they'd all been eating for days. He found a quiet table in the back of the hall. But he need not have bothered, he thought. *I'm invisible now that the Duke has returned.*

He leaned back against the wall after doing nothing more than smelling the coffee. He pushed the sandwich away, no longer feeling hungry. He closed his eyes, and perhaps he dozed for a moment.

"Commander?"

He looked up as Justin Sortek slid into the chair across the table from him.

"You fought well. I wish I could have been at your side."

He nodded. "Thanks for noticing." He closed his eyes again.

"They rally around the light, Commander, not the man. The light is drawn to spectacle and ceremony, but without you, it would have been extinguished. The troops haven't forgotten you. They're merely . . . distracted."

Erik looked at him through heavy, half-opened lids, saying nothing.

"The light knows nothing of pride, but it knows those who wield it well. It returns to them again and again. Your day will come, Commander."

"Perhaps."

Sortek leaned his elbows on the table and sighed. "I bring a message from the Duke. You're invited to dine with him in the *Tyrannos Rex,* and to take the hospitality of its guest rooms while it is here."

Erik felt his empty stomach twist into a tight knot. "The Duke can take his hospitality straight to hell, and the devil can have my dinner."

Sortek half-smiled. "Well then, can I have your sandwich?"

Erik pushed the plate across the table to him. Sortek grabbed it and dug in as though famished.

Erik stood. "Justin, you're a good soldier, and a good friend. My anger is with the Duke. I would never betray you."

Sortek put down the sandwich and looked at him, a puzzled expression on his face. "Of course not, my Lord."

But Erik was already walking away. Then he stopped and turned back. "Justin, wait. Scratch what I just said. If the Duke is willing to dine late, after I take care of some pressing business, I'd be happy to take dinner with him."

Sortek seemed relieved. "You're sure?"

"What kind of fool would I be to sleep in a hovel,

when I can have a palace?" They both shared a chuckle. "I'll sleep in the Duke's soft bed, I'll eat his fine food, and I'll drink his best wine. After all, I am a Sandoval. Aren't these all *my* things as well?"

Sortek smiled, assuming he was joking. "I'm not sure the Duke would see it that way, Commander."

"How the Duke sees things is less important than how *I* see them. I'm starting to understand that now."

His "business" finished, Erik managed to find a dress uniform and an operable shower before heading for the Duke's ship. He showered, shaved, and groomed himself as though headed for an affair of state, which, in a way, he was. He checked himself in the cracked mirror, adjusting his collar and the ceremonial dagger on his belt

He emerged from the barracks to find his uncle's limousine waiting for him. Ulysses Paxton was at the wheel of the otherwise unoccupied car.

He entered without a word and sat down.

The short drive to the *Tyrannos Rex* took only a few minutes, and Erik would have been content to pass it in silence. It was not to be.

Paxton looked at him in the mirror. "I've been reviewing the events before our landing, Commander. I compliment you on a brilliantly fought defense against overwhelming forces. One for the textbooks."

"They write books about generals who claim victories, Paxton, not soldiers who fight wars."

"For the masses, perhaps. But the warriors will hear about this one. They'll know."

He leaned back in his seat and nodded. "They will, and for now, that's all that's important to me. For now."

Paxton looked at him but did not respond. The car pulled to a halt. "We're here," he said.

Erik waited as Paxton came around and opened his

door. He walked up the red-carpeted steps, past the guards and through the grand entrance. But instead of proceeding into his Duke's quarters, he took a side service door out of the lobby, leaving the theatrical façade behind.

He took a lift to the upper decks and wandered the corridors aimlessly, not even sure himself what he was doing. Until he saw Captain Clancy, and Clancy saw him.

They were alone in the corridor, one deck below officers' country, in an area dominated by mechanical gear for one of the weapon turrets.

Clancy gave him a sour smile as he walked past. "Guess we pulled your fat out of the fire, eh, pup?"

Erik spun, one hand grabbing the front of the captain's shirt, the other reaching for the dagger at his belt. Erik was more than a head taller than Clancy and far heavier. He slammed the little man against a row of power conduits, pinning him, and put the knife against his Adam's apple. He leaned in close to Clancy, until their eyes were inches apart.

"Listen to me, Clancy. I don't care how you treat my uncle, and I don't care what you think about me. But understand this. If you *ever* call me 'pup' again, I will kill you. I don't care if the Duke is standing behind me, I don't care if he's standing between us. I don't care if the ship is plunging into a star and you're the only person alive who can save us. I—will—kill you."

Clancy looked at him, licked his lips, and to Erik's surprise, smiled. "Well, well, the young Sandoval shows some backbone after all. Bravo . . . Commander." He said the honorific slowly, and precisely. "I was beginning to wonder if you had it in you."

"Do we understand each other, Captain?"

"Oh, I understand very well, Commander. Since you feel so strongly about it and all."

Erik released the captain who, his feet still off the floor, dropped as Erik stepped back and sheathed the blade.

The captain just grinned at him and nodded. "Now this," he said, "could make things interesting."

Erik turned and walked for the nearest lift. *It could, indeed.*

Erik and Aaron sat at opposite ends of the long mahogany dining table. Music from a string quartet played softly through hidden speakers, buffering the silence between them. There might have been a time when Erik would have found such a silence awkward— a sign of some disapproval on Aaron's part. There might have been a time when he would have felt compelled to inject himself into that silence, seeking some sign of validation or approval from the Duke.

Not today. Not ever again. The Duke was no longer the center of Erik's world, the focus of his attention. Aaron was merely a force to be reckoned with—one that could not be ignored, but which, when taken into account, could easily be maneuvered around, as a DropShip maneuvers around a star.

A pair of stewards entered the dining room bearing plates with the main course. Though both stewards seemed to move in timed unison, Erik noticed that Aaron's plate was placed just a second or so before his. Erik glanced at his plate. Palm-sized circles of thinly sliced red meat in a dark sauce, surrounded by intricately carved steamed potatoes, radishes, and carrots.

Aaron picked up a knife and fork, and began to slice his meat. He glanced up at Erik. "Rare medallions of Geef in a burgundy sauce. Delicious, and all the more so as spoils of war."

Erik considered his plate for a moment. It did smell delicious, but he was determined not to be like a loyal dog, diving immediately when his food was presented. Taking his time, he reached for his utensils, cut a small bite, and tasted. He chewed thoughtfully, then nodded. "It's excellent."

He took a sip of wine, a fine Tikonov vintage. Marvelous stuff. Erik made a mental note to remove a case from the Duke's cellars before they parted company. He did not intend to ask permission. "What news from the rest of the front?"

Aaron put down his fork carefully and dabbed at the corner of his mouth with a lace-trimmed napkin. "We believe that House Liao stripped many of their forward units of 'Mechs in order to build up the invasion force here. They took heavy losses at Ravensglade and at Georama, and we were able to destroy one of their departing DropShips. Though they've advanced past St. Andre on two flanks, my hope is that we've stemmed that advance, and that they may even have to withdraw and regroup. That will give us time to build on our momentum, to extend our coalition, and use the resources we've gained to expand our forces."

"It will also give House Liao time to rebuild their forces," said Erik. "When we next face them, they'll be stronger than ever."

Aaron looked it him, seeming to sense that something was different. "That can't be helped."

"No, it can't. You'd best focus your efforts on building the coalition. We desperately need allies, and clearly you're the better diplomat. But our forces will need to be honed to a razor's edge—coalition units trained to mesh with our SwordSworn troops. You can leave that to me."

Aaron raised an eyebrow. "Really?"

"It's where my skills can best be put to use. You already know that. And there's another matter."

"Which would be?"

"We've captured or salvaged a good deal of House Liao hardware, between here and the main continent. I think that by the end of this operation, we may be able to put together a full brace of assorted 'Mechs. It's not going to be top-grade equipment, but it would be a good starting point for an independent combat group under my direct command. It would be the first step to building a second army. Liao is already advancing on multiple fronts. We need to be able to fight on multiple fronts as well."

Aaron took another bite of food, but he seemed to be too distracted to taste it.

"You know I'm right," said Erik firmly.

Aaron swallowed. Sniffed. "Good ideas. I was thinking along similar lines myself. Only I was thinking Justin Sortek would command the second army."

"I was thinking he would be *my* second in command."

"Really?"

"Really."

Aaron sipped his wine, then the corners of his mouth twitched up just a little. "I'll consider it," he said.

"You do that," said Erik. He watched Aaron, imagined the wheels turning inside his head. *There's something else, Uncle—something else you're waiting to drag out. What is it?*

"I've heard some curious reports," he said finally, "about a woman. That this woman had somehow followed you halfway across the Prefecture, and that you have her locked in an isolation cell here somewhere."

Erik smiled slightly. *There it is, then.* "Not anymore," he said. "I don't have her in a cell anymore."

"What happened to her?"

"She was a Cappie operative. I played her for a while and extracted what information I could from her."

"So where is she now?"

"I personally eliminated her as a threat," he said, just before popping a piece of Geef into his mouth, "and cast her into the sea."

"Just like that?" He chuckled. "Erik, I didn't know you had it in you."

Erik smiled knowingly, remembering how it had happened. *No, Uncle, you don't know me at all.*

Elsa Harrad huddled miserably in the little cell, watching a drop of condensation slide down from the corner of the ceiling to water the crusty lichens growing on the wall. She'd heard the sounds of battle outside, even through the thick, reinforced walls. Several times, dust fell from cracks in the ceiling, and she wondered if the cell was going to fall in on her.

But then the explosions faded, and she heard the happy, celebratory voices. It could only mean that the SwordSworn had won.

Won!

She didn't see how it could have happened, how they could have survived against such an overwhelming attack. But they had, and she had one more woe to add to her list of many: She had picked the wrong side.

She was cold. She was filthy. She was hungry. She was lonely.

Bedding down on the tiny bunk was like sleeping on a slab. It seemed that no matter how she tossed and turned, the hateful thing tried to push some part of her skeleton out through her aching flesh. Yet when it came to the malice and evil of inanimate objects, she saved her true hate for the cold and exposed toilet standing in the corner.

Was it better, she wondered, to die an old woman in prison, or a young woman in front of a firing squad?

A tough choice—not that anyone was likely to allow her to pick.

"Elsa?"

Erik? She looked up, angry at first. Had he come to gloat? Then she saw the look in his eyes. Despite the obvious fatigue, there was something different about him: the dead-ahead thousand-meter stare of a hawk. But there was also a grim coldness there that made her shudder.

He produced a set of keys and fumbled them in the lock. "Come on, we're going."

"Where?"

"Look around you. Does it matter?"

"No, I suppose not."

He went first, leading her out through the twisting corridors. The guards were nowhere to be seen. They finally emerged in a vast tunnel where a hovercar waited. He pushed her onto the floor of the backseat and threw a blanket over her, then climbed into the driver's seat.

They drove for perhaps ten minutes, several of those traveling steeply downhill, stopping three times so Erik could confer with guards. Finally the car stopped, and Erik shut off the turbines.

"You can come out now."

She cautiously drew back the edge of the blanket. It was dark. Erik opened a door, and she heard the gentle roar of surf. The air outside was bitterly cold, and she wrapped the blanket around herself. She looked at him. "What are you doing?"

"We're taking back this planet, Elsa. Ravensglade is ours. There's still fighting on Georama, and the capital may take a few days. But the Cappies are on the retreat, and we're taking it all back."

"What has that got to do with me?"

"If I let you go back to the Capellans, you know

things. You'll tell them things. To even consider letting you go would be treason. On the other hand, you know things that could damage me here as well, should my uncle learn them. You're a danger to me, Elsa—a liability no matter what I do."

She looked at him nervously, feeling her stomach knot. "What do you intend to do about it?" There was a snapping sound, and she suddenly realized that he had a pistol in his hand.

"You said people like us don't have choices, Elsa. Well I have choices, and I'm giving you one. The first choice is to stay a Cappie spy"—he pointed the pistol between her eyes—"and die."

"Good Lord, you're serious aren't you?"

The look on his face said everything.

"You said I had a choice. What's my other option?"

"I let you go back, but on my terms. You like excitement, Elsa, danger? I'm offering you the biggest thrill there is. You become a double agent."

"A double agent?"

"You'll go back and tell them that, while you couldn't sway me, I'm vulnerable—that I might be compromised. I want you to learn everything you can from them, and then convince them you need another chance with me—that you are so close to seducing me into betraying the Duke." He smiled grimly. "Hell, there might be some truth to it. I'm keeping my options open." The smile quickly faded. "But let me make this clear: if we do this, you work for me. Not the Duke, not the SwordSworn. You will pledge your loyalty to me."

"I should do this why?"

"Because it's one way out of the situation you've placed yourself in. I've told you what the other one is. But I assure you: As long as you remain loyal to me personally, you will be under my protection. Your mother as well. That may not mean much right now, but it will. If I'm going to control my own destiny— and that is exactly what I'm going to do—I need certain resources, I need certain assets. Many of those I can simply plunder from the Duke, but some of the more intangible things I'll simply have to build myself."

"And you want me as your first intelligence asset?"

"The first of many."

She sighed. "They'll probably kill me, you know."

"Better them than me."

She looked at Erik, and thought wistfully of love lost, and opportunities gained. She smiled sadly and shook her head. "What the hell." She pulled herself up straight. "Commander Erik Sandoval-Groell, by the blood of my ancestors, I pledge my life and loyalty to you, now and forever."

"Good," he said. He threw her a key. "It's for the car. The weather looks good, so you can probably make Georama in about two hours at top speed. You stand a good chance of hooking up with Liao troops before somebody else decides to shoot you. Get yourself off the planet."

She looked at him for a moment, then climbed into the driver's seat of the car and started the turbines. The heaters immediately began to blast at her, for which she was grateful. She closed the door, and engaged the lift fans. It took all of her willpower to keep her eyes ahead, to not look back, to not think about what she'd lost.

But she would be back, and there would be other days.

The icy wind plucked at him as Erik pulled his heavy winter coat tight and pulled the hood up over his head. He watched the car slide down the dune, along the beach, then over the surf and out to sea. He could still see it for a minute or so, but then it was lost against the dark water.

He turned and began walking back toward the road. Perhaps a vehicle would pass, or perhaps he would have to walk the two kilometers to the tunnel entrance. He could tell the guard there his car had broken down, that he'd come back for it in the morning. After the confusion of the battle, it would be a long time before the car was missed, if ever.

It was dark, and Erik was alone with his thoughts. Was this how Aaron had felt, when he'd publicly announced their allegiance to House Davion? He'd knowingly, and with his eyes open, taken a step down a dark road from which there was no turning back.

He was a man of many secrets. He felt giddy, powerful, dangerous. He felt like a man with a live grenade in his hand, and the pin was pulled.

He could still damage Aaron's alliance with what he knew—still exact some kind of revenge. Yet it wasn't the deadly responsibility of the secret that bothered him; it was its already fading power. Soon, it would be history, irrelevant except to those who already called the Duke their enemy.

His safety, and his plans for self-determination, depended on having leverage against his uncle. Fortunately, Aaron Sandoval was a man who had no end of dark secrets.

Erik knew now, he had to have them. He had to have them all. Knowledge was power, and if he knew Aaron's secrets, he would be in a position to damage the Duke, or, alternately, to protect him, depending on which best served *Erik's* interests.

Right now, he wasn't sure which would be the better course. He wasn't sure he cared.

Erik smiled grimly and quickened his pace, sand crunching under his boots. Dinner awaited, and he had business to discuss with the Duke. Things would be different now.

For the first time, Erik felt firmly in charge of his life, if not his destiny, and soon that would come as well. But Erik's aspirations did not stop there.

He was no longer content to control his own destiny. He would control Duke Aaron Sandoval's as well.

About the Author

J. Steven York has written and published novels, short stories, nonfiction books, and software manuals. He's also written for computer games, radio, video, and film. He's dabbled in *Star Trek*, Marvel Comics *X-mutants*, and several universes of giant combat robots. Someday he should really figure out what he wants to be when he grows up. He lives on the Oregon coast with his wife, fellow writer and occasional collaborator, Christina F. York. They share their living space with two cats, several hundred toy robots, and a regiment of GI Joes.